# FUNERAL OF A GOOD GIRL

A girl/Mistress story

Cyan LeBlanc

**Posies & Peacocks**

Copyright © 2022 Posies & Peacocks

All rights reserved

The characters and events portrayed in this book are fictitious. Any similarity to real persons, living or dead, is coincidental and not intended by the author.

No part of this book may be reproduced, or stored in a retrieval system, or transmitted in any form or by any means, electronic, mechanical, photocopying, recording, or otherwise, without express written permission of the publisher.

ASIN: B0BF5PWZ84

Cover design by: Jae Morgan
Printed in the United States of America

# CONTENT WARNING

This book (and series) will contain BDSM elements that will be descriptive and possibly graphic. All acts are consensual but may not be the model for healthy and sane BDSM relationships*.

Other trigger warnings may include explicit sex scenes, poly-romance, age gap relationships, unfaithful partners, domestic abuse, and implied child abuse.

*Protected sex is automatically assumed in this story and safe words are in place throughout all scenes, except where indicated.

# AUTHOR NOTES

I started the girl/Mistress series in 2008 with a fanfiction piece called "I'm Not A Girl, Not Yet A Mistress." The BDSM narrative was about Megan, a young girl who had been groomed to be a submissive and wasn't looking for a new Mistress but discovered someone she liked. Unfortunately, she was not a Mistress. To reach an agreement, the two protagonists had to strike a balance between love, pain, and addiction.

During the drafting of that huge 200K word novel, I met someone who not only inspired the work, but also introduced me to characters and combinations I would not have imagined. Amanda Rohwedder's incredible creativity and support for my work helped me bring this lifestyle and epic love story to life.

Years later, I decided to tackle the task of rewriting the original story as well as completing prequels that had been sitting on my hard drive for over a decade. I've gone to great lengths to flesh out significant characters in the series, such as Trixi, April, and Oliver, who ultimately effect the relationship of our two major characters, who you don't actually meet until book two. *Okay, we do officially meet Megan in this book.

Trixi VanPelt's journey into the BDSM community after falling in love with an older woman and her wife—a submissive and willing participant in this polyamorous affair—is the subject of the novel *Funeral of A Good Girl*.

Characters in the first edition were inspired by characters from Disney's Hannah Montana, as it was written for fan fiction. That motivation altered as the tale and characters evolved. Cate Blanchett served as the model for our lovely Agatha. Amanda Seyfried was Justine's inspiration. Finally, how about Trixi VanPelt? Despite my efforts, the only face that came to mind when I penned the character was the original: Romi Dames, who played Traci Van Horn in Hannah Montana. Romi will always be Trixi to me.

I hope you enjoy the first book of my girl/Mistress series with more one the way.

# MUSICAL PLAYLIST

## BOOK TITLE BY: BIF NAKED
## SONGS BY: GARBAGE

1. #1 Crush
2. Why Don't You Come Over
3. Breaking Up The Girl
4. Cup of Coffee
5. Stupid Girl
6. Drive You Home
7. Not Your Kind of People
8. I Think I'm Paranoid
9. Sex Never Goes Out Of Fashion
10. Sex Is Not The Enemy
11. Automatic Systematic Habit
12. Get Busy With The Fizzy
13. Blood For Poppies
14. Alien Sex Fiend
15. Fix Me Now
16. I'm Only Happy When I Rains

# #1 CRUSH

Trixi benefited enormously from being the daughter of one of the top music moguls by owning automobiles, clothes, and jewelry. Things she never cared about as she grew older. She knew half of the people in the music industry, or rather, they knew her. Martin VanPelt's daughter, Trixi VanPelt stayed at home rather than running charity events or going dancing like her older sister, Traci.

Nothing Trixi ever did could ever outshine Traci's merits, which is why she stopped doing anything. Trixi spent half of her time in Los Angeles under her father's roof, where there was a constant influx of singers and bands. While he had an office in downtown Los Angeles' new Warner Music building, he preferred meetings where he could wine and dine them at their residence in the Hollywood Hills.

Trixi spent the other half of her time in New York in her mother's loft-turned-design studio, which took up an entire floor of an apartment complex overlooking Central Park. Her father, whom she affectionately referred to as Daddy to keep him convinced she was still a good girl, discovered musicians on the west coast and shipped them to the east coast, where Trixi's mother created their look and style. In the music industry, they were a force to be reckoned with.

Trixi had gone to New York. IShe hadn't chosen a college yet. She had no ambition and knew that whatever she did, Trixi's parents would judge it as inferior to her beautiful sister, who appeared to be perfect in every way.

The rain poured outside. Dark pendulous clouds declared the day a total washout for any outdoor activities. Trixi sat in the window seal, leaning against the wall, staring out at the sad city as her mother's employees bustled around her. The annoying buzzer rang. Someone was at the door.

She might have run to answer the door for her mother while she worked in another world but there were butlers to do that in this one. Everyone did everything, including bringing Trixi drinks, so she never had to leave her perch on the window seal. They'd even shit for her if it was possible.

Trixi glanced to the door to see who had entered her domain. Trixi admired the beauty of a mature ginger woman who seemed all business and no fun, and a chump whose arrogance overpowered his baby face.

Trixi sucked in a gulp of her Mocha Frappuccino, pressing her lips around the green straw while watching her mother greet them and welcome them to her office. Their house, once again.

The smug lad smiled as he looked at Trixi. He strutted into the room, tossing his head up at Trixi and acknowledging her presence with confidence. With an endearing smile, the woman also looked in her direction. Trixi's resting bitch face should have deterred them from paying any further attention to her. Trixi returned her gaze to the window, tracing the raindrops in front of her.

The suction echoed around her as she slurped the last of her drink's contents. Trixi rose from her perch and walked through the room, tossing the empty cup into one of the many trash cans scattered among their living room's desks and workstations.

Fabric draped over the desk in front of her. Her mother yelled as she was about to step over it. "Trixi, be mindful of that there. That came straight from Italy."

Trixi danced around it, passing the pompous singer in the process. He turned around and said condescendingly, "Your name is Trixi?"

She extended her middle finger without caring what he thought of her. "And what's your name, fuck you?"

Trixi made her way around the corner, through the flurry of hurried workers. The photo studio was set up outside her bedroom door. Cameras, lights, and scenery. Mr. Charming Pants was most likely photographed as something he wasn't. Charming.

Trixi noticed the beautiful redhead walking down the hall with a stiffened back and a confident demeanor as she opened her door, ready to lock herself inside. Her heels clicked on the wooden floors, and her hips bounced side to side with each step in her tailored black business suit.

Her gaze was fixed on her phone, which she was texting. Her eyes widened as she approached Trixi's space. Green like emeralds; her eyes met Trixi's with a wide, vivacious grin, and she gracefully extended her hand. "You must be Trixi. Your father talks about you with such fondness. It's nice to meet you, finally. I'm Agatha Helvete. But call me Aggie. Everyone does."

Trixi took her hand in Aggie's firm but refined grip. "Nice to meet you. My father hasn't mentioned you once, even though I don't meddle in his affairs."

She stood at the door, staring at Trixi from head to toe. That was common in that industry. A harsh first impression for the daughter of a fashion icon and music mogul. She did not conform to society's expectations of what she should look like or wear. Trixi refused to be labeled as a rich Hollywood kid stereotype, preferring old jeans and tee shirts from the Gucci tracksuits for lounging around the house.

Trixi asked, "Who's the kid with the enormous ego?" to divert Aggie's attention away from her basic blue jeans and black tank top, which accentuated her breasts.

It was successful. "Davey Paris," she said, as she turned her head toward the design room. "Your father apparently believes he will be the next big thing."

Her opposing tone certainly contrasted with Martin's assessment. "Daddy is usually right, but you appear to believe otherwise?"

Her mouth released a small giggle. "Is it my place to question my boss?"

Aggie looked at Trixi again, as if she needed to decide whether she wanted more from her. Trixi had felt this look many times before. Aggie strode off, each step assured. Trixi's eyes drew downward to admire her form as she swayed her ass.

Trixi stood outside her door, watching as Aggie smiled and boasted about Davey's every move. That's how Martin VanPelt elevated his celebrities to the status of royalty. He showered them with compliments at the first sign of talent, only to see if they had the personality to rise above and seize success by the balls. Martin must have taught him well, because little Davey had a firm grip on arrogance's testicles.

Trixi sealed herself in her room and plugged in a pair of earbuds. She listened to music that her father did not make. Classical. She sat at her desk, searching for her father's employee list on his website. She scrolled down and saw Aggie's face on the page. Her beautiful green eyes glowed on the screen as if someone had painted them with the brightest emerald color they could find. She read aloud and added her own commentary under Trixi's breath. "Agatha Helvete. Artist liaison. She's a lion tamer for the rich and famous."

Memories flashed in front of her face as she scrolled through the faces of the past. She blew some and fucked others. Trixi despised nearly everyone who worked for her father. The scroll bar lowered and stopped on Michael Stuart with a flick of her finger. She cringed as she remembered an old memory, but then laughed as she commented on Michael's photo on the website. "Washed up country star turned song-writer, pumping out generic music like gasoline. Thank God you only fucked one of the VanPelt girls."

She rolled her eyes and clicked the X in the corner to close the computer browser. Trixi grabbed her chest with a start as she closed her screen. The presence of the imperious little prick in her room made her heart race. "Excuse you? What the hell are you doing?"

He walked further into the room, closing the door behind him. "I thought this was the restroom and wanted to say hello when I saw your cute face. Let me introduce myself."

Trixi stood her ground, her feet firmly planted on the floor and her hand on her hips. "No, it isn't. Davey is your name. Done. Get the fuck out now."

"Come on, Trixi. Don't be so stand-offish. I'm gonna be in town for the next week. Here mostly. Wouldn't it be nice to hang out? Be friendly? I thought about heading down to Echo one night. Maybe you're down with that. Show me some other hot spots in the city?"

Echo was a new club that opened and featured celebrity DJs. If you could afford the expensive cover charge, it was the place to go for celebrity stalking. Trixi was knowledgeable, although she had never been there. Her sister did regularly.

"Hard pass," she said to him as she opened the door for him to leave her room.

He picked up on the hint, albeit not very well. He ran his index finger over Trixi's lips as he exited the bedroom. She swatted him away, puckering her lips as Aggie walked past the door.

Aggie leaned in to Trixi once Davey was out of earshot. "I apologize. I'll tighten his leash so he doesn't bother you."

Trixi admired her poise as she walked away from the bedroom, so tall and assured of herself. She wasn't the first older woman to pique Trixi's interest, but she was the first to bring out the timid side of her she hadn't felt in a long time.

Trixi usually spent most of her time in her room. When Rachel VanPelt had clients at the house and she needed to be out of the way, this was her usual spot. Trixi would come out of her room to eat or take a breather on the patio. She mostly stayed in her solitude fortress, away from the chaotic worlds of music and fashion. Curiosity never allowed her melancholy to set in, since she focused her attention on Aggie. Her presence in the loft tortured Trixi deliciously.

Trixi hopped out of bed every fifteen minutes to peek out the door. Her head bobbed around corners, looking for Aggie. Trixi eventually gave up and returned to her window perch, where she had a bird's-eye view of everything that was going on. Trixi and Aggie exchanged glances and cautiously guarded smiles while in the same room.

Aggie hovered near the window wall, close to Trixi's perch, but far enough away from prying eyes that could see the seductive look in her eye.

Aggie's lustful expression thrilled Trixi as she neared. She detested that look on others and knew it all too well. In high school, Trixi fell prey to the perverted male teachers' ravenous eyes who desired a young, precious thing. Ms. Olivia Ryan was the only teacher Trixi desired that level of attention from, but Olivia showed no interest.

Trixi favored women. They were less callous with their touches and more tender, squishy, and soft. Not that she hadn't encountered men before. Trixi lived in the heinous rock and pop music world. By no means was it earth shattering for her to sleep with a member of the B2B Boys. Trixi didn't mind even opening herself up to sexy men who were twice her age, as long as they were attractive. When she discovered the pleasures of a woman, that stopped.

The first woman Trixi encountered was extremely sexy and full of conceit, much like Davey. Cherry West. She was Trixi's age and sang songs about getting back at her ex-lover after a breakup. Who that other half was —a man or a woman—no one could tell. The genius of Martin VanPelt's label, ViP Music, was their ability to conceal information they didn't want the public to know. Cherry West identified as straight to the real world.

Cherry had a late-night session at the Hills house one night. Trixi and Cherry found themselves making out in Trixi's bedroom, while producers argued about the right sound and vibe of her upcoming album. To live a normal life, Cherry wore a wig on stage, but when Trixi had her sprawled out on her bed, she wore nothing but a smile.

After a few nighttime adventures, Trixi invited Cherry to one of Traci's infamous New Year's Eve bashes, where Trixi would choose her victim for the night. She wanted it to be Cherry. Trixi decided not to ring in the New Year that evening by eating Cherry's pie; instead, she dumped Cherry and blocked her because she was too needy. Since then, they hadn't seen one another.

While reminiscing about her past conquests, Aggie seduced Trixi with her eyes. Emeralds on display for Trixi to admire and crave. Harry Winston had nothing in their cases that were as beautiful as those dramatic and brilliant green eyes, Trixi thought as wanting a close-up view of them.

Trixi sat on the last window sill on a padded seat, looking around the room, while Aggie leaned against the wall directly in front of her. Aggie had her legs crossed and her arms on the window seal behind her, causing her breasts to puff up in her high chest. Trixi admired her, thinking she had a good rack for an older woman.

Trixi could do whatever she wanted with whomever she wanted at twenty-years-old, though she was certain that didn't apply to her father's firm's employees. While her father would not approve of his employees finding their way into Trixi's bedroom regularly, Trixi did it anyway.

After Aggie's eyes darted between Trixi and the rest of the office, making sure they did not catch her ogling the boss's young daughter, Trixi did what she did best when she wanted a suitor's attention. Trixi went on the prowl. She breathed deeply as she stretched her arms upward, her ample chest puffed, to show off the pair of lovelies that God had blessed her with.

Trixi observed Aggie's lips pressed together, enjoying the show, but there was another emotion Trixi witnessed with Aggie. Maturity. Aggie shuffled away, immune to Trixi's advances, shaking her head at Trixi's childish game of cat and mouse. The cat walked out of the room.

Trixi would not easily give up. She made it a point to accompany Aggie wherever she went. Trixi walked by, leaning on a nearby pillar, and watched as Aggie lingered behind the photo shoot. Trixi would enter the kitchen after Aggie if she went there for coffee to get some water. Aggie played the same game as Trixi, meeting her on the patio by taking a phone call just so they could grin at each other.

As the day came to an end with Davey completing his photo session, the room bustled once again to clean and make the house appealing. Trixi entered her room to use the bathroom. She discovered a piece of paper stuffed beneath the door of her bedrom as she walked out. Trixi took it and read the scrawled text: And you have the most beautiful legs I have ever seen.

She brought the paper close to her heart, knowing Aggie appreciated her even if it was only in secret. Trixi dashed from her room to tell Aggie that she had gotten her message, only to discover that she had already left.

Trixi shook her head as she approached the door, disappointed that she couldn't say anything until she noticed Aggie's umbrella resting against the wall. Her eyes widened with excitement. She had an opportunity. Trixi snatched it and dashed out the door, down the elevator, hoping not to miss the lovely woman getting into a cab.

Her pulse pounded as she ran faster than ever, squeezing past the occupants in the lobby of the New York high rise, till she broke through the front door before the doorman could help her.

Her gaze flashed along the crowded Manhattan street. Trixi discovered her. "Aggie!"

Aggie hesitated as she approached a taxi, her gaze drawn to Trixi's voice. Trixi called her attention with a wave. She pushed the taxi away, leaving Davey inside, and headed toward Trixi, covering her head with her raincoat.

When Trixi walked in front of Aggie, she flipped open the umbrella and draped it over Aggie's head. The rain poured down on Trixi as she peered into Aggie's stunning green eyes, which belonged to an equally exquisite woman.

"Thank you so much, Trixi. I discovered I'd left it when I stepped outside into this dreadful weather. I would have gotten it tomorrow, but thank you," Aggie said precisely.

Trixi suddenly remembered the letter. She pulled it from her pocket where she crumpled it. Trixi held it up, a gleam emanating from her eyes, signaling to Aggie that she had accepted her advances. "And this. I found it. Thank you."

Aggie's brow furrowed as she took the paper. "What

exactly is this?"

Trixi's cheeks flushed as she assumed Aggie was the author of the flattering remark. "You didn't write it?"

Trixi's eyes dimmed as Aggie gently shook her head and said, "No, Trixi. I apologize. Even if I agreed with it, I would never leave a paper trail of emotions leading back to myself."

While it disappointed Trixi that Aggie did not write the words, she restored Trixi's hope when Aggie stated she agreed with the contents. Trixi looked down at her legs, as immature as the action appeared. Not long, but not too short. Firm and athletic. Trixi flushed as her gaze rose to meet Aggie's, who stood a head taller than Trixi at five feet.

Trixi's attention darted around Aggie's face, first to her eyes, then to her lips, and back again. Aggie did as well. Trixi didn't mind that her hair had flattened because of the storm above them.

Aggie shifted the strains of hair clinging to Trixi's face with her hand. Aggie leaned in and pressed her lips against Trixi's, their eyes still locked on each other. Soft, rosy lips took Trixi's breath in.

"I prefer to show my thoughts rather than leave them for the world to find," Aggie's soothing voice said as they parted, barely audible over the rain.

Aggie's kiss showed Trixi every image she painted in her head upstairs with her alluring glances that were true. Trixi was unconcerned about their age difference. Aggie was clearly older and more mature. Trixi breathed into Aggie. "Show me."

She tapped Trixi's nose as if she were a mere child who made her happy. Certainly a sign of her authority. Aggie hailed a cab and stepped into it as it arrived. Trixi ran her finger over her lips as she drove away, longing to feel Aggie again.

Although Aggie and her wife weren't actively looking for someone to fill the void in their marriage, Trixi had shown an interest in Aggie. Actually, it was more than a passing fancy. Aggie found herself instantly drawn to someone extremely off limits, just as Justine had done to her more than ten years before.

If it hadn't been for that kiss, Aggie might have dismissed the flirting as the work of a horny young lady with spare time. Trixi's eyes betrayed a desire to be loved, and it drew Aggie to her like a magnet. Aggie could have invited her back to the hotel for drinks and an impromptu roll in the sheets with her and Aggie's wife if she were any other person.

As Aggie entered the hotel room, her wife, Justine, greeted her naked and on her knees. Aggie was pleased to see her lovely wife in her natural submissive position. She patted her head as she passed, signaling to Justine that she could rise. After ten years together, Justine understood every command Aggie threw at her without saying anything.

"How was work, babe?" Justine asked.

"Work? I've worked with some narcissistic assholes, but this Davey kid is a douche. In terms of things related to work but on a more... recreational scale, I believe I have found someone for us," Aggie said, tossing her purse on the counter and removing her jacket. "Or possibly."

Justine shook her head at the thought. "We don't

need a third. I'm perfectly content with just being me and you in life, but I know it's not enough for you, so who is she?"

Aggie did not respond right away. Aggie needed Justine back in a submissive position before she could discuss her boss's daughter, so Justine wouldn't argue and protest as much. She extended her hand, which Justine accepted, and led her back into the bedroom. Aggie sprawled Justine on the bed, her limbs attached to each corner of the bed.

Justine inquired, "You're really doing this now, so can you tell me? I will not like this person, will I?"

She took a silk scarf from the drawer and wrapped it around Justine's head, stuffing it in her mouth to prevent her from speaking. "Yes, I demand your attention. Remember that piece of paper we signed? It states that I know what is best for you, and that is for someone else to please you."

Aggie also knew that even with a scarf in her mouth, Justine would continue to oppose the idea. She then grabbed the vibrator and climbed on top of her, pressing the pulsating device against her clit. Justine moaned, although Aggie heard her protest.

As the vibrator rumbled in the room and Justine's moans increasing, Aggie explained, "You know I have a hard on for cute young things, like you. And ones that I shouldn't be falling for, but I did. She's a little firecracker, tenacity, and I can see her holding you hostage. She's petite but has a figure you just want to wrap yourself up in."

"Martin and Rachel's daughter, Trixi," Aggie said as she pressed two fingers inside Justine's body.

Justine's eyes widened as she shook her head,

canceling out the protest and satisfying moan. Aggie continued. "I gave her a kiss. Or, more accurately, we kissed. She melted in my hands the same way you did when I first met you. If only you could see the look in her eyes. I could have had her in the back of the cab and brought her here, but I wanted your approval first because she'll be your Mistress as well."

Justine groaned and bucked her hips into Aggie's hand after another deep press into her sex. If it hadn't been for the scarf, Justine's orgasm would have sounded like an aria to Aggie.

Aggie tossed the vibrator to the floor but didn't get off Justine's body, only slipping the scarf from her mouth. "Please. Let me see if I can mold her into something wonderful."

Justine gave in to Aggie's plea as she caressed her face and pushed her hair away from her face. "I'd have you committed if I didn't love you so much. I'm putting my foot down; if I feel even the slightest bit unsafe, I'm out. No more. Agreed?"

Aggie kissed her passionately before leaping off of her and untying her arms. "Put on your clothes. I'll have to get her a phone. I don't need my personal information in her cell."

When Trixi's mother's employees arrived at the loft, their disregard for her irregular sleep schedule woke her up. She shuffled out of her bedroom in her pajamas and pink bathrobe, unaware that one of those employees was Aggie. Trixi heard the deep and sultry voice as she crossed the dining area into the kitchen, oblivious to the common sight of worker bees. "Good day, Trixi."

Trixi jumped out of her skin when Aggie startled her. When Trixi walked through the house in the mornings, no one spoke to her. Trixi's voice cracked as she clutched her robe closed; not that she was showing anything revealing. "I didn't expect to see you so early."

"Do you usually know who comes and goes from your mother's studio?" Aggie cocked her head, one brow furrowed.

Trixi concluded her stroll to the coffeepot and poured a large mug full of steaming and wonderful morning beverage, her face flushed with embarrassment at her remark.

Aggie approached the young lady, her shoes clicking on the clean marble floor. Aggie inquired with a low, hushed voice and a small slant toward Trixi. "Do you still want that, as you said the other day? To show you?"

Trixi could not forget their departing moment, no matter how much she slept. They kissed. Whoever left the love note beneath her door didn't matter to Trixi. She wanted Aggie to express her feelings to her. Trixi said, "Yes," with a heavy sigh.

Aggie went into her work suit jacket, grabbed something from it, and placed it in Trixi's bathrobe pocket. She placed her cheek to Trixi's ear. "Dress. Always put on your finest face, regardless of who is around."

Aggie strode out of the kitchen and out of Trixi's sight, tall and poised. Trixi took the object from her pocket when she was alone in the kitchen. A mobile phone. She unlocked the screen by pressing a button. Nothing out of the ordinary, nothing special. Not even a branded phone. There was only one contact on the list. The letter A.

Trixi trudged back to her bedroom suite, coffee in hand, after dropping the phone in her pocket, and slammed the door behind her. In the restroom, she looked at herself in the mirror and remembered Aggie's comment about looking her best.

In that environment, appearing her best meant putting on her nicest evening gown. Trixi laughed at the thought of slipping into a form-fitting little black Gucci dress and relaxing around the home.

Trixi stood naked in the closet after a fast shower and shave of her lady bits, hoping to seem beautiful but yet seductive enough for Aggie to desire her. Trixi believed her attire was dreary, with little flair, for a mother who was a fashion designer and image consultant. She had evening attire in case her parents made her attend one of their work parties or galas. The rest of her drab closet had been primarily made up of jeans and shirts, yet anyone outside of New York's penthouses or Beverly Hills homes might not think her closet lacked pizazz.

Instead of being plain-faced with a ponytail, Trixi

spent time blow-drying her hair and applying her make-up after choosing an outfit. She turned heads as she exited her room to present herself to everyone, especially Aggie.

Even her mother had a comment. "Well, look at you. Off somewhere? Finally, leaving the house?"

Trixi cast a glance in Aggie's way, who had turned her head toward her while talking on the phone. Trixi never desired that much attention when she came into a room, but when she got it, her face flushed.

While walking through the room to her window bench, she addressed her mother loudly enough for Aggie to hear. "I might have plans later."

Aggie turned away from her and hovered near the door, clearly talking business with her planner open. When she concluded her call, her gaze became drawn to her phone, which she quickly pressed against the screen before tossing into her pocket.

The vibration shocked Trixi since she was holding her cell phone in her hand. It had to be the other one. She took out the phone Aggie had given her and opened it to see a text message: *Café Luxembourg on 70th. Lunch 12:30 p.m.*

Aggie stood next to Davey, who was there for another fitting when she glanced at the phone. Trixi waited for Aggie to turn around and look at her, but she never did. Aggie moved to the door and out with a firm spin on the ball of her foot.

Trixi wasn't sure whether Aggie expected a reaction from her. The message was more of a demand for her presence than an invitation. So, at midday, Trixi hailed a cab outside the apartment and asked the driver to take her to the location Aggie had given her.

As directed, the cab drew up outside the café. Her head rotated and her eyes flew about as she walked out, hunting for Aggie. A tented area with tables lined up outside the restaurant situated adjacent to the street. Trixi noticed a stunning lady seated at a table just inside the tent.

Trixi arrived at the table barely five minutes late, with no wave to greet her. "You're late!"

Trixi's look questioned Aggie's absurd remark. "It's New York. There's traffic."

"I expect promptness," she stated as she urged Trixi to sit with an impersonal gesture. "Arrive early and wait if you know there may be traffic."

"Okay. I apologize." Trixi's joy at spending time alone with the lovely redhead vanished as she reprimanded her. The dangers of dating an older woman.

The waitress arrived and took their drink orders. Aggie eyed the young lady dressed in a black skirt and a white starched dress shirt. She grinned, clearly satisfied with the waitress's appearance. When Aggie ordered beverages and appetizers for both of them. When the waitress moved away, Aggie's attention followed her until she was out of sight. She drew her focus back to Trixi. Her elbow rested on the table, her palm beneath her chin, her gaze fixed on her raven-haired partner. "Tell me about yourself."

Trixi shrugged, perplexed by the traditional classic blind date inquiry. "I'm sure you've already learned a lot from working with my folks. What exactly do you want to know?"

Her back tensed as she sat up, clearly irritated by Trixi's interrogation of her query. She sat back in her chair, waiting for a response.

Trixi stammered as she spoke, as if she had irritated her. "I became sick of Los Angeles and returned to New York. I can't decide whether or not to go to college, so I'm doing the not-college thing, which is nothing." She then threw up her hands, attempting to be amusing. "I also like long walks on the beach."

Aggie leaned forward, elbows on the table, both hands gathered in front of her mouth, brow down. Her solemn expression appeared shortly after. "I value my space. My personal life is mine, and I control who enters it. That implies I will not defend it to anyone, so don't expect me to acknowledge us to your friends or family if something happens after our lunch date. What happens in my bedroom is none of anyone's business."

Trixi instantly nodded, comprehending what she said, though she felt it was very hasty to go into bedroom details so early. She had no intention of telling anybody about Aggie, especially her parents. She'd told no one in her father's workplace, especially somebody his age, that she fucked them.

"You look stunning." Her solemnity faded, giving way to a seductive look in Trixi's direction.

While Aggie may have thought Trixi was being coy, her words sent feelings through Trixi's body, resulting in a flush on her cheeks. She lowered her eyes, her attention fixed on anything but Aggie. Her prior male equivalents were polar opposites. "Thank you," Trixi said.

Aggie reached across the table and raised her chin. "When someone compliments you, maintain eye contact. Accept your attractiveness. Own it. You have advantages you should be proud of."

Trixi was certain she meant her breasts were her

asset, a part of her body she exploited when she needed something and hid when she didn't want to be seen. When people saw her, their gazes drew directly to them. Trixi would show them if Aggie wanted to see them. Aggie's eyes didn't droop as she tightened her backbone, elevated her breasts, and sucked in her stomach. Instead, her gaze shot upward to Trixi's face, where she smiled. "There you have it."

The waiter served them their lunch, which they ate while asking each other a series of questions, similar to a speed dating encounter. "How did you end up working for my father?"

"You don't get into this business unless you know someone who knows someone. In the sixties and seventies, my father worked as a studio musician for Gamma Studios, which was purchased by ViP. Martin retained my father for years, and when I returned to the United States, he introduced me to your father."

"Returned from where?"

"After high school, I studied in Spain and then spent most of my twenties traveling across Europe, staying in hostels."

"You don't look like you've ever lived in a hostel," Trixi said.

"A different era, yet it helped me find myself and what I wanted out of life. I was raised in a pretty sheltered, conservative environment that still doesn't understand my choices. So, why are you doing nothing when your parents have given you everything?"

"Perhaps I need to trek throughout Europe and live in hostels to find myself. I'm not sure why I can't make up my mind. Maybe it's just that I've been living beneath my sister for so long that it doesn't matter what I do. So

I don't do anything."

"You sound bitter," Aggie said, her gaze fixed on Trixi as if she were searching for the reason of her existence.

Trixi sat with her elbow on the table, her palm massaging the back of her neck. When it came to Traci, she was a little bitter. "Can we not speak about her?"

"Sure. So what do you want to talk about then?"

Trixi smiled. "You."

"Aren't you a little inquisitive one?"

Trixi flirted, "When it comes to stuff I like."

Her creamy white complexion became flushed, exacerbating the redness in her cheeks. "Do you like playing with fire?"

"Is that what they call redheads?"

Her fingers glided across her lips, her gaze fixed on Trixi's. They challenged one another to make the first move. Trixi sensed Aggie wanted to fuck her brains out, and she masked the giddiness that ached between her legs.

If she'd allowed them, any other member of her father's firm would have had her holding on to the toilet tank while getting banged from behind. Trixi felt tangled up in knots because of Aggie's secretive and guarded personality. She wasn't one to toss her on top of a table to go down on her. Aggie rather analyzed her to determine if she was worth her time. She deliberated about whether she wanted to venture into the prohibited region of her boss's twenty-year-old daughter.

Aggie may have spoken, but the waitress who had caught Aggie's attention interrupted them as she cleared their emptied dishes.

"Thank you, sweetheart," Aggie murmured, a grin

on her face that made the waitress flush. She had that impact on everyone, and Trixi was no exception. That's why she was there. Aggie had bewitched her in less than a day just because of her confidence and her expression that told anybody she was worth the attention.

Trixi's heart pounded with jealousy as she desired to be Aggie's whole focus. "I'm starting to feel like chopped liver here."

Aggie returned her gaze to Trixi, waving the thoughts away from her. "Oh, hush. I admire the female form, especially when it is as attractive as her. Are you saying you don't like window shopping?"

"Not when my eyes are already on the prize."

"Are you saying you're the prize?"

"No, you are."

Trixi's audacity stunned her to another blushing moment, and her eyes lowered for a brief period. Their next interruption occurred when her phone chimed again. It had occurred a few times throughout their meal, but this time it demanded a text response.

Trixi's phone never rang once during lunch. A depressing sense of being disconnected from any kind of status. Other than her tits, which Trixi had not seen Aggie glance at once since sitting down, she believed her lack of intrigue might hinder Aggie's interest in her.

The waitress dropped the bill down. She thanked her once more and called her love. Trixi grabbed for it, but Aggie pressed her hand against Trixi's, which was holding the check. "There is no chivalry. At this table, we're both equals, and I invited you."

Trixi flipped her palm up, thereby ending the debate. Aggie's hand crossed the table after she moved the check to the edge. She pressed her warm palm on Trixi's hand. "I don't need to return to your house for a few hours to pick up Davey. Would you like to accompany me back to my hotel?"

"Are you asking me to have sex with you?" Trixi inquired, her eyes wide with anticipation of an afternoon romp.

"I'm not asking you to do anything, and we need to work on your couth."

Trixi's head hung low. Her gaze rested on the table, and her face burned with shame. The words slipped out before she had time to think.

As she threw the napkin onto her soiled plate, Aggie stood. "I'm gonna catch a cab, if you're in it… great."

She stepped out of the patio area with a graceful sweeping stride. Trixi leaped to her feet, eager to follow. Her petite legs came close to catching up. Faster than her legs could carry her, the cab arrived. Trixi grabbed hold of the door and pulled it open as Aggie was about to close it.

Aggie moved across the backseat's flat bench seat to make room for the young lady to get in. Aggie leaned toward the driver as the door shut. "The Conrad, Midtown."

# WHY DON'T YOU COME OVER

The Conrad's entrance was stunning. Elegant and brilliant. The wealth of Trixi's father allowed him to provide his staff with the best. He gave even the peons nothing less than five stars, according to Trixi. Not implying that Aggie was a peon.

Aggie walked with a broad stride, her heels clicking with each step. The workers acknowledged her presence and addressed her by last name as she passed them in the foyer. Trixi trailed behind her, her tiny legs hurrying and her Doc Martens keeping her presence from being apparent.

She jumped through the elevator doors just as Aggie handed her key to the elevator operator and said, "Penthouse one."

"Certainly, Ms. Helvete." He pushed the button, and they soared up quicker than most elevators Trixi had been on.

Aggie had said nothing since leaving the cafe, so the silence was oppressive. She'd spent the whole cab trip on the phone, discussing business while keeping her planner open and taking notes. She said nothing inside the elevator, either.

They arrived at penthouse level one and entered a beautiful entryway with an east and west wing. Aggie took a right, walking down a corridor that ended at the single door on the west side. She came to a halt when she got there, instead of inserting her magnetic key into the lock. She turned to face Trixi, her back to the room's entrance.

Her demeanor reverted to sincerity with a cocking of her head. Trixi didn't think she had done anything wrong because she remained silent the entire time. Trixi became perplexed by Aggie's expression.

Aggie commented, "We will not be alone."

When Aggie stated that, Trixi scrunched her brows, unsure of what she'd gotten herself into with this lovely woman.

"There are just a few people that I find completely captivating. My darling, you are one of them. You've piqued my curiosity by being someone I'd like to get to know well. Both inside and out. That implies I must let you into my life." Aggie took a deep breath and shook her head as she finally told the woman something personal.

Trixi's thoughts turned to her meal and Aggie's demand for seclusion. While she didn't believe her father had been concerned about his employees' sexual orientation, it was a male-dominated industry. Aggie required respect in order to thrive in the harsh environment. "I swear no one will ever find out."

"We play by my rules. I despise drama, and I have no time for jealousy or childish mental games."

"Sure, whatever you want." Trixi desired Aggie so badly that she would succumb to any demands Aggie threw at her.

Aggie brushed Trixi's hair out of her face, then delicately brushed her lips to Trixi's. The lock behind Aggie clicked as they kissed. Aggie took a step inside after turning and opening the door. Trixi followed, and she found herself surprised to see a nude and blindfolded lady kneeling in front of the door.

Aggie brushed the woman's hair as she walked inside

the hotel room and set her purse on the counter. Trixi warily stepped by this woman, her gaze cast down at the motionless woman, a tickle stinging her center. She joined Aggie in the living room as the woman remained still. They both rested on the back of the sofa, the kneeling woman in front of them rigid and erect.

"Justine, go to the bedroom. Wait for us," Aggie said in a mild but direct tone.

Justine rose from the floor, not removing the blindfold, and walked out of the living room and along the corridor with ease, just raising her hand once to prevent colliding with a wall.

Aggie glanced to Trixi when Justine had gone out of sight, as if waiting for her to say something. Trixi was not stupid. There were several films and books that discussed Justine. She hadn't seen it in person, but she was aware of its existence. Trixi assumed Aggie wanted her as another submissive member in her hotel room, so she kept her inquiries to herself until she knew her role in this game.

When she said nothing, Aggie extended her hand to Trixi, who took it. Aggie guided her down the same corridor Justine had taken to an enormous bedroom with a king-sized bed, a table, and two armchairs. Justine kneeled in front of the window overlooking New York City, her blindfold still on.

"Up, Justine," Aggie ordered as she shut the bedroom door, which Trixi thought was strange because they were the only ones in the hotel room, until she noticed straps dangling from the top of the door.

Trixi had thought incorrectly that Aggie intended to place her there; Aggie approached Justine and brought her to the door. She stretched Justine out, lifting her arms above her head, drawing them into the straps, and forming an X with Justine's body. Aggie ran her hand around Justine's torso, delivering a gentle caress with a few kisses along her body.

Aggie caressed Justine's beseeching body with light fingertips across her skin, sinking into her core. Justine's pelvis craved more than Aggie provided. When Aggie's hand returned, she licked her fingers clean from a delectable dessert.

"Trixi, have you ever been with a woman before?" Aggie said, her back to Trixi.

She stammered with her answer. "Yeah. Of course. A few times. Sure."

Aggie glared over her shoulder at her, her eyes indicating Trixi she didn't believe her. It wasn't a lie, even if Trixi had never been with a lady attached to a door.

"Come here."

"I promise I did. I'm not a virgin by any means," Trixi stated emphatically as she approached Aggie's side.

Aggie held her finger to Trixi's lips, stopping her from saying anything further. Aggie's fingers slipped once more between Justine's thighs, trying to moisten them as much as possible. When her hand lifted, her fingers glistened in the light from Justine's wetness. She extended them to Trixi's mouth.

As Aggie's gaze penetrated her, Trixi swallowed hard, gulping for a breath of air. Aggie pushed her fingers inside Trixi's lips with a small dip of her jaw. Trixi wrapped it around them, sliding her tongue over them and tasting Justine like Aggie had. Sweet and salty. Trixi sucked them with her eyes closed, enjoying the sensation of the long manicured fingers into her lips.

Trixi desired more when Aggie took her hand away.

"I love the taste of a lady in heat," Aggie murmured, her voice oozing with carnal desire. "Don't you think so?"

Aggie stepped aside, opening Justine to her. "Have another taste."

Trixi was unsure of everything at the moment, so she assumed a lot and prayed she wasn't wrong. She pushed between Justine's warm folds, stroking her clit and gracefully gliding around the pooled wetness of her center. Trixi's touch warmed Justine's body as she lathered her fingers and brought them to her mouth. Trixi licked Justine's secretions from her fingers, only to have Aggie yank them from her lips and devour them.

Aggie swirled her tongue around Trixi's fingers, sliding the delectable digits across her teeth. She dipped down to Trixi's height and devoured her mouth, attempting to expel any remnants from her lips. Her hand wrapped behind Trixi's neck, holding her on her lips till they needed to breathe.

"Are you going to let me taste you?" She inquired, her face still near to Trixi's.

Trixi's spine tingled as a result of their kiss. "Yes," she said.

She quickly unzipped her jeans and yanked them over her hips with a hasty wiggle. Her panties accompanied them. She'd let Aggie do whatever she wanted, regardless of anyone else was in the room.

Trixi's skin became covered in goosebumps as Aggie's fingers delved inside her scorching sex and flicked her clit. Aggie reached deep into Trixi's core, pressing as hard as she could. Trixi let out a breathy gasp as she entered the pleasure zone of her sex.

Trixi's womanly essence of sex dripped on her fingers as Aggie withdrew her hand. "Open up, Justine."

Trixi opened her eyes to see her fulfill Justine's hunger with her fluids. The nude hungry woman devoured Aggie's fingers as if they were her only source of nutrition. Aggie inquired, "Worthy of my mouth?"

Aggie removed her finger from Justine's mouth. "Yes, Ma'am. Definitely."

Trixi's lustful passion desired her hand once again. Her entire body did as well. Trixi's prior experiences had her flirting with everyone she was with and purring like a kitten, so he would desire her. Trixi didn't believe her coquettish ways suited a lady like Aggie, who knew what she wanted and wasn't afraid to go after it.

Aggie removed her jacket and draped it neatly over the arm of a chair, while Trixi stood in the center of the room, her trousers about her ankles. "Get undressed for me. I dislike having to work for it."

She complied, taking off her boots, pants, shirt, and bra. Trixi turned around and displayed her naked body to Aggie, hoping that she would appreciate her.

Aggie turned around with a huge smile on her face. She appeared happy, and her gaze immediately pointed to Trixi's breasts, then to her groomed sex for the first time. "Very wonderful."

"Thank you," Trixi murmured, hoping Aggie would fling her on the bed like her former lovers did.

Aggie approached Trixi. Trixi's hair gently brushed away from her face by her fingers. Trixi had to remember to tighten her hair into a ponytail. Or not, she thought, as Aggie reached around her head and untied her hair, allowing it to cascade over her shoulders. Aggie fluffed it out, smoothing the wave that had resulted from hours of confinement in a band.

"I want the freedom to explore your body without your assistance. I despise being disturbed by extraneous distractions, such as you trying to reciprocate my advances."

Trixi assumed she didn't want her to grope her, even though she had a strong desire to touch Aggie. She'd gotten a taste of Justine, which just fueled her need for Aggie. Trixi loved the salty taste of cum on her tongue, but she knew if Aggie wanted her as a bottom, she'd never be able to have her on her taste buds.

Aggie reached for Trixi's clit, teasing it with a few fingernail flicks. Trixi closed her eyes and took a big breath, elevating her breasts. Aggie's lips enveloped Trixi's nipple, sucking and biting on the tight buds in the middle of her dark areola.

Trixi masked the loud groan of delight from her mouth, a little embarrassed by the pleasure of her touch. Aggie raised her fingers to her mouth as she rose from her chest. Her tongue barely tapped her finger, as if she were tasting Trixi's favor rather than consuming her, as Justine had done.

She put her finger to Trixi's mouth, offering her the luscious fluids. Her sex burned as she extended her mouth wide to clean her.

"Don't conceal your pleasures by restraining your voice," Aggie murmured to her as Trixi tasted herself. "If it feels nice, share it with the rest of us. Never be modest in my or anybody else's company. You have the right to be satisfied and to express it loudly and proudly."

When Aggie pulled her fingers from Trixi's lips, her exhaled breath filled the room. She guided Trixi to the bed, oblivious to the panting lady who clung to the door. Trixi sat down, but Aggie pushed her backward so her back rested on top of the pristine sheets.

"Show me your sex," Aggie urged, nudging Trixi's knees to the side and coaxing them open for her.

Trixi raised her knees and buried her feet into the bed, welcoming the confident woman. The chilly air in the room surged over her sex, cooling her for a split second before Aggie's fingers fell over it.

Trixi caught her breath, almost choking, as Aggie tormented her with her touch. Trixi's nipples tightened, pressing the skin surrounding them firmly.

Aggie stroked Trixi's sex shape along the folds of her center, diving in and out along the way. She teasingly learned Trixi's shape and pleasure points for a few seconds. Trixi's sex called for her, her mouth open and relaxed. Aggie dropped her head between Trixi's knees, her fingers opening the soaked folds and letting her tongue to glide over the pulsing sex bud.

Trixi's mouth fell as she was free to express her desires, and a vocalized groan escaped her breath. Trixi heard a faint moan at the door. Justine approved of her Mistress's delight in satisfying another lady.

Normally, she'd place her hands on her seducer's head, but Aggie didn't want any distractions. Trixi clenched her legs, sinking her claws into her thighs, desperate for something to hold on to when Aggie's teeth caught her clit. Trixi's brain signaled a sting of pain, allowing her soprano voice to shout out in a delightful pleasure.

Aggie lifted her head from Trixi. She could feel Aggie's stare on her, but she couldn't look down at her. As Aggie's fingers delved into her center, tearing her open like a virgin all over again, her head sank back into the mattress. Aggie reached deep into the back of her core, pressing as far into the little, delicate hole as she could. As she exerted her magical touch within Trixi, the inside walls clamped around her fingers.

Trixi's body clenched, her eyelids squeezing shut as her sex pulsed around Aggie's persistent search for her soul. Trixi succumbed, shouting an aria of excitement as the warm flood of heat engulfed her.

Aggie gradually drew herself away from her center. As Aggie touched the sensitive pressure spots surrounding Trixi's sex, her body jerked. Trixi's gaze lowered, staring between her legs at Aggie. She wanted to know if Aggie had the same enjoyment as she did.

She sipped from the pool of Trixi's cum that coated her palm in her hand, admiring her trembling body. Trixi's head dipped backward once more as she inhaled deeply, enjoying the wonderful aftereffects of her most intense orgasm.

Aggie rose to her feet, made her way to the door, and let a perspiring Justine lick her hand. A reward for behaving and tolerating pleasure that wasn't her own.

Trixi raised herself, leaning on her elbows and lowering her knees to hang over the bed after her breathing had calmed. Aggie dried her palm on the submissive woman's chest as she hung from the door while she observed. Justine kneeled to the ground as soon as Aggie released her from the straps.

Aggie lifted Justine's chin. "To the bed, my love."

"Yes, Ma'am."

With her blindfold on, Justine made her way to the bed, feeling for her location by caressing Trixi's knees with her hand. She climbed into the bed next to Trixi, her head resting on the pillow.

Trixi cast a peek behind her at Justine, waiting for something or someone to gratify her. Her legs parted wide, oozing with desire to have someone touch her sex. The sexual heat of everyone raised the temperature of the room. Trixi's excitement resurfaced when Justine exposed her vaginal area without modesty.

"Do you think Justine is attractive? Beautiful? Is she your type?" Aggie inquired, reaching up her skirt and removing the pair of black lace panties she had worn.

"She's lovely, however, I'm not sure what my type is other than you." Trixi responded as Aggie stepped to the edge of Justine's bed and slipped her underwear into her mouth.

Trixi's eyes widened as she failed to realize that this truly occurred in reality. She was only familiar with that pastime from films. Aggie noticed her look of astonishment. "Unless you wanted me to insert them into your mouth?"

Trixi reddened and didn't respond. She never considered it, but she would like to know how that felt. She never even tried it with one of her father's lewd coworkers. Trixi shook her head, unsure of where she belonged on the bed.

"I didn't think so. In your loft, I watched you confront Davey. You are a resilient little one. Although you don't appear to be solely here for sex, I wasn't expecting you to succumb to me so quickly. You want more from me, I guess."

Trixi hated Aggie had brought up the conceited jerk amid feeling attracted to Justine's awaiting sex's musky aroma. Aggie teased Justine and kept Justine's passion stoked as she slid her finger over the outer folds of her core.

Trixi swallowed heavily, unsure whether she preferred Aggie's domination over Justine or the climax she gave her. A gasp of breath entered her lungs. "I want something beyond sex."

Aggie ran her finger over Justine's shaved skin, as if petting a domestic pet. As Aggie spoke, Justine whimpered. "You don't appear to mind or be afraid of Justine's bound state. I'm only sharing the mildest of my passions for her with you right now to ease you into it. I get the impression you're accommodating of my preferred method of pleasure?"

It was much more. Trixi desired to behold the majesty of her expertise and maturity. "Yes," Trixi said, refusing to return to the male-dominated sex she had previously lived in. "I'm completely prepared for anything you want to throw at me."

Her laughter filled the room, dampening Trixi's enthusiasm and intimidating her. "I'm not asking you to submit to me, but to share in my world," Aggie replied, her finger still stroking the bare skin of Justine's sex. "The desire for the finer things in life, such as a beautiful woman to please or not. Trixi, get up and come around here. Join me."

She jumped out of bed, her breasts bouncing with each step. Aggie took Trixi's hand and placed it on top of Justine's warm center. She led Trixi into teasing the woman, while Aggie's hand rested on top of hers. Trixi's gaze followed the lascivious submissive on the bed as she caressed and outlined the folds, not even dipping into her pool, which Trixi observed.

Justine clenched the dark gray duvet cover under the pleasures of their touch. "Can you make her come?"

Aggie asked in Trixi's ear.

The warmth of her breath on Trixi's ear created a layer of chills down her skin. "Yes," Trixi exhaled.

"Can you make me come?" Another sigh of hot, sensual air tingled her from head to toe.

"Yes." Trixi noticed a dribble of her own lust on her leg. Her eyes closed as she marveled at the forbidden lust of a trio.

Aggie yanked on Trixi's earlobe with her teeth. Aggie asked her final question as she let go. "Can you make us both come at the same time?"

Trixi had never tried anything like it before, never engaging with more than one partner at a time. Her chest heaved with assurance. "I'd like to try."

Aggie slipped her hand away from Trixi's and climbed to the top of the bed, lifting her skirt as she settled next to Justine. Trixi breathed deeply, perplexed as to how she could execute this sexual undertaking at the same moment. Trixi's lack of experience weighed heavily on her shoulders, as if it were a test of her ability. Fearing failure, her gaze raced between the two of them, devising a strategy.

Aggie's non-abrasive delight interrupted Trixi's thought of her internal suffering. She wiggled her finger at Trixi. "You are adorable, if I may say. Let me help you. Come to me and show me your talents. If I am pleased, I will please her. If not, Justine will not enjoy it either."

Trixi stood in front of the bed, marveling at Aggie's lovely, mature figure, anticipating her sex. Aggie placed her hand over Justine and waited. Trixi's heart raced as she felt the pressure of pleasing a woman with significant expertise who was far more eloquent than blow jobs and bend overs.

"Do I have to entice you? Need some foreplay?" Aggie asked, snapping Trixi out of her trance.

It resembled waiting to take the plunge while standing on the high dive during swimming class. Trixi crept up to her. Aggie's gaze followed Trixi's every move, assessing her every action.

Trixi spread Aggie's legs, taking her fingers up to Aggie's shimmering sex and opening her generous folds to expose her enlarged rosy bud. She'd only pleased a woman twice before, and both times the girl loved it, or so her body told her. Trixi blew slowly over her warm sex, expelling a stream of air from her lungs, cooling Aggie down.

"Delicious," Aggie said in a breathy tone.

Aggie rolled her hips into the bed. Trixi's breath warmed her rather than cooled her. Trixi peered over Aggie's pelvis to see if Justine liked her vibe, knowing that if she pleased Aggie, Justine would be pleased. Her attention returned to Aggie, tickling her engorged clit with her tongue before sucking it in and applying pressure around her bud, attempting to swallow her whole.

"Very nice," Aggie stated with a hip grind. Justine moaned, nodding in agreement.

Trixi flicked her tongue over the bud once more, then dropped to her center and back up. Trixi observed the absence of waves over Aggie's body to determine when her movements were common. There's nothing exciting about traditional oral sex. When Aggie's body limped under her, her confidence suffered. When she grabbed Aggie's engorged clit between her teeth, she sent her pelvis upward toward Trixi. Her confidence soared once more. Aggie demanded more.

Aggie's blindfolded submissive let out a deep roar of pleasure as her breathing deepened, long solid breaths exhaling from her chest. Trixi continued the moves she knew received the most delectable praise, praying she'd bring Aggie to an orgasm soon. Each minute she raced to the finish line, her neck and jaw tightened.

Trixi pressed her fingers into Aggie's sex, hoping to bring her to a climax, but she tired before they got to the edge. Aggie reached out to Trixi's bruised ego, raising her head in defeat. Trixi's tearful eyes begged for forgiveness. "I'm sorry."

"Nothing we can't work on, my precious." She got out of bed, removing her hand from Justine's crotch and pushing Trixi out of the way. Aggie put a pink vibrator in Trixi's hand and pushed her to the side of the bed next to Justine. "Finish her off. No need to make her suffer from your inexperience."

Trixi sulked over to Justine, deflated and disgusted with her performance. She turned on the vibrator and pressed it against Justine's still warm and saturated sex. Justine came by a vibrator as Trixi stared at the closed door while Aggie was out of the room.

Aggie and Trixi dressed before walking Trixi and her depression to the lobby, where she flagged down a cab for Trixi. Trixi's inability to bring Aggie to a climax left her sulking as she failed at the one thing she felt she understood how to do well.

When the cab pulled up next to them, Aggie held the door open for her. Trixi asked, "You're not coming?"

"Remember, I said discretion. If we show up together, then we were together. Not a discussion I wish to have with your mother. Even though you're of age, you are still a mere child next to me. And still her baby."

Trixi needed to know this lone cab journey home was a kick to the curb before she hopped in. "Did I blow it with you?"

Aggie kissed her with a tender touch, petting Trixi's hair down. "No, precious. Nothing I can't teach you if you will accept my guidance."

Trixi ducked into the yellow taxi, Aggie's palm shoving Trixi's chest backward and into the car. Aggie shut the door on her. With a wave, the car sped off down the busy afternoon streets of Manhattan. Aggie returned to the hotel room.

Justine wasn't in the living area, so Aggie went to the bedroom, where she discovered Justine in bed still. Aggie leaned against the door frame, watching her lovely wife, who remained stretched out in the tangled blankets. They didn't say anything for a while until Justine said, "She's cute."

"Beyond cute," Aggie remarked, still standing with

her arm on the frame while she awaited Justine's reaction.

"You didn't orgasm on purpose. I know you."

"She's cocky." Aggie said, leaning as Justine sat up on the bed with her legs crossed. Aggie held up her fingers an inch apart. "I was this close. Trust me, it took a lot to hold back."

"She didn't shy away from any of it, which surprised me."

As she moved away from the wall, Aggie sighed. As much as she wished she could take Trixi under her wing, she was aware of how difficult Trixi would be. Trixi was so stunningly attractive, youthful, complicated, and feisty that Aggie got a tickle between her legs just thinking about her. Trixi had both advantages and disadvantages, but her last name was by far the largest detriment. Aggie had to be concerned about her financial security because VanPelt was equal to her employment.

It had been a long time since anyone had piqued her interest, like Trixi had. Aggie's last strong connection with a woman was with Justine. Aggie and her former wife took Justine in and used her for their sexual games. After Aggie's first wife died, the relationship blossomed into love, and she married Justine. They had tried being monogamous, but Aggie enjoyed watching others please her wife and the heat of multiple lovers in the same bed.

Aggie stalked to the bed's edge and yanked Justine's ankles toward her. Justine slid over the sheets until her hips collided with Aggie's at the foot of the bed. Aggie leaned in, pressing Justine's legs against her.

"I want her," Aggie said, licking her lips and sighing

deeply as she pressed her fingers deep inside Justine's sex.

Justine laughed underneath her moan. "I know you do, babe. You're frustrated and deprived of release. Please take it out on me."

That sexual frustration of not allowing Trixi to please her only exacerbated Aggie's desire for sex. It was simple to sit back and let Justine do her thing, but this required more than a quick roll in the sheets. She needed the soothing sounds of a woman experiencing a painfully delicious orgasm. Two fingers turned to three, then with a deep breath, Justine took in four, hitting a soprano chorus. It wasn't enough. Aggie forced her entire hand into Justine's sex and broke her open with an ear-piercing scream for more.

Aggie made three deep reaches toward Justine's heart before removing her hand and lowering herself to the bed. Justine sprang on her as soon as Aggie's back struck the bed and ripped off her clothing to fuck her quickly and forcefully, exactly as Aggie loved.

Both of them laughed at Aggie's desperation and relief. Justine knew very well that Aggie wasn't thinking about her. Trixi's name was all over that intensely painful fuck and that orgasm. Justine didn't mind. When Aggie had been married to another, Justine had occupied her thoughts. Justine would benefit from Aggie's repressed sexual desires now that another attractive young woman had her attention until they established a rhythm with Trixi.

"We need to go to the club," Aggie said, talking about a private BDSM club for lesbian woman.

Justine turned over, running her fingers over Aggie's

chest, tracing the still erect nipples. "And bring Trixi?"

"I need to know if she is willing to submit to me so I can build her up to dominate you."

"And if she doesn't or won't?" Justine placed a kiss on Aggie's breast, licking the rosy bud.

With a slap to Justine's leg, Aggie got out of bed. "Not going to be an option. She will," she firmly asserted, grabbing her clothing and scurrying off to the bathroom to get ready so she could go back to the VanPelt apartment with Davey and welcome Trixi to her new life.

The surprise was Justine. Although she didn't think it was a deal-breaker, Trixi understood she wouldn't be special to Aggie, since she hadn't anticipated Aggie to have someone else in her life. The aching in Trixi's center triggered memories of her greatest orgasm, and it made her feel as though Aggie had torn her apart from the seams.

Sadness washed through Trixi as she exited the vehicle alone. A memory of the numerous evenings she had to make the walk of shame home. Her memoir should be called "Discarded in a Cab". In Los Angeles, Trixi would have gone directly into her bedroom to cry. In New York, she had to walk through a lobby full of staff members, all of whom were welcoming her while she looked used and sullied. The walks of shame in New York were ten times worse since she had to stand in the elevator with an old man who wanted to make small chat and ask her how her day was.

Everyone turned to look at the door when Trixi opened it and entered the loft. She hurried to her room with sex written all over her face, but Davey stopped her as she turned the corner.

"Hey, beautiful. Did you get my letter under your door?"

Trixi attempted to shove him away, but he restrained her by grabbing her arm. When Trixi swung back around, she said to him, "I'm not into dicks, you dick."

He pressed into her when she managed to free her

arm from his grip. "Perhaps you just haven't had one as amazing as mine," he said.

"Maybe you'd like yours broken by my father when I call him and tell him where you want to stick it."

"Ouch. So you're into pain. I can dig it." Trixi slammed the door on Davey while he leaned against the wall. She heard his voice behind her closed door. "Trixi, you are such a tease. I wish you'd talk to me. I'm not a dick. Cocky, yes. Dick, no."

She opened the door roughly, his face right next to hers. "Explain something to me, please, because this is what I don't understand about guys. I told you to fuck off and yet you, like most guys, continue to think women are just teasing and secretly want them. Why is that, Davey? Why is your brain such a void for common sense?"

He grinned. "Because you're so fucking hot and I seriously want to see those beautiful tits of yours."

Trixi slammed the door in frustration, but his hand caught it, and he forced his way inside, closing it behind him. Trixi hollered, "Get the fuck out of my room!"

"Come on, Trix. I know all about you. Heard you give good BJs. Just a little suck. No one will know." He entered the space once more. Trixi took a step back for every step he moved forward.

"Actually, everyone would know because I record everything in my room." Trixi pointed at the camera that was only there for show in the corner of her room. The loft was being frequented by too many individuals. Trixi was never at ease. "So they'd see how small your dick really is and how fast you'd come, too. I don't think it would be good for your image since they're trying to make you a stud when really you're a dud."

Davey retreated as Trixi spoke after following her finger to the camera. Trixi pointed to another one, which he also didn't notice, as he moved to where he believed he would be out of the camera. He opened the door before leaving the room. Trixi groaned. The only other occasion she had to use them was when a filthy bag followed her into her room after he delivered artwork to the loft.

Trixi collapsed into her bed and drifted off to sleep. She remembered Davey's statements about having a reputation for performing amazing blow jobs. Trixi wasn't sure where he had heard that, but she instantly wondered if Aggie hadn't heard something similar, being carefree and willing to get into bed with anyone.

Although untrue, it may have passed for truth. She had placed Aggie at the top of her sexual conquests, making the list resembling a baseball roster. The one thing Trixi might have excelled in over her sister was this.

About one hour after Trixi, Aggie arrived at the loft. Thanks in large part to Davey, who continued to stab her battered ego, Trixi's despair remained unaffected by her feelings of failure and whoredom.

Aggie entered the loft and looked around before moving near the window directly in front of Trixi while keeping her ear on her phone. Trixi gave it a quick glance before turning back to look at Central Park's rich vegetation.

Trixi missed Aggie's text because she was oblivious to what was going on in the room. She became aware because of the vibration in her pants. She took her phone out of her trousers to view the text: **Melancholy** *isn't a good look on you.*

She chuckled as she replied. ***What else do I have if I can't even please you?***

She answered another call. As Aggie walked near her, she took almost ten seconds between each step, and Trixi's eyes alternated between the window and her. Trixi counted while making increasingly louder clicks with her shoes. Her heart beat quickly with each stride. Still, Trixi could feel Aggie's hand squeezing her from the inside, a memory she'd didn't want to forget.

Aggie came to a stop in front of the window seal and leaned slightly to sit down with one foot elevated. Her skirt slightly parted, revealing her thigh. Her eyes lingered on Trixi as she spoke on her phone, before darting toward Trixi's mother, who was standing in front of a shirtless Davey. She turned to face Trixi, and the two of them exchanged a timid smile before repeating.

Aggie concluded her conversation, looked down at her phone, put it in her jacket pocket, got up from the window, and started walking away. A text message alarm rang on Trixi's phone. ***Kitchen.***

With Aggie's back to her, Trixi jumped off her perch and stomped across the room. Trixi looked through the empty kitchen cupboards, searching for anything to eat, and slammed each one in self-pity.

She heard the door to the kitchen swing open behind her. With a glance over her shoulder, she saw Aggie. She walked to her, leaning on the counter next to her.

Trixi yanked the phone Aggie gave her from her pocket and slammed it with a slide. "Take this."

Without saying a word, she put her finger on the phone and moved it back toward Trixi.

"I don't want it," Trixi stated firmly.

With a small pull on her pants' pocket, Aggie scooped up the phone and slipped it inside. "Don't act like such a child. It's so unbecoming of you."

"Are you only doing this because of some preconceived notion you have about me?"

"If I remember right, you ran after me. Therefore, no preconceived anything with you other than I knew you'd look perfect in my hotel room."

Trixi giggled with a bashful head drop.

Aggie turned and grabbed a Pierre from the fridge, opening it. As she made her way back to Trixi's side, her high heels clicked on the floor, making a loud pop and fizz in the quiet kitchen.

Aggie lifted Trixi's shirt, placing the cold bottle on the small of her back. Trixi's chest rose from the chill. Aggie whispered to her as she pressed her body extremely close to Trixi. Her entire body covered Trix's short stature. "You're so beautiful when you're not pouting."

Aggie lifted Trixi's hair off her neck, sinking her lips into the delicate flesh and nibbling on Trixi's skin. Her other hand was on Trixi's side, her thumb lightly caressing over her. Aggie pressed her breasts into Trixi's back as she breathed over her neck. "You're gonna be the death of me, little one. I want to take you here and now."

"I have a bedroom." Trixi expressed a confident plea for them to recreate their afternoon frolic.

"Very tempting and extremely dangerous for the both of us." Aggie took a step back, sighing as she removed the bottle from her back. She leaned on the island counter after a few clicks of her heels. "Trixi, dear. I'd like for you to follow me."

Trixi interrupted her with a dumb inquiry, her back still tense and her breasts boasting in front of her. "Follow you where?"

Aggie took a swing of the bubbly water. "To a world I'd like for you to discover. Something that would change your life; open you up to the possibilities of a new type of pleasure."

Almost loud enough for all of New York to hear, Trixi said, "You mean S&M?"

Aggie shook her head, her gaze swiftly falling to the floor, appearing disappointed at Trixi. She took a step back and got out her phone just as someone entered the kitchen. Davey.

Trixi scowled at him for disrupting their conversation. His presence made the hairs on her neck stand on edge. He raised his hands. "I'm just getting water. Geez, calm yourself."

Trixi motioned him to the fridge as Aggie typed on her phone. When Trixi's message signal vibrated, Aggie pushed through the swinging kitchen door and out of sight. ***Discretion. Ears are everywhere.***

Trixi fled the kitchen by pushing through the swinging door. She noticed Aggie stroll out onto the balcony as she walked toward her bedroom. She looked around to check whether anyone was looking at her. With no one in the corridor, Trixi opened it and closed the door to the patio behind her.

Aggie leaned on the railing and shot a glimpse over her shoulder before returning her focus to the city. "I'll have to teach you how to be discreet."

"Fine, but out here, no one can hear us. These doors are soundproof."

She didn't look at Trixi, simply stared straight ahead

as if no one else was in the area. "Just because I am a woman doesn't stop prying eyes from watching our every move."

"So what? I'm not allowed to talk to one of my father's employees. I mean, I can talk to Davey, but not you? Maybe I'm asking you for advice on boys," Trixi said, not seeing the problem with talking to her.

She laughed and turned to the young woman. "Do your parents know your preference for women?"

Trixi squinted her eyes, thinking about the question. "I don't know what they know. I've kinda never brought anyone home to meet the parentals."

"Don't think you'll start with me, Trixi."

Trixi narrowed her brow, serious in her words. "I'm not. I just want a—"

Trixi was mid-sentence when Aggie's watch beeped an alarm. Aggie responded, "I've got to leave."

Trixi waved her hand and moved away. But Aggie didn't move right away. She returned her attention to the city, while Trixi turned to look at Central Park in the distance.

Aggie didn't comfort Trixi, especially with the full glass doors looking out on the terrace where they stood in quiet. Trixi knew well that she had promised Aggie no drama, but it appeared to have found both of them sooner than planned.

Aggie pushed away from the railing. "Davey has an appointment. I have to go, Trixi."

Trixi remained silent while Aggie slid the glass door open. She received a text message on her hidden phone in her front pocket a few seconds after the door closed, with an address and time, as well as instructions to wear something seductive. Trixi groaned, smirking.

Aggie had not dismissed her.

When Trixi entered the studio from the balcony, she saw Aggie say goodbye to Rachel and Rachel's assistant. Trixi licked her lips and bit them when Aggie looked in her way. They made a mutual arrangement that Trixi would visit her later.

# BREAKING UP THE GIRL

The next evening at precisely nine o'clock, Trixi arrived at the secret address, but a burly woman at the door prevented her from entering. It was pretty apparent that the woman could pick her up with one hand and toss her over forty feet in the air. There was only the purple female gender symbol above the door and the address below it. As if they were hookers waiting for a trick, a few women queued up outside the door.

As the taxi pulled away, Trixi looked around to see where she was. Trixi was in the right place, but she didn't see Aggie. As she looked down, all she could see was the cleavage of her raised breasts, which were jammed into a form-fitting black designer dress. A popular choice among potential suitors before Aggie.

Trixi advanced into what she imagined being a nightclub, but a muscular woman with a hand out pressed her back. "Are you on the list?"

Trixi said with a deep breath, maintaining an air of familiarity as though she truly belonged everywhere. "Trixi VanPelt."

The woman checked off Trixi's name on the list, flashed a savage grin, and let her and the others in while locking the door behind them. On the other side of the door, another woman stood with a clipboard and paper. Trixi called out her name once more without waiting for an answer.

"Ms. VanPelt. Welcome. Ms. Helvete is awaiting your arrival in bungalow seven. Kitty will escort you." A scantily clad-dressed woman presented Trixi with her arm to walk.

"Thank you."

She made her way into the club, where women of varying sizes and appearances chatted and drank together in open rooms. There were no private areas because there were no doors. Each bungalow has its own unique wooden number that served as a street address. As they strolled to the seventh bungalow, Trixi began counting down.

Passing from room to room, she saw a wide variety of games being played. Women hunched over a table or hanging from a cross. Women getting lap dances from other women. Instead of the usual musky body odor that permeated the clubs Trixi visited, the dimly illuminated BDSM club smelled like lilacs.

As they approached the wooden number seven, they stopped. When Trixi entered the room, she saw Justine kneeled on the floor, serving as a footrest for Aggie.

Trixi swore she had arrived early when Aggie welcomed her with a kiss on the cheek in the center of the bungalow. Quite different from the passionate kiss they experienced in her hotel room.

"Yes. Actually, you are. Welcome, have a seat."

Trixi followed Aggie's gesture to the L-shaped couch that was built into the wall. Aggie returned to her original position and propped her feet up on Justine's back in a crossing position. "I appreciate you meeting us here."

Trixi, unable to focus on anything else while still in awe at her newfound surroundings, said, "I didn't know this place existed."

"I'm sure you don't know a lot of things exist,

precious."

A waitress entered, her breasts popped up and exposed in a leather corset. Trixi focused on her breasts and immediately became everything she detested in a man. Waitress smirked at Trixi's attention, so Trixi looked away, then at Aggie, who laughed at Trixi's naiveté.

As soon as Aggie saw that Trixi's humiliation was preventing her from speaking, she placed an order. "She's underage, no alcohol for her. I'll take a glass of red wine, Pinot Noir. She'll have a seven. Hold the bourbon. And a bowl of water for my pet."

"Coming right up." The waitress left with Aggie's order.

Trixi fumed. Her ears reddened by Aggie's snide comment about her age. Aggie scolded her for the attitude. "I don't care how mature you are. You will not drink in my company until you're over twenty-one."

There was silence from Trixi. An expression of displeasure remained, albeit she didn't resort to the stereotypical childish gesture of crossing her arms in front of her chest. "Fine."

After stroking Justine's hair, Aggie reclined in the corner of the couch, her arms stretched out on the back, and her bound breasts pressed against her corset. "Yes, Trixi, I do take pleasure in this world. Some people might call me a dominatrix, but I despise that label since it's often used to refer to kink performed for money. Though I have no problem with it, I am not for hire.

"Over the years, I have had many submissives. Not because they paid me, but because that is what I look for in a relationship, like Justine here. The reason you couldn't bring me to a climax is that I don't get off on a little tongue action. You couldn't have known that."

"So it was a test?"

"Far from a test. Rather, it's about fully grasping your thought process and your experience. As I mentioned before, I know you want sex but there's more you want from me. I need to know what it is, Trixi. What do you want from me?"

"I don't know," Trixi said, dropping her eyes to her lap.

"Not an answer. You're just afraid to say it."

That was correct. Trixi felt like a sucker for being frightened to express it. She said nothing more and continued to look at the floor while staring at the bottom of her dress.

"Let your guard down. This is a safe place to talk. In here, nobody will listen to what we're saying or see us together, so we can talk freely without fear of being overheard. It doesn't matter to me, Trixi; talk about anything you want. What is the popular phrase these days? No shade?"

Trixi giggled at the realization that their generations were so different. She found herself drawn to her sophistication and maturity. Trixi stared at her directly. The soft lighting accentuated the sparkle in her eyes. "You don't have to speak my generation's language. Hell. I don't either. All of my sexual experiences have been one-night stands, and they have all been with guys. In fact, you aren't the first of Daddy's henchmen I've agreed to meet. You exude an air of self-assurance without coming off as arrogant. I thought you'd be different and that you might see something in me more meaningful than ten minutes of fun."

The beverages they ordered from the waitress came out. Trixi lowered her head once more for fear that her staring at the waitress's bare chest would make her flush. Aggie reached for her wine and swirled the glass before taking a sip. "Delightful."

Trixi took a swig from her fizzy beverage while avoiding eye contact with the waitress. The server snickered at her self-consciousness. "It's okay to look. I'm very proud of them and if I didn't want people to see them, I'd cover up."

With a flick of her finger, Aggie motioned for the waitress to come over. She took a few steps toward Aggie, who'd bravely asked if she could touch. The waitress smiled and nodded as Aggie cupped her breast and flicked her nipple many times. She raised her head and encircled the waitress' nipple with her tongue.

Aggie leaned back and snapped the breast out of her mouth with her teeth before declaring, "They are exquisite."

"Thank you, Ma'am."

The waitress plopped a bowl of water down in front of Justine. She then politely requested Aggie's approval before petting Justine. Aggie indicated her consent with a nod. The bare-breasted waitress bent down and ran her fingers through Justine's blonde hair, which reached to her shoulders. "You are such a pretty little bitch, and so well behaved." The waitress stood up and lavished praise upon Aggie. "She is quite adorable, Ma'am."

Once they were alone again, Aggie took another sip of wine and went straight back to her authoritative yet relaxed stance. She immediately resumed their conversation without any pause for clarification. "I do,

Trixi and I'm looking forward to it but in order to really enjoy you, or for you to fully enjoy me, I must first break you. That is one of the great things about being a sadomasochist; both inflicting and experiencing a satisfying pain. I think it will be something you like, too."

For a moment, it seemed as if they were playing a game of chicken with their gaze, trying to determine who would back down first. Trixi mimicked Aggie's calm demeanor, making sure not to blink or exhibit any signs of concern about what Aggie proposed.

Trixi became quickly distracted by the activity outside their bungalow. How Justine could keep her cool and concentrate on the wall was beyond her comprehension. Apart from lapping at the water in her bowl, her gaze stayed fixed on the ground the entire time.

The club may have seemed dull from the outside, but inside it was everything but. The soft background music and the fresh aroma of flowers put at ease the guests. Women felt safe enough to walk about the club shirtless, and there were no obnoxious men to grope them.

Like Aggie, Trixi felt at ease in that setting. With her confidence soaring and her ample breasts heaving in the air, Trixi looked back at the attractive older woman and said, "Break me."

That was the beginning of her adventure into an universe that was significantly larger than herself. Trixi was a firecracker who stood just five feet and one inch tall, thus everything was bigger than she was. After reaching an agreement to let Aggie break Trixi's spirit, Aggie began her work. Trixi's objective was not to acquire a slave for herself; however, in order to play with one, she had to first submit to the position of a slave. The only reason she consented to go through the mental and physical suffering was so that she could send Aggie into a mind-blowing orgasm and bring her to her knees.

Trixi had lofty goals.

Aggie made sure that Trixi understood the safe words, the risk awareness, and the consensual agreement that they were entering with each other before she began Trixi's submission.

Once Trixi gave her consent, Aggie stripped her down to her underwear, then attached her to the ceiling cuffs using a brilliant machine with a cable that reached the floor and retracted using an electronic pulley system. She positioned Trixi in a stretch such that her feet were just over the ground.

After Aggie revealed Trixi to the club members, she invited them to experience Trixi's exposed torso with salacious touches. They petted her, rubbed their hands over her full breasts, squeezed and pinched them, and even sucked on her firm nipples. While many people continued fondling Trixi, others came in with paddles to slap her behind. The slaps weren't particularly forceful, but they were enough to catch her off guard and cause her eyelids to fly open.

Trixi's back stiffened as she sucked in air and attempted to maintain her composure so that Aggie would approve. She did not make any complaints, but she winced as women bit into her flesh. Trixi whimpered as the invitees slipped their fingers under her panties and felt the pool of pleasure between her legs.

"Oh, she's so impressive," one invitee said.

Throughout the entire process, Trixi made it a point to observe in on Aggie whenever she had the chance. When Aggie watched Trixi endure the obscenities of those invited into her den, Trixi saw the joy in her eyes. Trixi detested the fact that it wasn't Aggie's hands on her, but rather the hands of strangers whom she didn't recognize. She begged Aggie with pleading eyes to come with them and take control, but all Aggie did was laugh at her when Trixi winced and her skin turned red. Trixi's disgust wore her down and made her weak.

After what seemed like an eternity, Trixi only saw the people directly in front of her. She became exhausted from the constant bouncing that she had to do in order to determine who or what was behind her. It was possibly her greatest error because out of nowhere, a scalding hot liquid poured down her back, driving her into an emotional anguish. "Red! Red!"

And as soon as she yelled out her safe word, the touching stopped dead in its tracks. The groping ended. Trixi's body was finally freed from the licks of ravenous mouths. And she couldn't stop the tears from falling. Aggie quickly ascended from her throne and dashed toward Trixi to inquire about her safety. Although it wasn't exactly the attention Trixi had been hoping for, Aggie did finally pay her some attention.

Aggie calmed Trixi's whimpers by gently petting her head and running her fingers through her hair around her face. Although the temperature of whatever was poured on Trixi quickly decreased, the sting remained alive on her flesh. Trixi knew it was wax as soon as the liquid stiffened up quickly.

Guests left Trixi in the care of the stunning woman with the red hair, whose torment she craved mentally but did not receive physically. Finally, she was alone with the beautiful woman.

Aggie embraced the young and vulnerable woman, pressing her lips against Trixi and wrapping her arms around her. The body of Trixi, which was still suspended in the air, swayed from side to side. Aggie removed a chunk of wax from Trixi's back by flicking it off with her finger. "Are you still in the red zone, my love?"

Trixi let out a whimper. The discomfort caused by the wax became less intense. "Can we drop it to yellow?"

While maintaining her pressure on Trixi, Aggie lowered herself and licked one of the erect nipples for a calming and relieving effect. While she attended to Trixi's breast, which was still heaving, she flicked the wax off of her back as she discovered it.

After Aggie had finished scraping away all the wax, Trixi felt the soft touch of her hand as it slid her panties to the side. Aggie's fingers dipped back and forth between the folds of the slippery folds. She wiggled the tip of Trixi's clit in a rapid circular motion, which brought Trixi to the verge of ecstasy.

Because the scene was taking place in an open room, anyone who passed could see the writhing body reach for Aggie's hand. Trixi's hips attempted to buck into Aggie, but they were unsuccessful because of the restraints. Trixi's salacious howl of pleasure mixed with another round of tears, and it echoed in her chamber, bouncing off the three walls.

It appeared deliberate that Aggie's hand moved away from the center of her body just as Trixi began her climax. She lowered her head and put her chin to her chest as her sex burned for more. Trixi had no reason to believe that Aggie would ever let her come.

She inserted a straw into the soda and brought it close to Trixi's mouth. "Drink up, sweetheart."

Trixi, who was thirsty, did so. Aggie exposed her by leaving her hanging. Humility flushed Trixi's cheeks as the chills from the drink sent shivers down her skin. Aggie's friends came, peeking at her work, and then left. Every time someone left the room, Aggie would come back to Trixi and get her almost to the point of climax before stopping. She spent the whole night playing that game.

When the hostess entered the room, she looked around and then announced, "Twenty minutes until closing."

Aggie gave the woman a wave before rising to her feet and strolling over to Trixi. Trixi wanted nothing more than for Aggie to press her lips together one more time hoping to bring her to an orgasm.

Aggie asked, "Do you have anywhere to be? Need to be home for Mommy?"

Her lungs barely had enough air to speak. "No."

"When you are in this position, you address me as Ma'am."

Trixi tried again. "No, Ma'am."

"Much better. Show respect and you get respect."

Aggie freed her ankles by removing the cuffs that had been around them. Trixi's feet felt a tad more stable though her legs gave out from underneath her as Aggie unhooked the wrists. Trixi collapsed to the floor.

"You have twenty minutes to learn to walk again." Without another word, Aggie exited the room, leaving

Trixi to get up and, presumably, dress herself.

Trixi stood and stared down at Justine, who was still crouched down in a very still position. "How in the hell do you do this?"

Trixi was clearly talking to Justine, but there was no response. She didn't even move her head to look at Trixi. She was a well-trained submissive, and she didn't flinch even when her crotch was on display for the whole club.

Aggie's hand briefly touched the damp, uncovered part of her human ottoman when she returned to the room. She saw Trixi on her feet. "You rebound well."

Trixi, feeling blue-balled, scoffed as she yanked her dress off the sofa and slipped into it, wiggling as she tried to get it over her drained body. As she dressed, Trixi aimed a piercing glare at Aggie's heart, indicating that she was more angry than disappointed in the situation.

Her incredibly toned and athletic body strutted over to Trixi. Her fingertips ran over the smooth back of Trixi's jet-black hair, which fell over her back. "You're not broken yet."

Trixi twisted around, the red in her eyes intensifying. "I'm not broken—"

She repeated herself while placing her finger over Trixi's mouth. "You're not broken yet."

Trixi didn't bother to argue about it; instead, she rolled her eyes. She undoubtedly experienced feelings of shatteredness. She left Trixi feeling violated and robbed of her humility. Disappointed that after going through all of that, she didn't even climax. The moment Aggie turned her back on her, Trixi's temper reached an all-time high. "Are you serious? After everything I've done, I don't even get fucked?"

Aggie ignored Trixi's words and gestured for Justine to get dressed after she got up off the floor. Justine dressed herself in a pair of pants and a low-cut blouse without a bra, exposing her pert bosoms. Although Trixi never caught a glimpse of Justine dressed, her beauty was a perfect complement to the air of sophistication that Aggie carried.

When contrasted with them, Trixi's appearance was that of an elegant and alluring lady of the evening, thanks to her revealing black minidress and high heels. Once more, she had the impression that she didn't belong.

They waited for a taxi outside the club. Trixi thought she'd take the next one when it came, being discarded by a cab again. Aggie moved to the middle of the bench seat to make space for Trixi.

Aggie looked out the door when Trixi didn't come in and asked, "You coming or staying to sulk, which is really unflattering?"

It wasn't pouting as much as it was being annoyed. Trixi shook her head, but in the end she complied with Aggie's request and got into the taxi with them. The taxi hurried off into the misty darkness as soon as they shut the door.

During their time in Aggie's club, a rainstorm that had just passed through hit the city. The lights glistened as they reflected off of the wet streets. The city lights flashed into brilliant crystal colors as they interacted with the water drops on the cab window. Trixi leaned her head against the window, and despite the fact that she wasn't actually alone, she felt a sense of isolation.

When Aggie was discussing her forthcoming itinerary, she directed her comments more toward Justine than toward Trixi. During their talk, Justine offered her thoughts and opinions. When Trixi finally heard Justine's husky voice for the first time, Trixi's ears perked up.

During their conversation on Friday concerning their travel, Trixi learned Aggie had the intention of leaving both the city and her. "You're going back to L.A.?"

"Yes, I have work to do," Aggie said, directing her attention toward Trixi.

"And she's going with you?" Trixi referred to Justine without actually using her name. Aggie picked up on the jealousy. One more thing that Trixi vowed she would never have.

"Justine is my partner. She travels with me everywhere."

Trixi shifted her head and attention to the streets of New York as the cab drove through the traffic of the city that never slept. She watched the buildings pass them by as they traveled through the never-ending city. The vibrant nightlife reminded Trixi of Las Vegas with the dazzling lights emanating from all the signs and buildings. Trixi felt a knot in her gut as she paid attentively to the ramblings of a normal couple who were sitting next to her. It made her feel like a filthy whore. The lone squeaky wheel in their otherwise twisted playground.

Aggie realized Trixi's attention was elsewhere, so she gently tucked Trixi's hair behind her ear and brushed it out of her face before placing her hand on Trixi's knee and gently massaging it. Trixi's gaze slid to her hand, then traced her arm.

"What's going on in that pretty head of yours?" Aggie asked.

Trixi counted a million things in the car before saying, "I just don't see how I fit into the middle of this. You. Justine. Me?"

"Stop trying to find the answers to a problem that doesn't exist. You wanted to be in my life. Here you are. This is it, Trixi."

"But you're leaving? How am I in your life?"

"I guess I need to hold your hand a little more. When I said *we* are leaving Friday for Los Angeles, you didn't hear the word *we* in that. I'm still working on the logistics. Justine is easy to explain but you? You take a little more planning. The all-encompassing we means you, darling, as long as you are willing to take this journey with us."

Trixi looked past Aggie to Justine, who blushed and grinned shyly at her. Trixi experienced a surge of youth. Even though it made no sense, she felt like a child. Inwardly, she was burning up with embarrassment. The more she reacted negatively because she misunderstood Aggie's intentions, the less likely she was to become a significant part of Aggie's life. If Trixi wanted to stay with her and, presumably, Justine, she would have to grow up quickly.

Everybody got out of the cab at once and entered Aggie's hotel like it was a scene from a movie. Trixi's gait was brisk as she tried to keep up with the leader's long, gorgeous legs. There was never a time when Justine wasn't trailing her Master by a whole step. The pace was the same as Aggie's. Trixi had to put forth extra effort with her tiny legs to keep up with any of them.

After they were safely inside penthouse one, Justine undressed as she made her way to the bedroom. Trixi, confused as to what she should do next, stood in the midst of the living room. Aggie proceeded in the same direction as Justine.

Trixi hesitated in the living area before making her way to the window, and looked out at the city below. She didn't want to appear too confident by following. Trixi had not been paying attention to what was going on behind her when she felt someone seize her hand. Aggie stood in front of her wearing a black teddy, lacey and see-through.

Trixi gulped down as she tried to control her salivation brought on by the sight of Aggie's breasts. Even if they were not as perky as hers or even Justine's, they were still very lovely, with rosy circles surrounding the points of her nipples that were pressing into the fabric.

She lifted Trixi's chin with her free hand, the other still gripping her palm. "You most certainly require someone to hold your hand. Come to bed, darling."

As Aggie guided Trixi along, a shy smile spread across Trixi's face. With each stride she took, butterflies flit into her stomach, excited at the prospect of them playing together once more. Trixi wanted another shot with her so badly.

Justine, who wore nothing, arranged a line of objects along the foot of the bed. Trixi's suffering didn't appear to be done when she noticed there were two of each item. There were two sets of restraints, as well as toys, that are appealing. As they stood in a line in front of the bed, Aggie finally released her grip on Trixi's hand.

"Justine, love. Remove Trixi's evening dress."

She obliged with Aggie's request by taking the bottom of the dress, sliding it up Trixi's body, and raising it above Trixi's head in a gentle manner. She positioned it so that it elegantly draped over the top of the chair.

"If you thought she did a good job, give her a gentle touch and some kind words to show your appreciation. Not going crazy, but just something to indicate that you approve," Aggie said, instructing Trixi with Justine.

Trixi's mind kept going to the idea of giving Justine a high-five, but she knew in her heart that wasn't what Aggie meant at all. "Nice, thank you."

"On the bed, there is a waist belt, collar, and cuffs. Trixi, place them on Justine."

The cuffs were the first thing she adjusted. At this point, Trixi's reactions to the frightening things she had seen or even experienced had become less extreme. She picked them up with no hesitation and snugged them around her wrists as she watched Justine's eyes follow her and seem to judge Trixi's every action. Not too tightly, she buckled the collar around Justine's neck. There was enough space for two fingers to fit between Justine's skin and the collar.

Trixi couldn't figure out how to fasten the V-shaped belt around her waist, which was made of black leather and buckled in the back. Fearing that Trixi would touch her sex, she fumbled around with the buckles and attempted to insert the wrap-under strap. However, Trixi did touch her. Her lack of maturity was not intentional, but rather the result of her lack of experience.

Aggie helped when she witnessed Trixi's struggle with a simple buckle. Their hands worked in harmony with the belt.

"What are we going to do?" Trixi asked.

"Don't ask questions. Do you see Justine asking questions? Your submissive should trust you enough to wait and see; reap the rewards of whatever sadistic pleasure we want to bestow upon them," Aggie replied.

The end of Trixi's questions. When they finished, they laid Justine out on the bed with her head down on the pillow. Aggie snatched the spares and confined Trixi in the same restraints as Justine.

Trixi received a vibrator from Aggie. An old-fashioned looking grip with a big ball perched on the very top of it. Nothing like the one inside her dresser, underneath all her panties.

She first demonstrated to Trixi how to attach the vibrator to the strap between Justine's legs, then removed it and gave Trixi the chance to try it out on her own.

Trixi continued to make mistakes despite her best efforts to prevent her hands from coming into contact with any area of Justine's sex. As soon as the vibrator was in its correct spot, Aggie gave Trixi instructions to start the vibrator and set it to its lowest setting.

While Justine shimmied her way around the ball and covered her sex, there was a faint mechanical hum that mingled in with her purring.

Aggie whispered while trying to maintain the mesmerizing vibrations she tried to create. "Open her folds and let the magic wand sit on top of her clit."

Trixi's hands reached between Justine and the vibrator, opening her up and forcing the ball against her eager clit. Aggie secured the pleasure wand with a more snug strap. Justine's chest expanded, her nipples contracted, and a prickly sensation spread up and down her skin.

"Now attach the vibrator to yourself, in between your folds, tighten the straps. Just as we did our pet."

Trixi did not show any reluctance when Aggie gave her the command, and she hurriedly attached the second vibrator to herself before putting it on to the lowest level. Trixi, who had not yet laid down, thrust herself onto the vibrator in an eager search for pleasure.

Aggie pulled Trixi's body backward, causing Trixi to fall backwards into the bed, landing with her head on the pillow while the pulsating beat was on top of her sex.

Under the influence of the hypnotic hum, both Justine and Trixi let out groans. Trixi's eyes closed, her eyeballs rolling into the back of her head. This continued until she felt the weight of a third person joining them. When Trixi's lids opened, they revealed Aggie creeping toward them in the space in between their bodies. Both of them gawked admiringly at her breasts as they hung under the exposing teddy.

She drew the blankets up and over them, tucking them in for the night in the manner of a mother putting her children to bed. She fastened Trixi's left hand to her neck cuff and Justine's right hand to hers.

As Aggie snuggled into her pillow, she grumbled softly as she placed their free hands on her sex. "Please me, angels."

Justine and Trixi partnered to reach their respective climaxes while serving their Master. Trixi's groin pressed into the machine between her legs, eagerly anticipating the satisfying release that an orgasm would bring. Aggie sensed her natural impatience and urged her to take it easy and enjoy the ride. The hell with that, Trixi needed to come, and fast.

Trixi rubbed her crotch against the machine while making rapid circles with her fingers to Miss's love bud. The aching on her sex caused her heart rate to quicken and her breathing to become more rapid. Trixi graciously accepted the gift of the old-fashioned fuck stick, despite the fact that she wished it was Madame's hand doing the work. With a powerful grunt, Trixi throbbed beneath it.

Trixi's hips lurched, and as a result, she lost control of her fingers. The ones that should have been making Aggie happy. Trixi trembled and buckled as she attempted to remove the wand from her aching clit, but she was unsuccessful. In her state of extreme orgasmic ecstasy, she was on the verge of convulsing.

Trixi attempted to stop the vibrating wand by ripping her hand away from Aggie, but Aggie grabbed hold of Trixi's hand and used her strength to overcome the weaker girl. "I told you to breathe and wait. Your greed is your worst enemy. I will have mercy on you when you can please me."

What the hell? Trixi knew she had failed immediately. She was completely powerless over her own body. Her entire body trembled uncontrollably as her sex pulsed. The nausea caused her to regurgitate in her throat. Despite this, Justine maintained her composure, occasionally emitting low moans of ecstasy.

Aggie's grip on Trixi's wrist kept her hand between Aggie's legs. Trixi compelled her fingers to work for her in order to alleviate the pain she experienced.

Aggie whispered it so as not to disturb the calm atmosphere in the room. "Free your mind. Place your thoughts on the feeling of your fingertips, not on the pain you are in."

Trixi let out yet another shriek and then yelled, "I can't!" Her pain engulfed her senses in a wave of warmth as it remained in a constant state of climax. "Please, Aggie. Please."

"Are you using your safe word this soon? Are you not woman enough to handle a minor discomfort?"

Trixi's eyes well up with tears. The ones filled with

fear and pain, and the others with the shame of falling behind Justine, who let out her first beautiful shriek of delight.

"Just say the magic word, Trixi, and everything will end. Or let your thoughts wander freely and guide your physical being into this irresistible realm of bliss."

Inconsolable tears streamed down her cheeks and soaked her hair as Aggie's voice encroached on both her sobs and Justine's delight. Trixi loathed Justine because Justine was better than her and because Justine could persevere while she wilted under what was meant to be her rhapsodic overture. She despised herself, along with the predicament she'd made for herself. Trixi's rage clouded her judgment, as she could not remove her hand from between Aggie's knees. Trixi clenched her fist and gave Aggie's clit all the pressure she could summon by grabbing it between her thumb and index finger.

Aggie's voice rose, drowning out Justine's multiple orgasms. Aggie yelled, bursting in spasms as Trixi twisted her wrist. Her body jerked forward as Trixi squeezed her hard, pressing her swollen clit between her fingers and torturing her out of anger.

Trixi felt a sense of satisfaction wash over her, and she temporarily blocked out the physical discomfort caused by the unrelenting vibrating of her own sex. Aggie delighted in Trixi's tasty treat. Aggie pleaded for more torture, not relief, in between gasps for air. "Harder. Use your nails."

Trixi followed Aggie's instructions and sank her claws into the meaty flesh of her victim, acting as if she intended to pull it from her body. The shrieks of a lady, whose climactic cries Trixi previously could not bring about, became putty in her hands when she gave her a tight squeeze. Trixi gave Aggie a taste of her own medicine by continuing the onslaught.

Aggie's body trembled beneath Trixi's grip. Even though she had the power to, she chose not to stop Trixi. On the contrary, she yearned for more. Her voice was trembling and breathy as she commanded, "Bite me. Eat me. Hate me, Trixi. Don't hold back; show me torture."

Trixi used her rage to suppress her discomfort as the vibrator came along with her as she climbed on top of Aggie. With her clit still stuffed between the two fingers, Trixi wanted to taste the creamy discharge she felt around her. Trixi threw off Aggie's blankets and sank to her pleading sex, where she sucked on the sweet and savory cream while tearing at her abused clit with her teeth.

Aggie thrashed upward, her screams echoing off the walls in a resounding chorus of praise for Trixi as a torrent of scorching ejaculation spilled down Trixi's chin and neck.

As her body crashed back down, Trixi heard the inevitable words she knew Aggie would say. "Red, Trixi. Red."

Trixi released her torture. Her teeth and hands ended their assault. Trixi's hands trembled with rage as she switched off the vibrator, yanked it from her body, and hurled it across the room before she calmed down.

Aggie's body unwound on the bed, but her sex continued to quiver with little spasms brought on by her high. With her eyes closed and her head thrown back, her lips gaped wide. She radiated beauty. Trixi loathed Aggie for giving her so much agony, but she eventually understood that Aggie got pleasure from not only inflicting, but also experiencing such suffering herself. Aggie's sexuality not only sought the pain of others, but it required it in order to build up to a crescendo.

As the dynamic shifted, Trixi leaned quietly down. She had figured out how to keep Aggie in line and was no longer scared of using this knowledge. Trixi stroked Aggie's silky hair, moving it away from her face so she could give her an adoring kiss. Trixi desired her affection and the approval of her youth. As she rose, Aggie's lips yearned for Trixi's, peering into the eyes that eventually opened.

A warm grin spread over Aggie's face as she revealed how ecstatic she was about Trixi's ability to be dominant. Trixi paid little attention to the fact that Justine was there in the room as she carried out her plan to torment Aggie. Trixi kissed Aggie once again, this time drawing out of her the response she had hoped for.

Trixi's hands pressed into Aggie's cheeks, drawing her close. Their tongues danced with such vigor that Trixi fell in love. Regrettably, her lips had no restraint and said, "I love you, Aggie."

Trixi recoiled in shock as it came out, but Aggie quickly reached up and collected her. Aggie delivered Trixi a passionate kiss, leaving her gasping for air as she pulled away.

"I guess this was the funeral for your inner good girl, and it was a magnificent one," Aggie added with a chuckle.

Next to them, a writhing girl achieved a pleasant, euphoric high. Trixi withdrew her vibrator with another fling to the ground after turning it off. Aggie pulled Justine close and placed her head on her shoulder as the two of them relaxed.

Still on top of Aggie, Trixi shrugged. "What am I supposed to do with her?"

"Love her as you love me. And I'll love you as I love her."

Trixi bent down and softly kissed Justine on the lips as she slept, before turning back to Aggie, who showed no signs of exhaustion. Trixi felt her heart tugging her toward Aggie, so she went in that direction. As Aggie reached between Trixi's legs to ease the discomfort of the forced orgasm, Trixi's lips tenderly sucked the air out of Aggie's lungs and filled it with hers.

Aggie hushed Trixi as she pressed her pelvis into her palm while muttering into her lips. Aggie spoke to Trixi in a calm voice. "Don't be an eager little girl. The orgasm is just the bonus to something greater. Savor the journey and it will reward you twofold."

After saying that, Trixi shut her eyes, allowing Aggie to lead her into yet another satisfying orgasm in a way that took both of them a substantial portion of the night to achieve. During that time, they experimented with one other by exploring with their hands and lips as Justine slept peacefully next to them. What a lovely way to transition from one phase of life to the next.

# CUP OF COFFEE

The following morning, when Trixi awoke, she turned over in the bed, only to discover that she was alone in it. This was an unfamiliar scene for her to take in. In most cases, her escapades resulted in her being kicked out in the middle of the night; alternatively, if they invited her to sleep over, she crept out of bed and called an Uber. The sun had barely peeked through the luxury hotel drapes. It was unequivocally the morning.

Trixi propped herself up on her elbows and peered through the opening in the door. She strained her ears to pick up any signs of life, which she heard by the gentle clank coming from the other room. After quietly slipping out of bed, her naked body crept slowly toward the door and listened to the distinct voices, which easily distinguished Aggie and Justine from one another. At first, they discussed mundane topics such as their daily routines, their agendas for the day, and what Aggie needed to do.

After that, Trixi overheard Aggie referring to her by name. "I think Trixi will fit in just fine."

"She is adorable; I'll say that," Justine replied.

"Let her sleep. When she wakes up, give her a bath and a massage. Keep her satisfied."

Trixi positioned her ear closer to the opening in the door so that she could better hear Justine's response. "Yes, Ma'am. I'll take good care of her while you're gone."

"If everything goes as planned, I should be back by midday at the latest. After that, we will have time to grab some lunch and go shopping before we leave tomorrow morning. I still need to figure out why Trixi is leaving New York."

The sound of Aggie's heels clicking on the wooden floorboards became increasingly audible with each step she took. Trixi bolted away from the door in a hurry. The clicking grew louder. Before Trixi could return to their bed, Aggie opened the door. "You're up!"

Trixi sputtered, "Yeah," avoiding the truth about her eavesdropping. "I just woke up."

"Good. I've asked Justine to give you a bath, and she'll make sure you're thoroughly taken care of by preparing breakfast for you as well. Around noon, I should be back. We'll go to lunch if you're still here."

Trixi gave a curt nod, unsure of what else to comment on, given that she was speaking so quickly.

"Alright, it's time for me to leave. I'll hopefully see you later?" Aggie posed the statement as a question as she leaned in closer and gently pressed her lips into Trixi's. Trixi inhaled deeply as she accepted the treat that Aggie offered her.

Aggie turned to leave and Justine came in. Aggie gently kissed a nude Justine and murmured, "Take good care of our precious one."

"Yes, Ma'am. See you soon."

As Justine watched Aggie walk away, she cocked her head to the side and looked over her shoulder. Justine flashed a grin as the door closed, and then she went on into the bedroom. "I'll draw you a bath, Ma'am."

Justine, unconcerned about the fact that she and Trixi were both nude, walked by Trixi on the way to the bathroom and opened the tub's faucet. Justine called out from within the room, "Since I'm uncertain of your temperature preference, I'd like your guidance the first time, if I may."

When Trixi stepped into the room, she saw Justine on her knees, with her hand submerged in the water. Everything seemed quite strange and unfamiliar to her. Trixi positioned her fingers underneath the faucet as she bent over the woman. "Just a tad bit hotter."

After making another adjustment to the temperature, Justine waited for Trixi to test it again by placing her hand below the water. "Perfect," Trixi remarked.

It would take some time to fill the bathtub up completely. When Justine stood up, Trixi felt somewhat threatened by her presence due to her height and the impeccable stance she maintained. "Let me help you in."

Trixi made her way into the tub with the help of Justine's gracious hand, and once inside, she sat down in the water that was heated to a comfortable temperature. Trixi's favorite temperature, which left the skin with a little sting. Justine ambled over to the counter and snatched a few different things off it. When Justine returned to the tub, which was still filling, she inquired, "Would you prefer I bathe you from inside or outside the tub?"

Trixi shook her head, perplexed as to what action she ought to take, particularly in regard to Aggie's girlfriend or wife. Trixi was uncertain about the situation with them. When she couldn't decide, Trixi gave a shrug.

When Justine realized how foreign this world was to her, she let out a lighthearted chuckle. "I'm certain you'd be much happier if I were in the tub with you."

Trixi clenched her teeth and exhaled deeply before

waving Justine into the tub with her. Justine climbed in and sat down across from Trixi, back against the opposite side of the tub. Rising water surrounded them. Justine reached around to the back and turned the faucet off.

As soon as she turned her attention back to Trixi, a smile crossed both of their faces. Without a response prepared, Trixi simply watched as Justine hoisted her leg over her shoulder and lathered it with shaving cream. She carefully and slowly raised the razor to Trixi's skin and scraped it across her leg, erasing the very fine stubble. She extended her arm so far up Trixi's thigh that she came within a hair's breadth of touching Trixi's sex.

Trixi let out a sharp exhale of surprise at the near-miss. Just as she had done before, Justine repeated on the other side, this time grazing her midsection and making her gasp again. Justine finished Trixi's legs, then scooted up next to her in the tub, wrapping her legs around her. As Justine shaved under Trixi's arms, their sexes remained forced closely together.

The awkwardness of the situation, along with her sex on fire from being so near to another woman, prompted Trixi to speak so her mind could wander somewhere other than between her legs. "Are you sure Aggie is okay with all of this?"

"Yes, Ma'am. All of it." She stroked over the fragile flesh beneath Trixi's arm with the razor and gave her a little tickle as she went along.

As Trixi drew a breath, her nipples stiffened and perked to attention. "And you like this? Being a slave to her?"

She put her razor down before raising her other arm.

With her head tilted and a sweet grin, Justine reassured her, "I know Ma'am is guiding you into this world and I'm sure after a while, it won't seem so... foreign. Being a little bold here, Ma'am rarely likes me speaking during moments like this. We can chat after I please you if that's alright?"

As Justine leaned into Trixi to lift the other arm, Trixi lowered her head and felt the heat rise in her cheeks. Trixi caressed Justine's leg when she finished and gave her a soft touch. She did this because she remembered what Aggie had said about complementing Justine on a job well done. "Thank you."

"Would you like anything else shaved?" There was a tantalizing arch to Justine's brow as she smiled.

Trixi was on the verge of giving her a yes answer, but she realized she was not yet willing to have Justine and a razor that close to her intimate parts. "I'm good. Thanks."

After retrieving the shampoo and soap, Justine resumed the bathing process until everything, including Trixi's sex, which she tormented with her fingers, was clean. Trixi could get used to this life.

Trixi felt quite needy after her connection with Justine. It made no difference to Trixi that it wasn't Aggie. Especially after Justine had finished drying her off, she yearned for a release like there was no tomorrow. Trixi inhaled deeply into Justine after a little pause between her legs, and she came dangerously close to leaning into her hand so that Justine might take her. Aggie was accurate that Trixi's worst enemy was her greed.

In the final moments of her drying off ritual, Justine kissed Trixi on the belly before getting to her feet.

"Ma'am said you'd like a massage."

She let out a sigh of longing as her chest expanded. "Oh, God. Yes."

"Full body? With stimulation?" she whispered.

Trixi expressed her assent to the proposition by making a low humming sound. When Justine brought Trixi to the bed, she lay her down on her stomach. Her fingers dug deep into the muscle tissue of Trixi's neck and shoulders before moving on to her back and continuing the process. The moans were not sexual in nature; rather, they released naturally by the hard, tough grip Justine had on her.

After completing one side, Justine rolled Trixi over and began at her feet, working her way up to the thighs. When she finally reached the core of Trixi, she began massaging the warm folds to reawaken Trixi's desires. She then positioned a small vibrator on Trixie's clit and engaged it to deliver a low and steady hum while Justine's hands worked their way upward.

Trixi wiggled her way into the vibrator; however, Justine paused her greed with a gentle word and, by applying pressure to Trixi's yearning pelvis to prevent her from bucking into it. "Breathe."

After saying that, Trixi lowered her head and went into a meditative state, allowing everything to unfold as it should. She allowed Justine to finish the relaxation of her body, rubbing her breasts and caressing her nipples between her fingertips. The vibrator delivered the other portion of Trixi's massage, which led to her gradually reaching her peak.

When Justine completed her massage of Trixi's shoulders, neck, and temples, she turned her attention back to the one area still not satisfied. She hushed Trixi and asked, "May I ride out this orgasm on your stomach, Ma'am?" in a soothing voice.

Even though she didn't know what it meant, Trixi hummed her answer, and Justine climbed onto the bed. To Trixi's surprise, Justine had her very own vibrator perched atop her clit. Justine turned up both of them so they could roll through the waves of ecstasy in the increasing ambient heat.

Trixi slipped her hand between them to Justine's sex and pressed the vibrator firmly against the sensitive bud while simultaneously grabbing Justine's breast with the other hand. So the two of them were singing a wonderful duet together, Trixi gently squeezed her nipple between her fingers as they complimented each other in song.

After basking in the wonderful ecstasy for a short while, Justine eventually got up from the bed. "I'll prepare you breakfast. Do you have any allergies I should know, or is there anything you absolutely despise?

Trixi found it extremely strange to go on a talk about food so soon after they had sex, but she was speechless and could only murmur that anything would be acceptable. Justine left the room without covering her naked body with anything. In the next room, Trixi could hear the clattering of a pan being placed on the stove.

Before getting out of bed, Trixi took a moment to collect her thoughts over the previous two days by exhaling deeply. She desired to have a romantic connection with Aggie, but she later learned that Aggie was already in a relationship with a subservient partner. Aggie invited Trixi to join them in a naughty threesome in which she just had Aggie's sex slave make love to her in Aggie's absence. It was impossible for this to be her life. A few days ago, Trixi was a privileged brat who was wasting her life away by doing nothing productive. What a rapid pace life took.

Justine popped her head inside the room. "Are you alright, Ma'am?"

"Yeah. I'll be there in a second."

While Trixi got out of bed, Justine left her alone once more. Trixi had the impression that putting on her dress, which she had thrown over the chair, would make her appear as low-class as a prostitute. Though in that hotel, Trixi wouldn't have been very cheap at all.

After wriggling into her little Gucci dress and donning her soiled underwear from the previous day, Trixi joined Justine in the living room. It's hard to imagine putting on dirty clothes after getting cleaned up so nicely by Aggie's… Trixi was clueless about the true nature Justine's relationship to Aggie.

"Are you and Aggie married? Or just—" As Trixi entered the living room, she questioned.

"Married; engaged. Mutual commitment. It's all the same." Justine sat the plate of eggs on the dining table.

Trixi sat before the dish of eggs and freshly buttered bread. Justine set a glass of orange juice next to Trixi on the table. "Do you mind if I sit and drink my coffee?"

"Sure." Trixi stood as Justine sat, but Justine immediately stood back up.

"What do you need, Ma'am?"

"Coffee. If there's more."

As Justine returned to the kitchen, her head slumped to her chest. "I'm sorry. I should have asked. Let me get it. What do you take in it?"

"Black." Trixi sat down once again and took a taste of the eggs, which were surprisingly tasty.

When Justine returned with the coffee, she said, "Anything else, Ma'am?" before resuming her seat.

Trixi chuckled. "No. Because I grew up with maids and butlers, you might think I'd be used to the whole *Ma'am* thing and being served, but it seems a little strange when you're.... naked."

Justine sat down across from Trixi, ignoring the comment about her being naked. "Permission to speak freely?"

"Sure."

"Madame thinks that you will be a great addition to our loving family. So do I. Stick around. This will quickly become second nature to you."

"Am I allowed to ask questions? Talk to you. I don't know what to do with you, which might sound strange." Trixi's cheeks burned from how stupid her questions sounded.

"Ma'am wants you to be my second Mistress, someone to keep me occupied while she works. Now, with that out of the way, whatever you want. My hard limits are—" When Justine saw Trixi's eyes narrow at the words, she told her, "Hard limits are things I don't want to do. How knowledgeable are you about BDSM?"

"Pretty much nothing besides whips and chains."

Laughing, she propped her chin on her hand. It seems the student had become the teacher. Not to worry, Ma'am. As a starting point, I'll describe the kink that I really dislike. I'd want to remove my discretion filter and ask you not to pee or crap on me."

Trixi cut her off. "Good, because that won't ever

happen."

Justine laughed, their friendship growing with each bite Trixi took of her breakfast. "I'm not into knife play or suffocation, but I do love pain. I do better with servitude, here to please you with all the menial tasks like keeping the house clean. Ma'am likes her privacy, so most of her domination takes place behind closed doors, though she has teased me in public a few times. We don't discuss BDSM in public or in front of others, including friends."

Trixi slid the dish aside, pulled the coffee cup forward, and fiddled with the rim with her fingers. "How did you get into this?"

"With Ma'am? Or in general?"

"With Aggie," Trixi stated. She wanted to know their story.

"I was working for a woman in France at a club, similar to where we went last night, but for both men and women. Ma'am was in town for two weeks and spent most nights at the club. After our first time together, she requested me each time afterward. At the end of her trip, she offered me something more. Bought out my contract and I returned to the states."

"What did she offer you?"

"Her love and devotion for mine." Justine stood from her chair, still naked, as she grabbed for Trixi's plate and brought it into the kitchen. When she returned to the table, she remarked, "I'm sure it wasn't in your plans to spend the night; do you want to go home and change, or would you like to see if anything I have would be appropriate for the day?"

To which Trixi said, "You mean you actually wear clothes?"

"If I had a choice, no." She nodded and then pointed toward the bedroom.

Trixi accompanied her back to the room and watched as she opened a dresser drawer to reveal a few different outfits. Justine's attire comprised of jeans and cute tops, in contrast to Aggie's professional attire. Aggie wore business suits.

Trixi found an option that would work, even if it meant spending the day in heels, and she went with it. Trixi ditched the skintight dress she had been wearing in favor of a dress modeled after Justine's more laid-back style. However, it still wasn't Trixi's manner of dress. At least she no longer had the appearance of a prostitute.

# STUPID GIRL

A fter spending the better part of a day getting to know Justine, Trixi had the impression that the two of them made a better match than she did with Aggie. In addition to learning about Justine, Trixi had a strong desire to learn more about Aggie, the third and most crucial member of their trio. What gave her joy, what she loved, and what she disliked? Trixi had only a few vague ideas about Aggie's serious and complicated personality.

Close to two o'clock, Justine received a text message. When she finished reading it, she got up from the couch and kneeled in front of the door, much like she did when Trixi first entered the hotel room, but this time she did not have a blindfold on.

Trixi received a text as well. **Will you be at the hotel when I get in?**

She replied. **Yes, watching the naked woman waiting for you.**

There was another text. **Good, because I missed you.**

Trixi responded to that message. **Am I supposed to be naked on my knees too?**

Almost immediately after Trixi had pushed the send button, the door unlocked with a click. Aggie walked into the opening and secured the door behind her with a quick turn of the knob. She gently stroked Justine's head before bending down to give her a tender kiss on the cheek. She dropped her bag on the counter as Justine got to her feet.

As she walked toward Trixi on the couch, Aggie

said, "I might have liked you naked, but I'll take you just being here." She smirked as she saw Trixi's stylish clothes. "And you're dressed like our sweet Justine?"

She leaned over the couch and gave Trixi a kiss on the cheek, just like she did with her naked pet. Trixi quipped, "How was your day, honey?"

Aggie flicked Trixi's head at the comment, then stood up, pulled off her blazer, and gave it to Justine to hang up. The naked one took the jacket and walked out of the room, while Aggie sat down next to Trixi on the couch and put her hand on Trixi's knee.

"I am Davey-free and hungry as hell," Aggie sighed as she sat back on the couch. She was a far cry from the uptight, classy chick Trixi had seen at the loft the day before. Aggie cocked her head to speak closely with Trixi. "Did Justine please you today?"

"Yeah." To be honest, Trixi didn't anticipate that topic of discussion right away. With a wry grin on her face, she said, "Very much so."

"Good, and you rewarded her for a job well done?"

"Yeah. She—" Trixi's cheeks became a little pink.

"We have to work on your prudishness."

"I'm not a prude. This is just a little surreal, that's all. I'm still taking everything in."

"Did Justine have an orgasm?" With questions regarding Trixi's day with Justine, Aggie's frank honesty caught her off guard.

"Yes. I made her come."

She patted Trixi's knee. "Good girl."

Immediately after she had stood back up, Justine entered the room. Aggie brushed by her, her hand touching the woman's stomach. Aggie uttered a grateful thank you in a hushed tone before vanishing.

They both heard Aggie yell as Justine entered the kitchen. "Justine, get dressed. I'm famished."

She responded to Aggie in the other room with an inaudible "Yes, Ma'am," but Trixi heard it and it sounded almost as if she didn't want to go with Aggie. Justine made her way through the living room and then disappeared from view. Trixi patiently awaited their return, sitting on the couch.

Trixi's ears perked up when she heard the familiar groans. She crept down the hallway and peered around the door frame to see Aggie wearing a strap-on while Justine was bent over the bed and being taken from behind. Trixi bit her lower lip together so they wouldn't be able to hear her as she watched them indulge in a moment of fleeting pleasure.

"Don't just stand there like a peeping Tom. It's creepy. Come in if you want to watch," Aggie spoke up without so much as glancing in the doorway's direction. Her sole focus being on making Justine happy.

Trixi exhaled the breath she had been holding and entered the bedroom, where she climbed up on the bed to get a better view of Justine as she reached her peak from Aggie's rubber penis. Justine's head tilted upward, and she let out a series of low groans of pleasure as her jaw dropped. Aggie drew Justine's hair in her fist and pulled it back, kissing her and drawing out the last breaths of Justine's orgasm with two hard thrusts.

While Trixi watched them enjoy themselves, she fidgeted nervously and felt a prickling sensation between her legs. Trixi, not being greedy, enjoyed both the show and the aftermath, during which Aggie referred, "My beautiful Justine. You delight me so."

As she laughed, she smacked Justine on the ass. "Now, get dressed and stop making me wait for my food. You are not sustenance."

Justine and Trixi smiled at each other, understanding their respective histories and roles in the relationship, even as Trixi continued to vacillate between feeling like an integral part of the equation and being more of an observer.

Trixi wriggled her way out of bed and made her way to the bathroom, where she observed Aggie disrobing. It surprised Trixi to find a scar on the side of her waist, as she had never noticed it there before. She had little time to devote to exploring this woman's body, so whenever she had the opportunity, she marveled at it.

"Where did that come from?" Trixi asked, tracing her index finger along the scar.

As Aggie shooed Trixi's hand away from the scar, she planted a passionate kiss on Trixi's cheek. "Battle wounds from protecting my flock."

Trixi leaned against the door frame, which prevented her from having any privacy while she changed. "Did you mean it about traveling back to California with you?"

"If you'd like. I wouldn't bring someone in here for a night or two if I didn't think they'd stay. We'd like you to come but will understand if you don't want," Aggie said as she pulled a tank top over her head.

Suddenly, Trixi felt Justine's weight pressing up on her from behind. Snuggling up to Trixi, she wrapped her arms around her waist. "Yes, we both would like you to join us."

"I'll need to get clothes from the house. I don't know what to say to my mom—"

Aggie stifled Trixi's chatter by putting her finger over the younger woman's lips. "Seriously, my loves. I need to eat something. We'll talk at lunch. Now, away with both of you. I need to finish dressing."

Justine yanked Trixi away from the entrance by snatching her hand. As Justine led Trixi out of the bedroom, she remarked, "Aggie can get cranky very quickly when she is hungry and needs to eat. Just a friendly word of caution."

They waited for Aggie to come out, dressed pretty casually in some jeans, a tank top, and a jacket, and who was also extremely hot, if Trixi were to say so herself. "Wow. So this is what non-business Aggie looks like. If you weren't starving, I'd molest you."

"Later, love. First food. Please."

They followed her out, with Justine trailing her by two steps and Trixi coming close to matching Aggie's normal walking stride despite her shorter legs. They crammed into a taxi, with Aggie getting in first, followed by Trixi, and then lastly Justine. Aggie leaned toward the driver as the door closed behind her. "One Eleven Murray Street."

Aggie murmured, exhaling deeply as she leaned back. "I am so glad to be rid of that little prick."

"Davey? Yeah, he tried to push himself on me the other day. Any more forceful, I'd have made him a soprano," Trixi responded.

Aggie said, "You should have told me I'd have made his little prick even smaller."

The trip, which was less than a half mile down the road and took less than ten minutes in the car, was one that Trixi knew Aggie would prefer not to take on foot. They quickly exited the taxi and entered the restaurant, where Aggie placed an order for three fruit-infused sparkling drinks as soon as the waiter came to our seat. "And an orange muffin right away. I don't think I can wait for a meal."

Even before their drinks were ready, the waiter returned with a fresh muffin. After taking a bite, she moaned with pleasure as the food settled into her growling stomach. She started babbling about how Davey's new handler was late and completely disorganized.

Finally, she tossed up her hands. "I'm done bitching about work. Please tell me something that will make me smile."

"The Linhof Master Technika arrived at the house yesterday," Justine said, which sounded like a foreign language to Trixi.

Trixi remained quiet, listening to Aggie's reply with a laugh. "Baby, that makes you smile, not me. I am sure the camera will be a wonderful addition to your collection."

"But you're smiling, anyway." Justine tapped on Aggie's arm.

Trixi's sadness intensified as she watched them interact romantically with one another. She yearned for a special someone to share things with, the tender touches and adorable smiles. Being a third may have been advantageous for Trixi's sexual life, but she had no idea how to act around her romantic partners.

When Aggie turned to Trixi, she asked, "What do you have for me?"

"I'm wearing Justine's underwear and they are a little tight," Trixi said with a straight expression after scanning around for listening ears.

Aggie buried her face in her hand, giggling as she shuddered at the thought. She extended her hand and gently stroked Trixi's cheek. "Oh, baby. You're adorable." When their food arrived, Aggie took a big mouthful of her zucchini noodles with loads of peppers on top. "Let's talk about California now," she replied, with another pleasurable groan to settle her empty stomach.

She took another bite, chewing and swallowing before speaking. "I mentioned to your father this morning that you wanted to grab a ride home with us tomorrow. So, he is expecting you home. What you do after I get you home is essentially on you. Being an adult, I assume you come and go as you please?"

Trixi nodded.

"Good. We'd like you to stay with us. You can come and go as you wish. Stay as long as you'd like. Though I can't have you bringing your friends around our house. I worry about our safety. Plus, you're a VanPelt. I have that to worry about, too. If you weren't the boss's daughter, this would be a lot easier."

Trixi grinned, happy to see she made an impression on Aggie. "You want me to move in?"

"That makes you all too happy. We need to keep this arrangement under the table. Whatever you need to do to keep the questions off where you're spending your time. Too many questions usually will cause a slip-up and you'll forget what you said two days prior."

"Got it. I'm gonna need to go home to pick up a few things. Nothing much. Shouldn't take more than five or ten minutes."

"You should probably spend the night at home. Tell your mother you're leaving. Not make it too worrisome about you running back to California on a moment's notice," Justine added.

"Good thought," Aggie agreed.

Trixi got the impression that they were trying to distance themselves from her after she learned their plans included a contradiction, and that they intended for her to spend the night somewhere other than with them. Throughout the remainder of the meal, Trixi maintained her silence. When the check arrived, Trixi did not even attempt to take it. Neither did Justine. Aggie took out her card, tossed it in the wallet, and set it aside.

As Aggie and Justine left the restaurant, they discussed where they should stop for some quick retail therapy. When the cab arrived, Aggie got in first. Trixi ushered Justine in ahead of her by waving her in. After Justine jumped into the cab, Trixi closed the door behind her and started walking away.

The door opened, Aggie yelling from the inside. "Trixi, what are you doing?"

"Going home," she said, not looking back.

"Stop acting like a child," Aggie told Trixi as the taxi door shut behind her on a busy street in Manhattan. Both Aggie and Justine were back out of the cab and standing on the sidewalk.

Trixi flailed her arms around, fuming at the fact that she brought up her age each time something went wrong with them. Aggie stomped toward her as the cab drove away, but Justine didn't move an inch. Trixi pressed her fists into her hips. "Stop treating me like a child when you don't agree with how I'm feeling."

"You are acting like a spoiled brat because you don't like how lightly we need to tread with you. Do you think it wise to tell my boss that my wife and I are snogging his daughter, who is half my age? I think not. So stop the crap, Trixi. We all are trying to find the best way to include you, but I do think it would be wise for you to go home. Decide if this is what you want, truly." Aggie called for a taxi, which arrived at the scene almost immediately. She crammed herself into the cab, and Justine followed her. The driver then sped off.

The atmosphere inside the taxi was not at all what Aggie had anticipated for the rest of her afternoon. Aggie was absolutely overjoyed when she found out that Trixi had spent the entire day with Justine and that the two of them had the opportunity to get to know each other. She had spent the morning basking in the wonderfulness of a new love, and throughout the entire time, she had been thinking about Trixi.

What irked her the most was how quickly Trixi's disposition could change, as well as the fact that Trixi's immaturity had caused her to misinterpret a simple suggestion as a rejection. How incredibly mistaken Trixi could have been in this situation. Aggie knew that having Trixi in her life would make it extremely challenging to differentiate between their professional and personal relationships. Aggie decided to give it a try because she had developed such a strong crush on the younger woman that she yearned for her to join the household in order to feel more complete.

Without looking at anything in particular, Aggie stared out the taxi window in order to clear her mind. Justine placed her hand on Aggie's leg and gave her a very light squeeze. "Are you sure you really want to do this with Trixi?"

While she said yes, a ping of doubt entered her mind. Adding Justine to her marriage had not been a mistake; Aggie needed to trust her instincts with Trixi, who would be her greatest challenge.

After becoming familiar with the BDSM way of life, Aggie had a long history of inviting numerous submissives into her bedroom throughout her life. Over the course, she had shaped many into subservient ways of life. And women like Justine helped her pick up a few new skills along the way. Her first wife was just as dominating as she was, and she adored newcomers to the submissive world. A virginal and fearful submissive possessed a certain allure that was utterly captivating. On the other hand, Trixi did not exhibit any submissive behavior at all. Aggie accepted the challenge of eradicating that aspect of herself, despite the fact that she may not yet have accepted her position as dominant.

"Do you think she has it in her?" Aggie asked as she directed her attention to Justine.

"This morning, she was so unsure of herself. No confidence. The night before, I could see it, but it appeared to emanate from a darker place. Not from controlling the scene, but from an uncontrollable emotion. I don't want to say anger because I don't think she was mad. Something else."

"Did you feel unsafe?"

Justine shook her head. "No. Not at all. Honestly, I enjoyed our day together. I know you are quite smitten with her. She did bring you to your safe word. I'm sure that pleased you because I haven't heard you use those words since Melody."

Aggie made a motion with her hand to indicate that she did not want to hear that name. Aggie didn't like to talk about her first wife or what had happened to her, despite the fact that she loved her very much. "Don't. And yes, Trixi provided me with a blissful release. It has been quite a while since I felt something that intense. I do believe she has what it takes to be a good Mistress, if I could just reign in her impudent attitude."

Trixi hailed her own cab to take her home. And sulked. Just as she got into the cab, the sky opened up and rain poured. It did nothing more than slow down traffic and cause her arrival time to be delayed at the loft where Trixi's mother had been standing in the living area, hemming a stunning gown with a lot of sparkling embellishments.

Drenched from head to toe in clothes that were not hers, Trixi looked haggard and battered when she stepped through the door. Instinctively, her mother's focus shifted to her. "I was worried about you."

"I'm fine," Trixi exclaimed as she shook off the wetness like a puppy that had just come inside after being outside in the rain. "I'm going to my room."

"Hey, stop for two seconds." Rachel placed down her tools of the trade and walked toward her daughter. "Are you really fine? Your father told me you wanted to go back to L.A. You've been gone for two days. Should I worry?"

When Trixi should have nodded yes, she shook her head in a negative response. "No, I'm perfectly fine. I just miss the sun and the beach. I'm going to my room to pack."

Rachel yelled as Trixi headed towards her room. "A bouquet of flowers arrived for you. I put them in your room."

After she had finished entering the room, Trixi turned around and saw the bouquet of wrapped flowers that was already sitting on her bed. She removed the card from it and read the words scrawled on it. After seeing that Davey had signed the note, Trixi promptly crumpled it up and threw it away, along with the flowers.

After getting out of the shower and removing the lotion and traces of sex that Justine had left on Trixi throughout the day, Trixi felt revitalized enough to contemplate her future with Aggie. Sitting on the bed, she saw the discarded bouquet. Among the several posies, the bouquet had three white roses as its centerpiece. Trixi rescued the bouquet of roses from the garbage and arranged them neatly on the chest of drawers.

Up until that moment, it seemed like everyone was having a good time. Orgasms were shared by everyone, and Trixi had seen little of the BDSM world that Aggie said she lived in, other than how she hung from the ceiling at the club. If that was Aggie's idea of kink, then she needed some lessons since, despite the fact that she admitted to being a sadomasochist, she had experienced nothing that screamed pain since she'd been with Aggie.

Trixi took a glance at the flowers that were displayed on the dresser, and her mind immediately went back to the scene when she had been watching Aggie fuck Justine. Trixi took a photograph of the three flowers and sent it to Aggie, who immediately grasped the meaning of what Trixi had seen.

Aggie replied via a text message. *Yes, my love. The three of us. It pained me to scold your beautiful face, but you have to trust me and know I have your best interest at heart. We'll pick you up at 8 A.M. Be ready and no mile-high club. We have a full plane.*

# DRIVE YOU HOME

When Trixi got a text message informing her they were only 10 minutes away, she realized she needed to make haste. Despite the fact that Aggie was not her Mistress, she detested being kept waiting whenever possible. After her meltdown the previous afternoon, Trixi did not have the finest relationship with them. Aggie was difficult to please and insisted on getting what she wanted. While she was unapologetic about her rules, Aggie made one exception for Trixi about the no-drama rule. Trixi felt confident it wouldn't slide again.

Trixi was well aware that she needed to clean up her act if she planned on being a part of this, and she set about doing just that. She was on the razor's edge between staying and being kicked to the curb. Because of this, Trixi hurried.

Trixi kissed her mother on the cheek and said, "Gotta run." She had a few things in a bag and a change of clothes. "I don't want to keep Ms. Helvete waiting."

"Have a safe flight, baby. Call me when you get to your father's."

"Will do." Trixi ran out of the loft and slammed on the elevator's down button as if that would make it open quicker. When the elevator door opened, there was only a young girl inside. Trixi pushed the lobby button, and the door shut. The girl, who was only 14 or 15, reached across Trixi to press a floor number.

The button for the lobby glowed on the wall. It was unnecessary to press anything else at this point. Trixi put out her hand to halt the girl. "Stop. I'm in a hurry." The small girl smirked maliciously as she hopped around Trixi and pushed Trixi's hand away. The small girl flung her hands over all the buttons and pushed roughly half of the floors.

Blood boiled in Trixi's veins. "Are you fucking kidding me, you little shit?"

Trixi felt like kicking the girl back to the south because of the girl's laugh, which had such a strong rural drawl. "Imma just havin' some fun."

The elevator made a stop at each and every floor. The door opened and closed many times as it continued its journey down the shaft. If Trixi had lived on, say, the fourth level, things would not have been so horrible. There were over thirty of them that Trixi had to sit through, and this little brat smiled every time the door opened and closed.

"You do not understand the amount of crap I am going to get for being late because of you." Trixi said, while waiting for the door to open and close for the umpteenth time. She quietly pleaded with the building management to institute a minimum age of eighteen policy.

Her thick, raspy voice said, "My Daddy's important. He's a country singer. Real popular."

This young girl did not want to compete in a piss-off with Trixi. She did not care who this tall, lanky girl's father was, as music would not be where it was without Trixi's father. He was music royalty. "I don't care who your fucking dad is. You've made me late and I have a very pissed-off girlfriend right now, which makes me very pissed off too. So if you say another word to me right now, I'll kick your little scrawny ass all the way back to the swamps of Louisiana."

"I'm from Tennessee, not Louisiana," the girl said as she pumped her chest with confidence.

As the lobby door opened, Trixi pressed her lips together to stifle the temptation to strike the youngster. Instead, Trixi dashed out the door while dragging her backpack behind her. A girl's voice sounded off in the elevator. "Bye. Nice meetin' ya!"

Trixi hurriedly pushed through the lobby entrance and made her way to the waiting car. Trixi ducked inside as the driver opened the rear door for her. As she leaned back in the seat next to Aggie, her defense was already in motion. "Do not say anything about me being late. Some kid pressed every floor in the elevator. I swear I wanted to punch her in the face."

"Temper. Temper. It's fine, love. I am very glad you decided to join us." Aggie leaned forward and welcomed Trixi by pressing her lips to hers. She whispered before pulling away, "If Justine is to be yours too, show her love and respect."

Trixi nodded, then reached over and give Justine a gentle kiss like Aggie had.

Justine grinned. "Thank you, Ma'am."

They crammed as many people as they could onto one of Trixi's father's private planes. Michael Stuart, a songwriter who worked for ViP Music Group, accompanied them on their journey. After achieving success in country music on stage, he chose to pursue a career in songwriting instead. Alongside him were his two children, one of which was a young man of around seventeen years of age, and the other was the young brat from the elevator. When Trixi watched the girl gloating with a bounce in her step, it caused her to grimace.

"You've got to be shitting me," Trixi said as they were boarding the aircraft. In the two seats that faced forward, Trixi sat next to Aggie, while Justine faced toward the two of them.

The Stuart family boarded the aircraft on the opposite side of the cabin from them. Aggie welcomed the family. "Michael. Glad to see you again."

"Agatha. You know my kids, Mickey and Megan."

The young man made a casual gesture of waving his hand. Megan, on the other hand, stuck her tongue out at Trixi as she passed them. Trixi wanted to chase her down and smack her, but decided it wasn't worth her effort. She prayed that the young tween would be quiet and not make a ruckus. At the very rear of the plane, behind everyone else, there were guys dressed in business attire with their briefcases open.

Due to the large number of passengers, Trixi had to maintain her discretion. Putting in her earphones and listening to her favorite music, or more specifically, her favorite album of all time, Benjamin Britten's War Requiem, was the most effective way for her to keep herself from expressing any of her feelings toward Aggie. This was a beautiful classic opera with some very breathtaking choral passages that sent shivers up Trixi's spine. It nearly didn't sound human. It was far more pleasant to listen to this than the uneducated-sounding Southern speech coming from the person sitting opposite from her.

Aggie and Justine passed the time on their flight by reading. One of the most significant differences between their ages. Justine fetched a book from her bag titled *For By Grace*, written by Adrian J. Smith. The book's cover depicted a woman brandishing a firearm and appeared to be an entertaining piece of literature. Aggie, on the other hand, was carrying what appeared to be a more solemn book, written by Sarah Waters and titled *Tipping The Velvet*. Trixi's ignorance of literature meant she was unfamiliar with both, but she was a veritable walking encyclopedia of classical music.

Even if nobody actually spoke, Trixi might not have realized it because her favorite symphony was playing quite loudly in the background. Trixi cast a sleepy peek over her shoulder, which was directly across from her, and saw her adversary dozing out while resting her head on her father's shoulder. When Trixi shifted her attention back to her two traveling companions, Aggie came up close to her and removed one of her headphones so that she could give it a listen.

When Aggie heard something unexpected, her eyes widened and her forehead raised. In a low voice, she said, "I would have expected some rock music from you, not an opera."

Trixi drew nearer, her voice a perfect match for hers. "I am full of surprises."

Aggie's voice lowered even more. "I can't wait to discover them."

As soon as the plane landed in Los Angeles, all the passengers found automobiles waiting for them, including the Bentley that Trixi's father had arranged to have delivered to his daughter. Trixi's driver, Paolo, leaned on the car door as he welcomed her with a warm hug. Trixi waited until everyone else got into their cars, and then she turned her attention to Aggie and Justine as they dragged their own luggage to their middle-class vehicle, which did not have a driver.

Trixi snapped her fingers. "Paolo, go help them."

"Yes, Ma'am," he said.

Her driver and personal butler in Los Angeles hurried up to her favorite people and assisted them with their luggage, snatching it out of their hands.

Mostly from waiting in front of Trixi's room for someone to enter or for some idiot to do anything she didn't want, Paolo learned all there was to know about Trixi, including the list of her conquests. Over the years, he had been her go-to confidant whenever she sneaked in late or the time they caught her with illegal substances. Many times, he was the one to take the blame for Trixi. He was the person Trixi loved more than anybody else in the world.

While Paolo was loading the car, Trixi made her way over to Aggie in a self-assured manner. When Aggie saw how desperate and alluring Trixi's eyes were, she gave off the impression that she wanted to push Trixi away. Trixi thanked Paolo in his native language as he closed the trunk. "Obrigada."

He stepped away, and Trixi said to Aggie, "I know you said discretion and privacy, but when that man took the fall for much of my troubled youth, he is trustworthy. But... I will let you realize that on your own. I'll play by your rules and see you in a few days, I guess."

Trixi spun around and waved goodbye with an outstretched arm. "Paolo, let's roll out, Mister. How about a bucket of chicken on the beach, minha amigo?"

"Wait!" Aggie said behind her.

As soon as Trixi turned around to look at her again, a smirk formed on her face, and she took a step forward to approach Trixi head-on. "You sure?"

"Positive. They really should have deported his ass like five times already for the shit I have done."

She drew Trixi's attention to her own and gently kissed her on the lips. "You are going to be the death of me."

"I hear that a lot," Trixi said. As Aggie made her way toward her vehicle, Trixi trailed after her to say her goodbyes to Justine. "When you want my smart ass at your house, call me."

Trixi made her way back to Paolo's town vehicle with a brisk jog so that Paolo could take her to the beach where she could indulge in a bucket of fatty chicken while relaxing with her feet in the sand. Trixi needed to get away from the crowded and noisy metropolis for a while, since she desperately needed some beach therapy.

Trixi and Paolo ate their meal on the sand in front of her father's beach house after making a speedy trip through the drive-through lane at Kentucky Fried

Chicken. Trixi kicked off her Dr. Martens and buried her toes into the sand while pulling the bottoms of her jeans up higher on her calves. As had occurred several times in the past, Paolo sat next to her while wearing his suit and handed Trixi a thigh from the bucket.

"Paolo, it's nice to be home. I've missed you."

With a very heavy Portuguese accent, which Trixi had become accustomed to understanding over the years, even when he said words or phrases improperly, he said, "Is nice you are home, too, Ma'am. Is lonely without you in California. New York too big for a little girl."

"Paolo, I'm not a little girl anymore. You know that."

"Oh, I do. Two pretty girls you have. My, my. Too many to handle you."

"And we discuss neither of them. Like I'll cut out your tongue if you say anything about them. Aggie is one of my father's employees. It would not be good if he found out."

Paolo zipped his lips with his fingers. "I cut my own for you if I do. No, Ma'am. I no say nothing. Though I think they are beautiful."

Paolo filled Trixi in on the latest goings-on at home while she was away, including the fact that her father had invited a couple of women around for dinner. Her father would have gone out for his desserts if Trixi had been present, but since the house was empty apart from the maids and the butlers, nobody of whom dared to say a thing, he brought his delicacies home from his evening romps.

The fact that her father had extramarital affairs was common knowledge. There was no hiding it from them. It was the industry. Sex was more prevalent than the common cold. The only things that flowed faster than sex in the music industry were drugs and alcohol. Trixi was genuinely shocked by the fact that she avoided the latter.

Trixi had an insatiable need for sex. She despised and cherished it in equal measure. It was one reason she left California and went to New York, where she didn't know anyone, to take a break. She cut her brief period of abstinence short when she began a relationship with Aggie and Justine.

Rachel, Trixi's mother, had had her fair share of boytoys in her life. It confused Trixi as to why her parents continued to be married, despite the fact that both of them were involved in extramarital relationships. Her parents lived on opposite ends of the country, so she assumed that the only thing keeping them together was the mountain of paperwork required to dissolve their marriage. The more she contemplated it, the more appealing the idea of remaining married yet leading different lifestyles seemed.

As the sun dropped on the beach, Trixi found herself missing Aggie. Trixi recognized the symptoms of her compulsive tendencies and asked Paolo to take her to the waxing salon she frequented most often. She wanted to be ready for anything Aggie planned to do when she met her and Justine in a few days.

When Trixi arrived at her quaint estate in The Hills, a team of employees waited for her outside the front door to meet her. They gushed over the princess and made her feel extremely welcome in her lovely home. It was as if she were royalty, since everyone kept asking her if she needed anything or if she wanted to eat.

Trixi could hear the gravelly tones of her father's voice coming from the other room. "Is that my baby?"

"Yeah, Daddy!" Trixi said as she made her way through the rest of the home to the music room. Michael Stuart played the piano, and another of her father's proteges stood by.

When Martin saw his daughter, he walked around the room and embraced her with his enormous arms. "I hope New York did you well."

"You can say that," Trixi replied. Trixi took a long, intent glance at the girl who was standing next to Michael at the piano as she peaked behind him. "Who's the pop princess?"

He took Trixi by the hand and guided her toward the others. "Trixi, this is Miranda Valentine. She has quite of few number ones thanks to Michael here. Miranda, doll, this is my daughter Trixi."

Trixi realized why her father referred to Miranda as his "doll" when she saw her father's hand linger a bit longer than usual on Miranda's back. Trixi was not at all foolish, and if her father believed she couldn't see beyond the niceties, she would continue to entertain him by taking whatever she could get her hands on before he lost it all.

"Hopefully, these studs are giving you some fantastic beats." She left Miranda speechless when Trixi extended her hand to wave with a set of comments. Miranda was just a few years older than her, so she understood the backhanded comments, but she was still extremely naïve about the profession.

Trixi walked off, leaving them to their own devices, and called her closest friend as she made her way up the stairs to her room. "Cookie. I'm back!"

When Cookie VanBuren's father started working as Martin's financial adviser, Trixi and she had already been friends for quite some time. The girls were only entering their teenage years. Their fathers had a good instinct that they would get along, and they were correct. Mr. VanBuren would often bring Cookie along with him to meetings so that the two of them could socialize with one another and be... well, girls.

Trixi didn't have a lot of friends, but Cookie was like a sister to her. Trixi adored spending time with Cookie. She would be the ideal companion the next day while Trixi cashed in on her inheritance by charging up her father's American Express.

Trixi need a makeover, which included purchasing new clothing to accentuate her cleavage and hips, two attributes that Aggie admired about her. She needed to get rid of the old Trixi and replace it with the new and improved version.

Trixi took one last look at herself in the full-length mirror that hung in her ultra-feminine bathroom before retiring for the night. It was time to rekindle her relationship with the sex kitten she once was. Trixi undressed and struck a few poses, looking for the best angle. She took a picture of herself as soon as she discovered that seductive stance, and she immediately sent it to Aggie using the private phone.

She received a text reply quickly after. ***A delightful bedtime treat. Thank you, my love.***

At least Aggie hadn't forgotten about Trixi completely despite the fact that they were back in familiar territory where Aggie might easily avoid her.

A ggie passed Justine her phone with the snapshot Trixi had sent already open. Justine flashed Aggie a gleeful grin before sending it back. "She sure does tickle my fancy."

"Along with other things," Aggie laughed as she took her phone off the counter and dropped it in her pocket. She walked out of the kitchen and into the living room, where she sat down in her favorite chair and propped her feet up on the ottoman.

A bit later, Justine walked over with a bowl of the stew and gave it to her. "You sure you don't want to eat at the table?"

"Nope. I missed my chair." She reached for the bowl as she answered. Aggie took the spoon, blew on it, and then dove into the scrumptious food.

Justine, who was not wearing any clothes, sat down next to her on the floor with her own dish. The two of them ate their meals in complete silence, with only the sound of gentle ambient music playing in the background. They preferred the soothing sounds of music from the distracting sounds of television. Reading was one of their favorite activities, thus they often sought settings that fostered a peaceful, Zen-like mood.

Aggie read a book as Justine fiddled with the new camera that had come while they were in New York. Being a photographer, she found great joy in experimenting with new photographic equipment.

Once Justine had the camera's lens and film loaded, she headed back into the living room to take some pictures of Aggie, who was her favorite subject despite her strong aversion to having her picture taken.

After taking a few pictures, Aggie shooed Justine away. Justine put down the camera and declared, "I'd love to photograph Trixi. She'd be a terrific model for me."

"No!" Aggie insisted. "She's off limits to your photos. They get in the wrong hands. We have an issue that I don't need with my boss."

Despite her disagreement with Aggie, Justine bowed her head in submission to her request. Taking a photograph with her was in no way equivalent to engaging in sexual relations with her. Justine's job required her to shoot a lot of stunning ladies, but none of them ended up being sexual partners. "Yes, Ma'am."

Aggie witnessed Justine's dismay. She made a snapping motion with her fingers and then pointed to the ground next to her. Almost instantly, Justine made her way over to her and kneeled down next to her. "As much as you want to treat her like a new toy and play with her, Trixi isn't like others. You know that. So stop sulking. You know how I hate that."

She directed her gaze at Aggie, and a little grin crossed her face. "I'm sorry. I just don't see how taking a photo of Trixi is a problem."

"Would she be naked?"

"Well, yes. All my models are."

"That's the problem. I know you. You'll want to put it in a gallery somewhere and I should not be looking at my boss's daughter naked." Aggie gave a little shake of the head, indicating that she would rather Justine not think about Trixi as a model. "Neither should you."

Aggie dismissed Justine, who went to her studio that night to focus. There was still a lot to accomplish before her upcoming art show.

After returning from France with Aggie, Justine found herself with nothing to do other than serve as a TPE slave to Aggie and Melody, Aggie's wife. By agreeing to Aggie's terms of a total power exchange, Justine filled her life with meaning. It seemed perfect to give the gift of service to a Mistress who met all of her needs.

While Justine was cleaning out a closet early on in their relationship, she stumbled across a camera stowed away in a box. Since that time, she has let the camera become an extension of herself, much like her life of submission.

Her very first images had been unremarkable landscape shots with nothing noteworthy in them. She realized she had found her calling when she began taking photographs of various pieces of bondage furniture and equipment. After that, she became skilled at taking self-portraits while being under her Mistress's control. That led her to find other models to photograph.

It was happenstance that led to an art collector to a few images she had taken of a model. He reached out to Justine, intending to acquire some of her art. What started out as a pastime of capturing and developing prints grew into something far more substantial: a successful profession.

Justine loaded her developer, stop bath, and fixer chemicals into her trays while the red light illuminated the darkroom. She watched the print in front of her come to life before her very eyes. A white tulip clutched in the model's cleavage. The skin that encircled the breasts was taut and dark, and the breasts themselves were firm and plentiful. The nipples stood erect. With Trixi on her mind, Justine licked her lips. A tingling in her center prompted her to crave the sensual touch of delicate and feminine fingers.

After Justine had put the print on the drying line, she found she could not suppress her want for pleasure any longer. After she exited the darkroom, she made her way back into the living room, where Aggie sat attentively reading a book. Justine tossed an antique pair of handcuffs, which landed on Aggie's lap. She flashed a sly grin when Aggie dropped her book to look at the handcuffs, which caused Aggie to notice Justine's presence.

"Horny little bitch you are tonight," Aggie joked.

"And you're not?"

Her eyes widened. "You're calling me a bitch?"

She shrugged with a caring smile. "Trixi sure made you hers the other night."

"Jealous?"

"No, Ma'am. Just horny as hell and could really use your dominance right now."

Aggie set her book on the coffee table and rose from her armchair. They turned off all the lights in the home and gathered in the bedroom that they had previously converted into a dungeon.

# NOT YOUR KIND OF PEOPLE

Trixi and Paolo drove the Bentley to pick up Cookie, who accompanied Trixi. They spent the day strolling up Rodeo Drive, running up charges on the credit card, and loading Paolo with numerous bags and packages. Trixi took Aggie's advice to heart and always made an effort to look her best, even when she was sure no one was watching. This included wearing lingerie that not only made Trixi feel confident, but was also something Aggie would like.

Cookie gave her stamp of approval to Trixi's new sex kitten appearance, despite the fact that Trixi did not explain the transformation other than she wanted to torment others with her sexual allure, which was not a lie. Even the salespeople at the store couldn't believe their eyes when Trixi emerged from the dressing room wearing a figure-hugging leather outfit. And Trixi relished the attention, particularly that which she received from bisexual women who coveted a relationship with her.

And what Trixi liked best was that she finally felt like she belonged somewhere, with someone who would let nobody else steal her away. Trixi secretly took images of herself and sent them to the woman on the other end of the phone in an attempt to titillate her.

The girls crammed into the backseat of the car, which is full of enough garment bags to fill both her closet and Cookie's. While they talked, Paolo drove. An art gallery caught Trixi's attention. "Paolo, stop!"

Upon hearing her order, he abruptly applied the

brakes. "What tis it, Ma'am?"

"Back up. I want to see this gallery behind us."

Paolo placed the car into reverse, and without caring if he irritated other people, he parked it such that they would only have a short distance to go to the gallery. Trixi went because, for some reason, she felt the need to nourish her soul with anything other than pop culture. If she wanted to create a new version of Trixi, she needed to occupy her life with something other than the social media celebrities who dominated the news stream.

Cookie followed closely after Trixi as she entered the exhibition and wandered about, taking in the many paintings and prints. Cookie cocked her head as she examined the various works of art. "I don't get it."

Trixi discovered after devoting a significant portion of her late teenage years to listening to classical music, it was unnecessary to comprehend the music in order to enjoy it. As is the case with art, there were certain things that made almost no sense at all, yet were nevertheless extremely lovely.

In the far corner of the gallery, there was a display of dark drawings that drew her attention. Trixi took a few steps in their direction when she noticed an etching that depicted a naked lady being attended to by another woman. The exquisite piece that prompted Trixi to see Justine or even herself fawning over Aggie in her royal guise. Trixi had to acquire it.

She summoned the gallery's stuffy curator to the drawing, where she then questioned him about the cost of the piece. Because of her height, he thought she was much younger than she actually was, so he looked down his nose at her. "Where are your parents, little one?"

She gave him a sneering look before pulling out her platinum card for him to behold and told him, "Seriously, Jeeves? What is the cost of this baby?"

Instantaneously, he shifted his tone and began telling Trixi the narrative of the artist and the artwork, ultimately estimating that it was worth just under five thousand dollars. She had no doubt that her father would be furious when he saw the bill, but she decided it was well worth the risk.

Trixi threw the card at him while maintaining an air of superiority. "Wrap it, Jeeves!"

Upon their return, Paolo carried everything up to her bedroom. While Trixi made a place for the new wardrobe, he arranged for the new items to launder. She stored her go-to items on one side of the closet, casual items in the center, and her sexier items in the back of the closet. A secret stockpile of garments that she intended to reserve for Aggie.

Trixi sagged into the bed and reached for Aggie's cell phone as soon as it vibrated at her. *How was your week at home, my love?*

Trixi replied to her with a grin. *Very fruitful though, I miss hanging out with you.*

A reply arrived. ***Good. Dinner Tonight?***

Trixi grinned as she responded, despite the fact that her needs had not been met for the past few days. *Do I get you for dessert?*

On Aggie's phone, a picture of her breasts suddenly displayed. Aggie had honed her skills to the point where she could seduce someone of Trixi's age.

After confirming their date with a time and location, Trixi took a bath. She longed for Justine's carefree approach to bathing her as she relaxed in the tub. Trixi couldn't deny the attraction she felt for Justine, despite the fact that Aggie had a special place in her heart. It did not satisfy Trixi with only wanting Aggie; rather, she yearned for both of them.

Paolo drove Trixi to the ranch-style home in Glendale, where she stepped onto the wrap-around porch with two wooden rockers that stood in front of a wide floor-to-ceiling window with the drapes drawn.

Because this was Trixi's first time visiting their residence, she did not have the confidence to expect that she could enter. In the meantime, Paolo waited patiently by the car for her to give him the go-ahead before driving away. Trixi rang the doorbell while holding the work of art that she had recently purchased. Similar to how she felt the first time she entered the hotel with Aggie, her stomach was in knots. When the door suddenly opened, Trixi did not know what to anticipate or what was about to happen.

As soon as Justine opened the bright red door, she greeted Trixi and welcomed her inside. Seeing Justine lifted her mood immensely.

"Trixi, come on in." When in her element of safety and comfort, Justine nearly forgot about her subservient role and added, "Please, Ma'am."

Trixi bid goodbye to Paolo and entered the sleek and contemporary residence. The exposed wood of the vaulted ceiling created the impression of rustic elegance while still exuding a great deal of mid-century charm due to its minimalist simplicity; similar to Aggie, who was both seasoned and refined.

After Trixi had taken a cursory look around their living room, Aggie entered the space discretely from the adjacent hallway. Just as excited to see her as Justine was, Aggie greeted Trixi with outstretched arms, much like a mother would do for her returning child. "My love."

Trixi placed the work of art on the ground, where it remained securely encased in its original packing, and then leaned it up against the chair. While Trixi hugged Aggie and kissed her longingly, she glanced over and saw Justine tilting her head to the side as she pondered the package.

As they parted, Aggie said, "I made reservations at DAMA tonight. It's downtown. We have awhile. Come in and sit."

After living in New York for the past half a year, Trixi couldn't even fathom the idea of driving in the city's downtown. She spouted out, "Do you want me to call Paolo back? He'd be happy to drive us."

"No, darling. We're fine." She brushed off the gesture and took Trixi by the hand, leading her through the remainder of the home.

Trixi quickly thought of the piece of art, let go, and ran back to it. "I got you two something. Yesterday. I found it while shopping. I immediately thought of you. So I bought it."

Trixi gave it to Justine, who took it while Aggie again waved her hands away from the gift. "Seriously, darling. Don't spend your money on us. We appreciate it, but totally unwarranted."

Trixi looked at the artwork on the walls of the living room, knowing what was in the package. It wouldn't go with their style. Justine sat on the white couch and put the package on the table so it would be easier to open. She tore through the craft paper to get to the bubble wrap, and as she removed it, her eyes widened and her jaw fell in shock.

She put her palm over her lips, and a muffled voice murmured, "Trixi? This is an Escoffier. Oh, my—"

Aggie, whose reaction was quite similar to that of Justine's, sat down next to her on the sofa to take in the etching, but she found herself at a loss for words.

As their feelings became more complicated to interpret, Trixi's face twisted in response. "Yeah, that's the name the guy said. Daphne, or something like that."

"Delphine Escoffier. A brilliant artist from France who drew and painted the female form, mostly nudes, in the thirties." Justine picked it up and turned it around so that she could read the information and the certificate of authenticity attached to the back of the frame. She mumbled under her breath as she continued to have a stunned expression on her face. "An original? Trixi? This is amazing, thank you."

Aggie sprang to her feet, made her way over to Trixi, and grabbed hold of her hand. "We don't deserve you, my sweet. Thank you, but you really should not have spent money like that on us."

Trixi shrugged. "I saw it in the gallery and it reminded me of you, so I had to get it. Didn't know it would be a big deal."

Justine chuckled. "Big deal? This is an early work of hers, very controversial at the time because of the hints of sadistic undertones."

Trixi expressed her excitement in Justine's great understanding of the art that she had given them by saying, "You seem to know a lot about this."

"Delphine Escoffier is the inspiration for my photography." She got up from the couch and motioned for Trixi to come with her. "Come on, let me show you."

They didn't hang their controversial artwork in the drably furnished main living area, but rather in one of the more interesting private spaces. Black and white images of stunning ladies in their naked glory adorned the walls of the living room, dining room, and corridors.

Justine reached up to a shelf and took down a book, revealing that it was a huge art book with Escoffier's name on the cover. They stood in front of a beautiful photograph that had a really noir vibe to it. The shot had lights and shadows on a wet street corner. The picture showed a naked lady splayed on the sidewalk like a dead prostitute discarded after her usage. Justine held up the original piece from Escoffier in the book. "I tried to copy her painting because this is one of my favorite pieces."

Another part of Justine emerged when she saw how similar her image was to the original artwork. "Wow. That's incredible. It looks almost the same."

"I shot most of the art in the house, trying to evoke similar emotions while trying to embrace a style of my own."

Trixi paused in front of a photograph of a woman's leg restrained by a heavy chain and rusted metal cuff. Quite macabre and sadistic. Trixi admired it. "I didn't know you were a photographer. I'm going to have to look at these all again, but so far, this is my favorite."

Justine gleefully retrieved it off the wall and presented it to her. "It's yours."

Trixi remarked, "You don't have to do that," despite the fact that she was pleased to have it.

"You can have any of them. I mean, you bought us an

Escoffier. These do not even compare to what you gave us. My work is worth nothing."

From the far end of the hall, Aggie added her two cents. "Stop negating your self-worth, love. You are an incredible artist, trust me." Aggie continued as she walked forward to them. Aggie talked to Trixi while she stroked Justine's back when she joined them in front of the painting. "She has her first exhibition with other artists in a couple of months."

"That's great!" Trixi said.

"You'll have to come with us. I'm so nervous about this."

Aggie said, "She is too modest. She'll have to show you her portfolio." Then she said to Justine, "You've been working years for this moment. You'll be great."

At that moment, Trixi seemed so inadequate. Aggie was busy with her job, which demanded a significant amount of her time and energy. A photographic exhibit resulted from Justine's efforts. And Trixi had nothing other than going shopping with her father on their family's money and purchasing art that she didn't realize was significant at the time. Trixi was under the impression that it was a mere painting of a naked chick.

Aggie gave each of them a passionate kiss with the same amount of intensity. "We should get going if we want to make our reservations."

When Aggie left the room, leaving Justine and Trixi alone, Justine said, "May I thank you with a kiss?" Trixi nodded her head affirmatively.

Trixi moved closer to Justine and enveloped her in an affectionate hug before giving her a kiss that left Justine gasping for air. At the point when they parted ways, Trixi walked away, leaving Justine breathless and hungry for more.

Because art and Justine's pastime took up the most of their time, they were unable to give Trixi a thorough tour of the home when she first arrived. So when they got back to the home after a great supper during which there was no drama at all, they invited her to join their inner circle. While Justine secured the residence and closed all the drapes, Aggie showed Trixi around into the common areas of the house.

When Aggie and Trixi had reached the rear of the home and were ready to look at the bedrooms, Justine walked up to them wearing nothing but a smile. She kneeled down in front of them.

Justine asked, "Have you decided which room you'd like to use?"

Trixi cocked her head to the side and looked at Aggie for clarification, since she did not know what it meant. Aggie answered, "If Trixi doesn't have anywhere to be, all of them?"

Still not understanding, Trixi replied, "I'm yours until you cast me aside again."

Aggie poked her with her finger while giggling subtly. "Oh, stop it. We did not cast you aside." Aggie gently stroked Justine's hair and encouraged her to continue, saying, "Go on, we'll follow."

Trixi didn't want to enter another quarrel, so she squeezed her lips together to suppress the temptation to have the final word. However, Trixi mentally said to herself: *You did cast me aside, which is why I have been alone for the past few days.*

Justine dashed quickly down the hallway and opened the door to a room that Trixi had not yet visited. Instead of following, Aggie grabbed Trixi's hand, holding her back for a moment. Her worried gaze moved slowly over Trixi's face.

Trixi asked, "What's the matter?"

Aggie's head sprang up in response to the query, but she maintained her focus on the ceiling. "Trixi, New York was only a taste of what I want you to be a part of with me. A tame taste of what I enjoy, and what Justine craves. It was only a tease. I don't want to hold back at home. In this private domain, we are free. Does that make sense?"

Trixi dragged Aggie down the hall, stating, "We're going to make Justine scream."

But before they entered the room, she turned to Aggie and stated, with a smart-aleck grin, "And I'm not going to piss, shit, cut, or choke her. I got it, Aggie. Now let's have dessert because I've missed this."

When Aggie brought Trixi in for a kiss, she placed her hands on her cheeks and pulled her in close. Trixi's breath caught in her throat. While gazing intently into Trixi's eyes, Aggie said, "I am so glad I made the right choice with you."

When Trixi stepped into the room, she took aback by what she saw and immediately skid to a halt. Chains. Very much like the ones in the photos that Justine took, gave life to the cement floors. They were thick and heavy, and they lay on the ground waiting for the limbs of someone. They adorned the walls with various implements of corporal punishment, including paddles, whips, chains, and floggers. All of these items were both on display and ready to be used. And there was Justine, kneeling with her head down and her gorgeous blonde hair falling over both of her eyes.

Trixi's sex burned with intense desire. It was necessary for her to collect herself. Justine cast her eye upward after seeing that they did not enter the room fully. Aggie leaned towards Trixi and wrapped her arms around her as she forced herself up against Trixi's back. Trixi gazed straight into Justine's eyes, and what she saw was someone who pleaded with her to be punished.

Next to Trixi's ear, Aggie whispered, "Don't be afraid."

It didn't scare Trixi; just wary since the only time she had ever seen something like it, was in a movie or as a joke using props or costumes. She moved her thumb up to her lips and pressed the nail between her teeth as Trixi's interest piqued by the notion of Justine's legs being tied to the chains on the floor. With the thought of Justine's legs being bound, Justine's cries were audible in Trixi's head even before Justine carried them out with her voice.

As Aggie nuzzled into Trixi's neck, her hands crept higher and cupped Trixi's breasts. At the same time, Aggie took a little bite of skin from Trixi's neck. This caused a tingling sensation all over Trixi's body, and a covering of goosebumps appeared on her skin. Deep and rapid breaths emitted from her body as pulsations between her legs begged for more.

At long last, Trixi drew a deep breath and declared, "I'm not afraid of this. Show me everything."

Trixi felt as if she were being engulfed by the world's eroticism, which caused her head to spin. As Aggie moved in front of her toward Justine, Trixi had a momentary episode of dizziness. Aggie extended her hand to Justine, who gracefully accepted it and then got to her feet. Both of them made their way over to the massive wooden X in the corner.

"I had this custom made for her stature. Come around to the back, Trixi." Aggie motioned for Trixi to come closer as she saw Justine go onto the platform that supported the crucifix.

Trixi positioned herself behind the cross and peered through two holes at the level of Justine's breasts to see her figure while she hung there. Aggie pushed her hand through one opening and then drew Justine's breast through by its nipple.

Justine hissed as Aggie passed it through the opening while twisting it hard so that it would rest on the outside. "Would you like to do the other one?"

In the following of Aggie's demonstration, Trixi reached through the opening and grabbed Justine by the breast. As she battled, Aggie's words served as a guide for her. "All you have to do is pinch her nipple and yank for it to go right in."

When Trixi did as she was told, Justine exhaled a thick, roiling pocket of air as Trixi pulled the nipple up and out of the hole. Aggie gently stroked the exposed mounds which settled in front of them.

"Are they not exquisite?"

There was no way that Trixi could deny how lovely it was to look at a set of breasts that were not connected to a face. She knew her large breasts would need a great deal more pulling and squeezing in order to fit them into those openings. "I can see why you love this."

"Join me." Aggie dropped her head as she devoured the perky nipples, her tongue teasing them before she consumed them with her full lips. Trixi imitated her and put the other breast of Justine's to her lips. Her periphery monitored Aggie, which piqued her interest because of how close they were to each other when they were enjoying their third.

When Aggie let go of Justine, Trixi did the same but swiftly seized Aggie with such need that she drove Aggie against the wall and raised up on her toes to reach Aggie's lips with force. Because of Aggie's exertions, she threw Trixi backward and slammed her into the cross. While doing so, Justine's breasts were being compressed by Trixi's back, while the two of them engaged in a lustful battle for dominance.

While they were kissing, Aggie moved her hand behind Trixi's back. Trixi first believed that Aggie wanted to remove her clothing but, when Justine screamed, Trixi realized that Aggie really wasn't concerned about her at all. As Trixi turned away from Aggie, she saw Justine's nipple being held in a vice by a small chain fastened to the cross's wooden platform.

She reached over Trixi once again and pushed the other nipple down before attaching a metal clamp to it. Justine shrieked as the clamp crashed into the delicate skin.

Aggie's finger gently stroked over the pinched bud, and she gave her ache a small lick to ease the discomfort. Aggie maneuvered her way past Trixi where Justine's body crushed up against the wooden cross and was only connected to it by her nipples. Trixi followed and watched Aggie work. Cuffs made of steel that were attached to the base using short chain links. Trixi followed Aggie's lead and lowered herself to Justine's level before attaching the chains to her ankles.

Nothing about it was fluffy and soft like the lingerie offered in shops; instead, Trixi's mind wandered to a prison torture movie with the hefty, worn steel.

As they rose to their feet, Aggie shackled Justine's hands to the cross's highest point. There was no step stool available for Trixi to utilize; but, if they had been playing by themselves, climbing up Justine's back may have been a possibility. Trixi's throat constricted as she admired the artwork that depicted Justine's body being stretched into the shape of an X. What a lovely sight. Trixi secretly wished that she had a camera on her so that she could capture and preserve the moment forever.

"What do you want to do to her?" Aggie spoke the words in a low tone.

Trixi did not dawdle in her speech in any way. "Make love to her."

"That's for later, beautiful. Right now, we make her scream in pain. Later, she'll scream for pleasure."

Aggie took a blindfold made of black leather from the drawer, put it on top of Justine's head. Upon her return to the dresser, she retrieved a ball gag from inside it. Aggie gave Justine a violent yank on her hair, which caused her neck to stretch back, and then she shoved the ball into Justine's mouth and secured it around her head.

Aggie finished preparing their victim and leaned against the counter next to Trixi to inspect her again. Justine waited helplessly, unable to speak or see. Once again, as they gazed in awe at the stunning appearance of their captive lover, Trixi felt a tingling sensation go through her veins to her core. Loving the bound feminine body to such a profound degree wasn't even on her radar until that moment.

The scars on Justine's otherwise flawless skin caught Trixi's eye. Some are really profound, while others were more subtle, but still very noticeable. Trixi pondered whether they were Aggie's handiwork or the result of the years she spent working as a lady of pleasure. Trixi felt an overwhelming urge to take Justine into her arms and console her for the abuse that had resulted in the scars; but she knew she could not be kind and compassionate as long as Aggie maintained her position of authority in the room.

Aggie said, "First and foremost, she cannot say her safe words while wearing the ball gag. Her hands serve as our pointers and guides throughout the process. She will elevate two fingers to indicate a slower speed, and three fingers to request a complete halt."

As Aggie talked, Justine showed her hands to Trixi by lifting her fingers. "If she has no voice, we will never bind them. It is imperative that we maintain open lines of communication. If she could talk, she would tell us *Jaune*, to slow down, and *Rouge*, to stop us."

Aggie interpreted Trixi's perplexed expression as a sign that she was having trouble keeping up, so she continued speaking. Her voice became irritable. "Safe words. Jaune. Rouge. Keep up."

"I get it, just wondering why we're speaking French. Continue."

"She learned about BDSM in France. It's easy for her to remember when safety is a priority. We don't want her to have to think in a moment of crisis," Aggie explained.

Following Aggie, who had paused for a minute to lavish her affections over Justine's body, Trixi made her way toward their love slave. Trixi moved closer to Justine and kissed the scarred skin very lovingly, knowing her guide, teacher, and lover wanted her to learn the acts that caused the permanent memory of those before her.

"We make her feel safe. Show her we adore her," Aggie remarked, as they lavished Justine with affectionate touches. She then asked, "Have you ever used any sort of impact object? A flogger? Paddle?"

Of course, Trixi hadn't. "Not enough to say I have experience."

Aggie took Trixi to the wall, where they displayed all the punishment weapons. Aggie continued to explain as the atmosphere remained calm and subdued. "This is called impact play because we are going to send an impact to her body. You could call it flogging or spanking, but that narrows a focus to an object or area. Pick an item, Trixi."

Trixi chose an instrument that had a lengthy leather handle and braided leather trails dotted with little barbs throughout the instrument.

Aggie snatched it out of Trixi's hands as soon as she removed it from the wall. "A girl after my own heart. Such a sadist. I knew I found my kindred spirit in you. A little advice: if you start hard and intense from the beginning, you'll end the scene faster. Work up. Remember, greed is your worst enemy."

Aggie replaced the item of punishment with a leather paddle, which in the BDSM world was analogous to using training wheels. Just a few minutes before, Justine screamed into their ears as Aggie squeezed steel clamps around her fragile nipples. Trixi's ears continued to ring with that sound, which caused a surge of adrenaline to run through her body.

Aggie grabbed an older paddle from the wall, one made of wood that seemed like it had seen better days. She demonstrated to Trixi how to handle the paddle properly, as well as the accurate tactics for where, when, and how hard to spank. These things served to stoke Justine's already raging passions as she whimpered and writhed beneath their swats. A foreshadowing of things to come.

Aggie gave off the impression of being extremely patient. Trixi wanted to dominate the willing submissive, but Aggie took her time as she took Justine's gag off, kissed her, and left the room. Trixi continued to follow Aggie around like a puppy and kissed Justine before rushing to catch up with Aggie.

"Why are we leaving?" Trixi asked.

"Because I wanted to change into something a little more comfortable. Don't you want out of your restrictive clothing?"

She tore out of her casual clothes and changed into a black teddy that revealed more of her figure in order to emphasize her seductive appearance. Trixi's one and only desire was to wrap her arms around her and devour every last bit of the woman's flesh. "Is tonight all about Justine?"

"Oh no, my love." Aggie reached around Trixi, easily unzipped her dress, and then tossed it to the ground, leaving Trixi wearing nothing but her black lace panties. "I plan on teaching you how to last the entire night."

Aggie reached for Trixi's sex and delighted her with twenty seconds of foreplay as she slid her hand between the lace and Trixi's heated flesh. This thrilled Trixi immensely. Trixi crept her hand in between Aggie's legs and enthusiastically pressed herself against her. When Aggie's twenty seconds were up, she yanked her hand away from Trixi and sucked the girl from her fingers before releasing her grip on the whimpering pupil.

"I think this is a great look on you."

Trixi lowered her gaze to her breasts and panties. "What is?"

"Lust." Aggie swept Trixi out of the bedroom without so much as giving herself a chance to look around or become acquainted with her surroundings.

As they returned to the dungeon, Aggie asked. "Are you doing well, my Justine?"

"Yes, Ma'am. Very well."

After that, she gave Justine another kiss and then replaced the gag over her mouth once more. "I took off the gag because we left the room. I can't see her hand if I am not here, therefore we need sound. We remove the gag. Safety, Trixi. Always remember the safety of your pets."

Aggie played soft ambient music in the room, reminding Trixi of a French cafe. Aggie said, "Edith Piaf, her favorite. Remember, when your submissive feels safe, she'll relax and enjoy the ride."

Aggie gave Trixi the handle adorned with leather tails, which was similar to what Trixi had chosen initially, but gentler on the skin. Again, Aggie guided her with the correct posture, hand-eye coordination, and a ratio of the amount of pain to aftercare, which allowed Justine to feel her caring touch. The leather tassels had never caused Justine to let out a single scream. She moaned with delight at each flick of their wrists because being flogged was a pleasurable experience for her.

After allowing Justine's body to rest for a while, Aggie switched back to Trixi's body and proceeded to provide pleasure for another twenty seconds.

As Aggie again withdrew her hand from her clit, Trixi pleaded with her, "Please don't stop."

"Patience, my love. You will come ten times over by morning."

They increased the intensity of their pain against Justine, which caused Justine's vocals to become progressively higher as they worked their way through each weapon until Aggie gave Trixi permission to use the barbed flogger under her supervision. As Trixi's hand came down over the small of her back, Justine screamed so loudly that it drowned out all the other sounds in the room, including Edith Piaf's voice. It sent a shiver down Trixi's spine.

That was the only confirmation Trixi needed to realize that BDSM was indeed her vocation. As she tore her hand away, tiny beads of blood oozed from the cuts in the skin. As Trixi prepared for another wail onto Justine's body, Aggie snatched her hand and held it high while whispering, "Aftercare."

Aggie snatched the whip out of Trixi's hand and replaced it with a small, warm towel. Trixi leaned in close to Justine and planted a peck on her cheek as she placed the towel against her skin.

Because she was so near to Justine, Trixi saw a tear dripping down from the corner of her eyelid. She asked, "Red, Justine?"

Justine shook her head, unable to utter a single word due to the gag placed in her mouth. Trixi continued to caress her for a few more seconds before returning to

Aggie's side, where Aggie gave her the whip once more. Trixi's eyes widened as she considered the possibility that it would not be prudent to continue to whip Justine, given that she had already caused Justine's skin to be broken.

After observing Trixi's hesitation, Aggie spoke her question out loud. "Justine, do you want more?"

Justine signaled to them she approved of extra punishment by holding up one finger and then giving a thumbs up with both hands. On the cross, Justine inhaled deeply as she braced herself for the additional force to be delivered by Trixi's wrist. Before Trixi could lift her arm to the sky, Aggie swung her around. Aggie left Trixi feeling lightheaded and deeply in love after kissing her in a way that was both passionate and salacious.

As Aggie pulled away, she placed her head next to Trixi, talking only to her ear, "Learn your slave's limits. Test them over and over. I know Justine's very well. You get three more. The next one will be soft, a tease only. She is expecting hard, you give her soft on the ass. The second one is a little harder across the shoulder blades. The third, low to the cheeks, full force. Remember, watch your placement."

Trixi put her newfound knowledge to use by tormenting Justine at first with a light touch, and then progressing to a more forceful prod, which forced Justine to stifle another scream.

Under Aggie's guidelines, Trixi committed one more assault on Justine's body. Trixi delved into the recesses of her mind and connected it with her hand as she encounter the bitch within her. Trixi lifted her arm and let the sharp thorns of the whip to cut into her skin. The impact awakened her all the way to her core. The shrieks emanating from Justine drowned out the quivering alto wail the French singer made in the background. Even muffled, the cries of the beautiful woman rang through the room.

The sound of her agonizing voice caused Trixi's breathing to become more labored and shallow, and she came dangerously close to having an orgasmic experience. Trixi hurried toward her, intending to cradle and comfort Justine. Aggie climbed onto the platform behind Trixi, reached between Trixi's legs, and took her to a climax as Trixi squished her body against Justine's while clutching the towel to her back.

Trixi ached with exhaustion, so she rested against the slave on the cross while Aggie scurried out of the room. She kissed Justine's back and all the places she had reddened. Trixi, who fought back her own tears, had an overwhelming feeling of guilt since she had experienced sick pleasure from providing such a cruel act of abuse to a woman.

Trixi overheard Aggie's authoritative voice coming from behind her and saying, "Let her down. It's time to move on."

While Trixi assisted Justine from the X, she became cognizant of a photograph of a blonde woman, bound and crying, hanging in a black frame behind the wooden X. Her tears, like Justine's, may have been tears of pleasure or they could have been tears of misery. In that room, between these two beautiful ladies, the feelings were quite similar to one another. Trixi used her fingers to wipe away Justine's tears, and then she removed the gag in her mouth. She kissed Justine with such fervor and enthusiasm that Trixi couldn't tell who she wanted more: the instructor or the slave. The kiss left Trixi unsure of who she desired more.

From one of the five bedrooms in the house, they went to another. Trixi escorted Justine into a room furnished with a variety of tables, benches, and chairs that had a sense of antiquity, thanks to the chains and shackles that were fastened to them. It seemed one pair was of a fuzzy material and the other of rough leather; it was almost as if one pair was for Justine and the other was for Aggie.

The evening progressed with the use of clamps and spreaders and other devices designed to bring one person pleasure while causing another person anguish. Aggie demonstrated to Trixi how to distort Justine's body into these incredible angles, which enabled Trixi to see Justine's body in ways that she had previously only imagined.

Trixi mastered the wonderful skill of gratifying a lady by the means of physical torture, with a lot of grunts, groans, and screams that were so loud that pierced Trixi's ears. After what seemed like hours of play, they eventually gave in and let Justine climax.

There was bondage in every single bedroom. For them, this was the only way to exist. After tackling each room, all with distinctive sadistic themes, they finally made their way to the master suite. They furnished the room in shades of brown, gray, and dusty blue, and it included side tables from the mid-20th century on each side of the immaculately made bed. It would be suitable for use as a bedroom if not for the pulley system that is reminiscent of the one Aggie used on Trixi at the club and the puppy cage that is situated in one of the room's corners.

After securing Justine inside the pulley's shackles, Aggie lifted her until her body was dangling in midair above the floor. Trixi couldn't even begin to fathom the amount of suffering that Justine had to go through while being restrained by nothing but her wrists due to gravity and weight. Aggie lavished Justine's body with loving kisses, licks, and pets while Justine hung helplessly in the corner.

Trixi soon followed her and imitated her interactions toward Justine until Aggie looked straight at Trixi. Trixi inhaled deeply into Aggie as she reached beneath the teddy she wore and discovered the sweet spot of her love. She cherished every caress that Aggie bestowed on her. They had spent hours placing various delights across Justine's body, but as she hung from the ceiling, she had to endure the agony of watching Trixi explore her wife with wild eagerness.

Aggie melted when Trixi touched her, her chest rising and falling as she pressed her fingers into her. The other wrapped around her neck to keep her lips pleading for Trixi's. Justine groaned along with them, but when Trixi heard a high-pitched shriek emanate from Justine, she wrenched her lips away from Aggie and saw that Aggie had dug her claws over Justine's body with her nails.

While Trixi's fingers enjoyed the warmth of her drenched folds, Aggie moved in close to Trixi's ear and spoke, "I absolutely adore it when she lets out a bloodcurdling scream."

Trixi's chest tightened as she gasped for breath. "So do I."

Aggie inhaled deeply into Trixi's neck, her words so light and airy that she could hardly hear them. "I know you do. Make love to me. Make me scream red."

Aggie's words engulfed her whole body in a chilly sensation. As soon as Trixi recognized the desperation in Aggie's tone, her nipples clenched. Trixi would have tossed her onto the bed and buried her head in the space between the sexy thighs if she had been with another woman. For Aggie, it just wasn't enough. Trixi lacked the ability to make love to her or any other woman. Making love was not a concept she was familiar with. Sex, she knew. Love? It wasn't a word in her vocabulary. "I don't know how."

Aggie pushed Trixi's body so that it leaned on Justine's while still suspended from the ceiling. As soon as her lips touched Trixi's, she sucked all the air out of her lungs. Aggie ran her lips over her flesh and nibbled at the sensitive areas. The tingling feelings spread throughout her whole body. When she finally reached Trixi's breasts, she took her time biting down on the apex of one until it was so painful that the sensation was utterly gratifying.

Trixi's hands dug into Aggie's head as they moved through her flaming red hair, securing Aggie's position and holding her in place. Her groans caused her to tighten her grasp on the delicate nipple, which she held between her teeth. When she pulled on it and let it to come loose from her lips, Trixi growled a breath from her chest.

Aggie pushed herself upward from Trixi's chest, snatched another kiss, and leaned down to whisper in her ear. "That is how you make love; with your whole heart. Go find some toys for us to use."

Trixi, still dripping from the overwhelming delights, sprinted from the room to the others and grabbed everything that seemed both delightful and torturous in the hopes of using it on Aggie's body. She returned to find Aggie's hands roaming over Justine's body.

From the threshold, Trixi watched as Aggie passionately kissed her slave. She kept her mouth shut as she saw Aggie marveled at the presence of the shackled slave. Trixi wished she could have one for herself.

Despite the fact that Aggie had her back turned to Trixi, she was conscious of the presence in the room in the same way that a skilled soldier might feel danger. Aggie barely removed her lips from the surface of Justine's skin before calling out to Trixi, "Join me."

Trixi's heart throbbed from the dagger that Aggie thrust into it when she turned her attention back to Justine. Trixi yearned for someone who she could call her own. They gave Justine another round of delightfully painful suffering, much to Justine's delight. Trixi felt the screams of Justine vibrate up her spine, which gave her the courage to force Aggie back onto the bed and take her along with the wonderful toy collection she brought back with her.

Trixi frantically combed over her body, grabbing at any and all pieces of flesh that she could find. Aggie silenced Trixi and held her down rather than greeting her with equal quantities of passion, as would have been appropriate. "Slow. Breathe. Feel your heart."

And that she did. Trixi had been so used to being in a rush to do the act that she hadn't stopped for long enough to appreciate it, to embrace it, or even to wallow in the ecstasy of being loved. Even though there were times throughout Aggie's enjoyment time when Trixi had to remind her excitement to simmer, the end result was absolutely magnificent when it did ultimately happened. Aggie shrieked her own lullaby, which only included a single phrase for the chorus. "Red."

They both laid on their backs to relax. The ecstasy and gratification of a torturous orgasm had caused a surge in their heart rates. Trixi cocked her head to the side to look at Aggie and watched as her worn-out body eased farther into the blankets, ready for slumber.

Trixi roused herself from the bed and walked to their slave. She didn't say a word as she lowered the pulley far enough for her to unhook Justine's arms from it. Trixi was not ready to give up, so she led Justine to bed and put her through the same gratifying movements that had exhausted Aggie. Just as Justine sang another aria, slivers of sunlight broke through the partially drawn curtains and illuminated the room. She then tucked them under the blankets to let them rest after their wonderful world of Trixi.

# I THINK I'M PARANOID

Exhaustion had set in for Trixi. Needless to say, it completely wiped her out, yet she still wasn't in the least bit drowsy. In fact, Trixi was so stimulated by the high that she couldn't go to sleep. Trixi wandered, about taking in Justine's stunning artwork. Trixi studied the paper with calligraphy fountain pen writing displayed in a frame. It read:

*With mutual love and respect, this parchment is to be signed in ink and in blood to bind two souls, one as master and one as slave, until their last breaths.*
*Justine Duval will accept the role of wife, lover, and dog. To completely relinquish herself body and soul to Agatha Helvete. To have no will beside that of her master. To accept all forms of cruelty, be that of mutilation, she will accept without complaint. Be that who is trampled upon, must kiss the foot that crushes the soul. To have nothing for the master is everything. And if the chains became too heavy to bear, shall be tossed below the sea, for slave may never have back freedom.*
*Agatha Helvete will accept the role of wife, lover, and owner. To dominate without restraint the body and soul of Justine Duval. To relish in the cruelty be that of mutilation, given without remorse. To crush the soul for purpose of being cherished. To have the conviction never to free her slave.*
*And only in death will this parchment burn.*

And there it was, prominently visible to everybody who entered their domain to see. Without a shadow of a doubt, Justine was Aggie's, and the only thing that can ever come between them was death. A place where no one else could fit. Trixi sneaked a second look inside the bedroom. Justine had her arms wrapped so gently around Aggie's that Trixi couldn't bring herself to break up their peaceful embrace.

Trixi cautiously entered, gathered her belongings, and immediately dialed Paolo's number to ask him to bring the vehicle while she got ready. She waited for Paolo on the front steps. Trixi hurried to the vehicle as soon as he drew up, carrying her bag. He hardly had time to get the door unlocked before she hopped in.

After taking the wheel, he faced her. "You had good time, Ma'am?"

"Delightful. Drive."

Having furrowed his brow, he questioned, "Where to, Ma'am?"

Without intending to continue the conversation, Trixi growled at him. "Canada. Mexico. I really don't care. Just drive."

For the most part, Paolo followed her directions without inquiry. Despite not making it to either Canada or Mexico, Trixi answered Aggie's call, which arrived about two hours of driving along the coast. She saw no reason to refuse her conversation.

"Where did you run off to, my darling?"

"Home. Away. I came for dinner, stayed for dessert."

"You didn't need to leave."

"Aggie, as much as I want this, at the end of the day, you two are still married. And to death, for that matter. There may be a place in your bed but—"

Aggie interrupted her. "Trixi, don't say that. I thought we went over this in New York, this drama—"

That's when Trixi intervened and stopped her. There was no hostility in Trixi's voice; only a hint of regret at being an outsider in their way of life. Her voice was unruffled. "There's no drama, Aggie. I'm okay with it. When you want me over, call me. I'll be there."

Trixi overheard Aggie sigh loudly into the phone. Trixi reassured her. "I'm fine."

The call ended with a click. Perhaps she wasn't doing as well as she believed. In the nook of her eye, a tear swelled. In time to prevent it from falling, Trixi wiped it away. Trixi urged Paolo to drive her off at the most opulent hotel on the beaches of Laguna, and she would spend the night there, worried that she may not hear from Aggie again.

Of course, Trixi didn't bring any baggage, so she had Paolo go shopping for some new threads and have the hotel bring them up to her room. By the time Trixi's replacement wardrobe came, she had already left the room. With each step, she dug her toes further into the sand as she reflected on the meaning of her reality.

Trixi watched the sun dip below the ocean's bed, alone on the beach. She had not yet decided whether she wanted the kind of life Aggie offered her. Although sexually gratifying, the relationship was not.

During their first rainy kiss, Trixi really wanted Aggie to adore her. Trixi knew well that the majority of her friends were actively hooking up using dating apps like Bumble or Tinder. Although Trixi enjoyed hooking up, she preferred to do it by physical contact rather than a mobile app. Ninety percent of the time, it worked. After seeing the commitment that Aggie and Justine had (although, in a very sexual way), Trixi yearned for the same.

Imagining Aggie and Justine together made her feel like crying. Trixi gave her cell a quick peek. There were no missed phone calls. No texts. Her mind envisioned them having dinner, sitting on the sofa watching a movie into the night, and then adjourning to the bedroom for a little foreplay before—the sound of Justine's piercing scream reverberated in Trixi's ears. She felt a sudden icy sensation as the vibration penetrated to her very being. After a moment of silence, she got to her feet to shake off the thought.

Trixi had just turned to make her way back to the hotel when she collided with an older woman. More the age of Justine, ten or twelve years her senior. She had a habit of staring at the person for a bit longer than necessary whenever she spotted someone she liked. Trixi smiled sincerely and offered her apologies.

"No, it's fine. I wasn't watching where I was going," remarked the lady, brushing her auburn hair out of her face. The lights on the beach cast the perfect glow on her. It emphasized her hair's natural red undertones. There was a look in her eye that Trixi had seen before; it was one that she had gotten used to seeing. It was that of enticement.

"I was just going to grab dinner at the bar. Care to join me? My treat," Trixi asked.

She smiled sheepishly when Trixi was so direct. "I'd like that. My name's Amanda."

Trixi lied and said that her name was Traci because she didn't want to hear the other people chuckle when they heard her real name. It wasn't like she'd see this woman again.

In no time at all, they were in Trixi's hotel room,

nude and panting heavily after a night of heavy drinking. Trixi forgot maybe Amanda might not have as thick a skin as her previous companions, while lost in her heaving bosom and vigorous caressing. Amanda whistled in protest as Trixi bit into her skin and felt the titillating pinch. "Not so hard."

When she realized Amanda preferred a more subdued Trixi special, she lowered the intensity of the performance, and Amanda responded in kind. Though they both came more than once, it wasn't Trixi's style. After her third orgasm, Trixi found herself staring at the ceiling and concluded that she did, in fact, have a style, and that it wasn't the standard lesbian vanilla sex. Trixi yearned to participate in Aggie's sexually charged lifestyle. The handcuffs and chains piqued her interest. Passionate screams pierced her ears like a concert by the best opera singers.

Amanda's departure from the bedroom after saying her goodnights made Trixi happy. To Trixi, BDSM was the last stop on her sexual road trip, even if Amanda had been a fun diversion along the way.

Trixi dialed her phone. "Paolo, pick me up in the morning. I'll be ready around ten a.m."

Then she switched to the other phone to send a text.
***Can we talk?***

She strolled out onto the patio under a dark sky, but the ocean's shimmering reflection made the night seem brighter. Trixi's phone rang in a matter of seconds. Following the polite greetings, Trixi inquired, "Is Justine with you?"

"She's inside. I stepped out by the pool."

"Aggie, I swear I am not mad. I didn't leave because I

was angry. I left because I'm confused and I don't know where I fit in with you."

On the other end of the line, Aggie groaned and sounded frustrated. "I've told you."

"You've told me you wanted to share Justine with me. That doesn't tell me about you. What am I to you?"

After a brief moment of silence, Aggie heaved loudly once again into the phone. "You're Trixi, my bright light of life. If I didn't want you too, I never would have shown you my world."

Trixi relaxed on the luxury hotel balcony. She drew in a lungful of the ocean air and exhaled slowly. Trixi, as she let it all out, said, "I want to move in with you."

Their call was met with a sudden hush. Trixi expected it to be the last straw between them, but it turned out otherwise. "This life is about communication. First and foremost. No matter how great the sex is for you and for us, if we can't communicate, it won't work. Having you live with us has always been the goal."

"Don't you think I should've known what the goal was?"

She sighed in a way that was almost funny and then laughed. "I don't want to throw your age around, so I'll throw mine. Trixi, I'm old. Maybe I haven't said those exact words. I've learned over the years not to be so blunt. Ride the lines, walk the fences. So I am going to say this once. Take it how you will. Get your ass home, and that means to Glendale."

The happiness in her heart threatened to overflow. Aggie may not have come out and said that she loved Trixi, but she certainly walked a line that was dangerously close to crossing it. It was sufficient for

Trixi. "I'll be there tomorrow, or you can come get me."

"Where are you, love?"

"At a very fancy joint in Laguna, with a beach view."

That being said, Trixi provided Aggie with the name and address of the hotel, and within two hours, Aggie and Justine arrived at the location. They spent the night under the covers, all three of them pinching and pulling on various tender body parts until each of them fell asleep, feeling completely content with their experience.

The following morning, when it rose behind Trixi, sunrise wasn't quite as warmly greeted. Her surroundings were just beginning to be illuminated by the dawn. Naturally, she was up before Aggie and Justine and stood on the balcony. She enjoyed the hustle and bustle of the city, but the beach was her true love. When Trixi was a child, she would follow along with her father whenever he went to a location near the beach. She had been to some of the world's best, but her personal favorite was right outside her house. Trixi made a note to inquire about her father's beach house plans.

She jumped when she heard the balcony door open. When Trixi looked over her shoulder, she saw Justine exiting the room without any clothing on and walking onto the patio.

Strangely, Justine encircled Trixi with her arms and nuzzled her head into Trixi's collarbone from behind. She then gave her a kiss on the neck and remarked, "I saw coffee and a maker. Would you like me to put on a pot for you?"

Trixi paused for a moment to catch her breath, and then she laughed as she exhaled. It was, in a sense, her new life. "Yes, thank you."

To get the coffee going, Justine left Trixi's side. Upon seeing Justine enter the room, Aggie stepped out onto the patio. Aggie did something similar, wrapping her arms around Trixi's diminutive self as if she were a blanket. She wasn't completely undressed like Justine, but she also wasn't wearing anything but her sheer nightdress. She felt safe in her embrace, sheltered from the outside world and from the many contradictions of her own thoughts.

Trixi desperately didn't want her to let go. She turned around and leaned in for a kiss on Aggie's lips, wrapping her arms around her neck. They continued to kiss passionately until Justine joined them on the patio holding three cups of coffee. Aggie and Trixi both snatched theirs away from her.

There were only two seats available on the balcony, so Aggie and Trixi occupied them while Justine sat on the ground between them. It was certainly a strange sight to see a nude woman sitting on the patio, but Trixi doubted anyone had noticed from so far away. They sat sipping their coffee in silence, perhaps still recovering from a passionate evening.

After seeing Aggie finish her drink, Justine rose to her feet and headed back inside to get another one. She returned with a fresh cup and positioned herself on the floor again. A very attentive slave who anticipated Aggie's requirements and served her accordingly.

As Aggie took another sip of her hot drink, she put the mug on her lap and said, "I have to swing by the office today for a bit. Other than that, I am free. We have a little rearranging to do, but you are more than welcome to bring over your things at any time."

Justine spoke up, no longer in a submissive role. "Would you like your own room, or would you like to share the master with us?"

That wasn't something that crossed Trixi's mind. Invading their territory looked like a really presumptuous move on her part. She shrugged, "Where ever you want me."

"I'll make space in the closet and drawers, next to ours. We seem to fit well in the King."

Aggie commended Justine for accepting Trixi into their family by patting her on the head. "Great. Trixi, I know you will be a loving addition to our family."

Aggie gestured for Justine to join her, placing her mug on the side table. Without words, Justine crawled in front of Aggie and lowered her head between Aggie's legs. Aggie sat back, opening up for Justine to deliver what Aggie wanted.

Trixi watched as Justine's tongue caused Aggie to melt and slump into the chair. Her chest tightened and her breathing increased as her hands pressed Justine's head farther into her sex, and soon she was gasping for air in an avaricious orgasm. Justine raised her head and body to kiss Aggie as she finished.

Trixi raised an eyebrow at Aggie, impressed and perhaps envious. "So, how does she get you off with oral sex and I can't?"

Aggie flashed a sinister grin in response to this. "It's all in the mind."

Although Aggie offered Justine to Trixi, she declined the offer with a firm shake of her head. When Trixi rejected the offer, Justine frowned. "Are you sure? I'd like to start your day off, right?"

Trixi cocked her head, but she put it down with a grin on her face. In a flash, Justine's tongue located her sweet spot and began drenching Trixi in a savory tongue bath that was the perfect way to begin the day.

When they were done, Justine brought their cups to the kitchen sink. Both Aggie and Trixi stayed out on the terrace. Trixi looked at her curiously. "So, you've been playing me all this time?"

"You'll learn that when you want to be pleased, it will be beautiful. And when you don't, you can manipulate the sensations of your body. It's like being with someone you dislike. No matter what they do, you won't get off because they disgust you. So, yes. I've been studying you and learning what makes you tick."

"How long have you been into BDSM?" Trixi inquired, approaching her for the first time like an actual person rather than a mere prop.

"College. I coerced my psych professor into an unethical romp in which she enlightened me on bondage. To this day, I get quite turned on by a woman tied with rope." Aggie licked her lips and grinned.

"Last night, before you came over. I was with someone else—"

She interrupted Trixi. "I know. I smelled her on you."

Trixi gave a shake of her head in utter bewilderment. Of course, Aggie knew. "It wasn't the same. While it was okay, it wasn't exciting. I wanted that control. I craved to hear her feel some sort of pain during it. It was boring."

"When it's inside you, it's inside you," Aggie said, puffing out her chest.

Trixi faced her, all straight and proper. "I'm here. I'm paying attention. Teach me everything. Please."

"First lesson. Let Justine do what she does. She will learn your desires and your needs. Accept it because it will be correct. You will learn who she is, too. It isn't about sex, Trixi. That is all a by-product of something greater. Her needs are to serve and once you learn that—once you accept that—your eyes will open."

"What's different from having a maid or butler?"

Trixi asked.

"It varies from person to person. BDSM is more than service. It's more than kinky sex. It's about finding the give and the take. The ying and yang of it. While Justine prefers to serve, she enjoys pain. While you pay your maid or butlers in cash, we pay Justine with torture. It's what she wants."

Stupidly but earnestly, Trixi questioned, "How do you know what someone wants?"

"Ask them."

So Trixi did. "What do you want from it?"

The woman laughed. Trixi admired the crinkles that appeared at the edges of her eyes. Aggie answered her, "Devotion. Love. Someone who likes it rough. And a drama-free relationship."

With a wink, she got up from the chair and went inside, leaving Trixi there by herself. Trixi had the dedication. In love already. She did like it rough. It was the last part Trixi had the most trouble with. Trixi had a soft spot for dramatic situations. Perhaps she made an effort to find it. Internally, Trixi grinned. Trixi followed Aggie into the hotel room where they all showered together, or at least Justine bathed them.

Trixi's relocation to Glendale was a slow process, although a radical change from her previous dwelling. Despite making an effort to be respectful because it was their home, Trixi still enjoyed the comforts of having a maid to wait on her and cleaned up after her. That was Justine.

Every time Trixi came back to the estate, her father had questions about where she had been and what she had been doing. All of it was enjoyable, and it was done with a friend. He constantly said the same thing that he hoped she took care of her. He knew.

Possibly he was unaware of Aggie, but he knew it was a female. Trixi's father had always thrown a tantrum whenever she mentioned having a male friend, therefore she had never brought one home. It didn't make a difference with the ladies. She brought them home and didn't think twice about having them on her arm at parties.

Did Martin mind she liked older women? No. Although he most definitely would care, if he found out that his daughter and Aggie were snogging several times a day. Trixi simply thought he'd be concerned because she worked for him. He wouldn't give a rat's hind end if Trixi took Aggie home, if she wasn't working for him.

All three of them were getting along well. Aggie worked, Justine spent the day as a housewife and worked on her photography, and Trixi looked for new kinky pleasures for the bedroom online. When Aggie got home from work in the evenings, a servile and insatiable siren stripped her to the bare skin and greeted her every time she passed through the door.

Trixi felt confident in the success of their polyamorous relationship. Their willingness to go along with wacky plans and outlandish circumstances resulted in success (sometimes) and laughs (other times). They happily welcomed Trixi's BDSM-related discoveries and developments. When Aggie was working late with difficult artists, it was usually just Justine and Trixi to do the wrangling of each other. Trixi had more sexual intimacy with Justine than she did with Aggie.

That could only make her happy for so long. Again, Aggie needed to work. Besides preparing for her show, Justine also had to take care of domestic chores. Except for sex, Trixi had nothing else. After a few months together, Trixi felt like an only child with no one to play with when her parents were at work. As Trixi's boredom increased, she realized she needed to get out of the house and find someone or something to keep her busy for a while.

◆ ◆ ◆

It was late at night when Trixi got a text from Aggie. ***Hey, love. Where are you? We're worried.***

Sitting on the edge of Cookie's bed, Trixi sighed as she read the message and watched Cookie show off the summer outfits she had bought for herself while Trixi was off enjoying her new lovers.

Trixi grumbled and threw the phone, prompting

Cookie to question, "Who do you not want to talk to?"

"No one." She could have stopped there. "I swear, she's like a mother hen watching over her nest. Am I not allowed to have friends and go out?"

"And who are we talking about?" Not having told her best buddy about her recent life changes, it intrigued Cookie.

Trixi rolled over onto her back, becoming too dramatic as per usual. "This girl. Woman. Ugh! I'm so obsessed with her."

"Oh, do tell! How have I missed this? Oh, wait. You haven't been around."

Cookie and Trixi both flopped down on the bed and looked at each other with smiles on their faces, but for different reasons. Trixi said to her, "I know. It's her. I think I am in love."

"Then what's the problem?"

"I feel trapped. We don't go out. We stay in and screw all the time. She goes to work, and I am stuck, literally all day."

"Is she hot?"

"Beyond hot."

"And you have incredible sex?"

"Beyond incredible."

Grabbing Trixi by the arms, Cookie jumped from the bed. "Then what's the fucking problem? Go get laid and be a kept woman."

She made a valid argument. And, in all candor, Cookie was usually right when she made her arguments. Aggie required nothing from her except that she help keep Justine entertained while she worked. As for Trixi, she enjoyed seeing Justine at work, both at home and in her studio. They had spent a considerable amount of time in the darkroom watching images develop. And the time spent in the dungeons had been every bit as pleasurable. She would discover the motivations and desires that drove Justine, just as Aggie had predicted. As for the afternoon debauchery, Trixi gave Justine a say in the matter.

Trixi did a lot of lounging around the house, just as she used to do in New York, with the relationship obviously unbalanced because they both had to work and Trixi did nothing.

Trixi finally said to Cookie, "I want to have a purpose, something other than being a gorgeous mantelpiece. Maybe a hobby?"

"Shopping. That's a hobby, right?"

Trixi grinned at Cookie, loving every second of her. "That's yours."

Cookie questioned, "We can share hobbies, right?"

# SEX NEVER GOES OUT OF FASHION

Trixi was of tremendous assistance to Justine in the weeks preceding up to her art show, doing anything she could to make Justine's life easier like putting the finishing touches on the prints and framing her artwork. When they examined it in its entirety, all three of them found that the work was impressive. When it came to her erotica, Justine possessed a keen sense of aesthetics.

Throughout the duration of the installation, Justine made daily visits to the gallery. Trixi tagged along because she still didn't know what to do with herself. The day before the event, Justine and Trixi went to meet the museum's curator. When Justine introduced Trixi to the curator, Justine paused after mentioning Trixi's name, as if she needed to justify Trixi's presence.

Trixi extended her hand to the curator when Justine hesitated. "Her assistant. Trixi VanPelt. Nice to meet you."

Trixi took on the role of a servant for Justine, attending to her every whim and ensuring that she had all she needed. By the time the exhibition opened, every single person in the gallery was familiar with her; Justine Duval's photographer assistant known as Trixi. Her attendance at the opening was almost required because of her involvement with Justine, despite the fact that she had no prior experience in the matter.

Trixi strolled in with Justine and Aggie as if she belonged with them, but she was stunned by the sheer number of people that were attending the event. Trixi cozied up to them when they arrived, but soon afterward she was off mingling on her own.

The word "sex" served as the inspiration for the exhibition, which featured works by photographers, painters, and mixed media sculptors who each presented their unique interpretation of what the word "sex" signified. Not all the pieces were extremely explicit, showing eroticism or nudity.

A ferrotype picture of two pairs of feet intertwined in each other was the photograph that Trixi fell in love with and eventually purchased. It was called "First Love," and Trixi bought it before anyone else could. Justine's work complemented the show with her medium format prints of women in service flawlessly.

Trixi grabbed a glass of champagne from the bar, and while she did so, she took a sip while watching Justine engage in animated conversation with art collectors, fans, and other artists. Trixi became accustomed to seeing her around the home with no clothes on. She worked naked and lived naked, but on that night, she dressed in a pair of black slacks, a white button-down shirt, and a pair of suspenders. She did not button her shirt all the way up, which exposed her perky breasts and drew everyone's attention to them.

If she had been Aggie, having Justine on her arm would have been a great honor for Trixi. She had a lot of talent in addition to being stunning. Aggie's presence captivated Trixi while others swooned over Justine. She wore nothing but black. A blazer and jeans. If she removed her coat, everyone could see her tits through her sheer undershirt. She had her tresses pulled back into a side split and fell just below her shoulders. Trixi's desire to kiss Aggie was so intense it caused an aching in Trixi's chest because she knew she couldn't.

Perhaps it was the amount of sexual tension that was permeating the walls of the museum, but Trixi really needed some time alone with her. After what seemed like an eternity, Aggie parted ways with Justine in order to search for the restroom, and Trixi followed closely behind. Alone in the room, Trixi shoved Aggie into the stall, trapped her against the wall, and pressed her lips to Aggie's.

Aggie giggled under her forcefulness. She'd never let Trixi take her to an orgasm in a bathroom stall, but she'd take Trixi. To satiate her hunger, she'd get thirty seconds of love.

As Trixi bit into her neck, Aggie joked, "All this sex is a little too much for you, I see."

"Shut up and kiss me."

That's what Aggie did, and Trixi crashed against the other wall under the force of Aggie's weight. She reached up Trixi's dress, moving her panties to the side and thrusting her fingers into her. Trixi's head fell downward as she leaned on the wall with her back against it. As she inhaled deeply into her neck, Aggie stated, "Now is the time to be greedy."

Trixi reacted swiftly, bucking into her hand and coming fast and hard as she bit her lips together to contain her ecstasy. After Aggie finished her assault and Trixi had calmed down, she helped Trixi adjust her dress and pushed her out of the stall. "Go. I need to pee."

As she emerged from the ladies' room, Trixi beamed, an afterglow of sex evident on her face. Justine strolled over to the restroom and leaned by the door to say to Trixi, "Either you met Aggie in the restroom or you masturbated in the corner."

Trixi's attempts to conceal her shame were futile. Her cheeks flushed as she exhaled happily and her hands remained calm. In light of the mounting sexual tension, she wanted to know how Justine managed to keep from feeling horny all the time.

Justine laughed and put her arm around Trixi's shoulder, as if they were best friends instead of lovers. "It's a very fine line, but I'll tell you this. I am always aroused. I live that way."

Aggie emerged from the restroom to discover her swooning suitors standing next to one another, arms slung casually over one another. She snuggled up close to them, one hand on each of their hips. Aggie put her head between theirs and spoke softly. "One big happy family. This is exactly how I envisioned us being."

A collector ushered Justine away from the group. Trixi accompanied Aggie as they made their way toward a group of paintings. Trixi remained by Aggie's side the entire time. They had a lengthy conversation regarding the artwork on display in the gallery, and art in general. Trixi regarded Aggie carefully and soaked up as much information from her as she could. The extent of Aggie's art-world expertise astounded her.

Trixi asked, "If you love art so much, why stay working for my father? You could totally own a gallery of your own."

"No. It takes quite a bit of money to own a gallery that I do not have. I was an art major in college, which was why I traveled through Europe. When I came home, I needed a job. You know, I literally started in your father's company in the mailroom."

Trixi laughed, "No, I didn't know that."

"Worked my way up. It's taken me a long time to get here," Aggie leaned close and whispered, "That is why I don't need your sexy body getting me fired."

Trixi wasn't the one who struggled to maintain her distance. Trixi felt Aggie's lips brush against her ear as she breathed in close. With Aggie's breath warming her cheek, Trixi's chest heaved. Trixi replied, her attention still on the painting. "You love my sexy body, and it will be your greed that exposes us."

Aggie walked briskly off. Trixi, alone with the painting, reflected on its evocative spiritual link to the male body. Lesbianism was not the exclusive subject of all the works. In this context, sex referred to people of both sexes, including lesbians and gays. Artists of all genders were welcome to explore sexuality in their works; one photographer even documented transgender people for her work.

As the night came to an end, the artists raised glasses in a collective salute of the evening's achievements. A collector whose interests lie purely in bondage and discipline purchased a number of images by Justine.

Trixi fell into a deep sorrow as she watched admirers fawn over Justine and the other artists' successes. She lacked talent. Trixi yearned for the praise of the people who were closest to her; she wanted recognition for something other than simply having a wonderful figure or being a fantastic fuck.

After Aggie broke the news to Trixi one evening that she would need to return to New York, Trixi immediately called her father. She needed to get back to the East Coast quickly, so she inquired if there was anyone leaving in the next week so she could catch a flight. When he said that Aggie needed to handle a press junket, Trixi found a way to get on the plane.

Even though Trixi spent most of her time in New York with Aggie and Justine at their hotel, she stopped by the loft to say hello to her mom. Justine found great locations for a shoot with a model she hired and brought Trixi along for the ride. They could quickly and covertly undress the model, pose her, and take the photographs. Although Trixi had a great time and appreciated being included in the creative process, it left her with a hollow sense afterwards.

There were many times when Trixi wanted to run away from them, which was easier than staying. Trixi, in need of some alone time, took a cab to Greenwich Village, where she met up with Casey Till, a cute little blonde she'd became friends with during their senior year of high school.

Trixi and Casey hadn't talked since Trixi met Aggie, so they spent the day taking a leisurely stroll through town and drinking mimosas at a charming cafe. While out for a stroll, they happened into a quaint local used bookstore. Casey dragged Trixi in with glee. Because Casey had a history of being a voracious reader, Trixi anticipated they would leave with a number of books.

While Casey gathered those armfuls, Trixi searched the aisles for art books she could give to Justine as a possible addition to her collection. Trixi discovered a tiny erotica area and browsed the titles and covers there. Trixi reached for a book with the title *Emmanuelle* and opened it to the back cover to read the description. Her curious brows curved and peaked. With the book tucked under her arm, she set out in search of more.

After checking out, Trixi brought Justine a book on a photographer named Mapplethorpe, who seemed intriguing enough for Justine to like. Trixi bought Aggie one as well. Djuna Barnes's *Nightwood*, which brought Aggie to apparent joy. Trixi plunged right into hers when she had the chance. Justine, who appeared to be well familiar with the book, assured her she would enjoy it.

Trixi felt a connection to the book as she read it. After finishing reading, Trixi looked up the author online to find out more about them. Because of what it inspired, Trixi went out and bought a laptop, which she used repeatedly throughout the day and even into the night.

They returned to Glendale from New York. Trixi didn't tell her father about her homecoming. She just joined Aggie and Justine on the plane. Would the pilot really be willing to disappoint his boss's daughter by telling her she couldn't come?

Once again, Aggie's busy schedule sent her to Miami a month later. The plane bustled with businessmen, Justine, Aggie, and Trixi, as well as four teenage lads who wanted a chance to get into Trixi's panties.

Aggie finally got their attention by threatening to turn them all into sopranos if they didn't stop pestering the voluptuous young woman. That was a new side of her that Trixi had never seen before, and it sent shivers down her spine and sparks to fly.

Because of Aggie's busy schedule, Trixi understood why Aggie hoped to pair her together with her wife. Aggie's long hours on the road were enough to drive anyone crazy with loneliness. Early in the morning, exhausted and desperate for sleep, she'd make her way back to the hotel. Even with her two women there, she had no desire for anything other than to lie in bed and sleep.

While they were in town, Justine suggested they check out a sex museum. Naturally, Trixi agreed after learning that Miami was home to an erotica art museum. It was enjoyable to spend the day sight-seeing and eating Cuban food with Justine before returning to the hotel to peruse the art books she bought. What they were to each other was unchanging, yet they were shifting from romantic partners to close friends.

Justine served as their slave and provided an outlet for sexual activity that was both safe and consensual for them. Justine had her routine. Each morning, ma'am would wake up with a session of oral sex. She poised their carefully curated wardrobe on the bed for them. Justine gave Aggie a bath, then Trixi before she gave herself one. And as soon as they emerged from the bedroom, she greeted them with freshly brewed coffee.

When Aggie wasn't there, Justine would get on her knees in front of Trixi with pleading eyes, hoping that Trixi would give her permission to do anything she pleased. If Trixi enjoyed herself, which she usually did,

Trixi would reward Justine with tasty treats: painful hisses of delight.

During the days that Aggie was at work, Trixi and Justine strolled hand in hand along the beaches of Miami. While the waves crashed against the shore, they talked to one another while kicking the water. Even though they spent much of their time talking about art and photography, somehow the subject of eroticism managed to sneak its way into almost every discussion. Trixi inquired about Justine's sexual history by asking, "Have you ever made love on the beach?"

"No. I think Agatha would be quite appalled at the thought of sand up her crack," Justine said, then asked, "Have you?"

"Once. With a guy outside my father's beach house. The sex wasn't great, but the feeling of the soft sand is quite a turn on."

Justine laughed. "Now I'm picturing you lying on the beach naked."

"Maybe we should have a covert beach photo shoot and you can photograph me? I'd love to be one of your models."

Justine dismissed the concept with a wave of her hand. "Mistress already forbade the idea. I actually wanted to photograph you, but she put her foot down. I'm not one to go against her wishes."

"Why? I'm not a mantel piece that might get broken. She keeps putting me in this box like I'm some fragile object. It kind of pisses me off."

Justine came to a standstill in front of Trixi. "It's not that she's afraid of breaking you. Trust me, you can handle your own. She's so worrisome over someone in the organization finding out about us, she wants to keep you—,"

Trixi finished her sentence. "Her dirty little secret?"

"Don't think of it like that, Trixi. Please. We love you and—" Instead of completing her thought, Justine leaned in close to her and planted a passionate kiss on her lips. As she stepped back, she added, "I know I shouldn't have done that without permission, but I feel like we are beyond Mistress and slave here."

Trixi savored the affectionate gesture by licking her lips and thinking about how much it meant to her. "That's because I spend more time with you than her."

"And that's a bad thing?" Justine added.

"No." Trixi gave a cheeky smile and a hushed laugh. "You and I are alike. We both love Aggie, but we're forced to be with each other because she's never around."

Justine clasped Trixi's hand in hers and stated with a calm expression in her deep blue eyes, "She's not forcing me to be with you. I'm here because I want you. You've brought a lot of life into this relationship. Trust me, when I kiss you, it's not because that's what Mistress wants; it's because I want it just as much."

Trixi pushed her way past Justine, who was following close after. Trixi said, "Being exposed to this world, it's all I want. It makes my past seem so... irrelevant and uninspiring." Trixi rotated her body so she faced Justine. "I want you. Or to say, I want someone like you. Aggie is so lucky to have someone who she can dominate any time she wants."

Justine laughed. "You have that too. You have me."

"You're hers. I'm just keeping you warm until she gets home. Justine, I have nothing. I don't have a person, or a job, or even a frigging hobby that makes me something other than a sex object."

Justine beamed as she gently stroked Trixi's cheek with the back of her hand. "You're lucky, even if you don't think so. We both are. Agatha is a loving provider who will take care of you like she has me. And you have a person. Two actually. You're looking at this relationship with a wall up in front of you. All you see is the smoke screen everyone else does; behind it all is a world where we are free to love each other without limits."

In this case, Trixi recognized Justine's validity. She was technically the third wheel, but she was anything but. To lighten the mood, Trixi remarked, "Well, there are limits. I mean, I can't piss on you."

"Thank you for that." Justine smiled as she put an arm around Trixi, and they continued their walk along the shore.

"I need to know. Has anyone actually done that to you?"

Justine shook her head condescendingly and rolled her eyes. "Yes, in France. There was a man that paid to come in, drink some beers, then would hire a lady so he could urinate on them and would leave."

"Gross! Were there only submissives there?" Trixi asked.

"No. There were two buildings on this little compound where submissives lived in one, and the Dominants lived in the other. Both men and women together."

"Have you thought about dominating anyone?"

"It's not in me. That is why Mistress likes other Mistresses. She's a switch so to speak. She learned as submissive and loves the pain. Maybe not as much as

I do; but she needs to be in control of the scenes. Doesn't like to be tied up at all. Another Mistress, like you, comes in and gives Mistress a taste of her own medicine." Justine laughed off the cliché nature of her comment.

They spent many afternoons in this manner; the girls talked and bonded over topics other than the BDSM scenarios that dominated their evenings. Without Justine, Trixi might not have stayed by Aggie's side.

# SEX IS NOT THE ENEMY

Trixi couldn't recall the last time she had spent any significant amount of time at the mansion. It was after dinner and drinks with Trixi's sister when she returned to The Hills. She did not want to return to Glendale in the middle of the night since she knew her women were sound sleeping and she did not wish to wake them up.

Paolo drove Trixi home. She shooed him away to his quarters and told him she could make her way into the house without his assistance. Because she had spent most of her life there, she did not require an escort. Trixi entered the residence discretely from the back entrance. As usual, a light in the music room stayed on. As Trixi walked through the open French doors, she turned her head and saw her father having a liaison with a starlet while perched atop the piano.

Trixi let out a gasp. Martin and Miranda Valentine, clearly taken aback, whipped their heads around to stare at Trixi. Martin tore his cock away from the vocalist, and Miranda did not appreciate the ripping sensation that he caused. After experiencing it herself a few times, Trixi recognized the sight of pain from a man's rapid retreat from her sex.

Trixi continued rushing toward her room, and Martin, who had just cleaned himself up, raced after her. As soon as Trixi reached the top of the steps, he followed after her and grabbed her arm. "What are you doing here?"

Trixi struggled to free herself from his grasp. "I still

live here, don't I? Or has Miranda taken my bedroom? Oh, wait. She's in Mom's."

With a swift motion of his palm, he smacked her across the face with a forceful blow. "How dare you speak to me in that tone!"

Trixi struggled to hold back the tears, but she refused to allow the situation to dampen her spirit. She was not ready to give up the battle just yet. "Whatever, Dad. I'm going upstairs, so you can go back to boning the next big star."

As she ascended the stairs, he played his hand. "Give my best to Agatha. Oh, and tell her I'd like to see her in my office tomorrow."

Trixi froze. She came dangerously close to suffocating due to a tightness in her chest. Slowly, as she turned, Trixi saw him waiting for her at the bottom of the stairs, glaring down at her with an air of authority. "I know everything."

After he left, Trixi went straight to her room and closed her door with a resounding thud as soon as she was inside. It wasn't even possible for her to inform Aggie about this situation. It would add nothing new to what he already believed he understood, which was most likely all of it.

The following morning, Trixi made her way downstairs. She walked normally until she reached the kitchen, at which point she noticed her father sitting at the table in front of the bay window, drinking juice and reading the newspaper. In order to fetch her coffee, she walked more gingerly, almost on her tiptoes.

He spoke without taking his eyes off the page in front of him. "Trixi, grab some coffee and sit."

The last time he said this to her, they got into an argument about Paolo's supposed drug use. Even though Trixi's father seemed to believe Paolo the morning he accepted the blame for his daughter's idiocy, Trixi knew better.

Trixi positioned her cup and herself at the opposite end of the table from him. Almost instantly, she said, "I don't give a shit who you screw, Dad. You've been doing it for years. Last night was nothing new. We both know that."

"Then we're done here." Even at this point, he hadn't bothered to glance up from the paper.

When Trixi got up from the table to go back to her room, she had a brief moment of reflection before continuing on. She turned around to address the situation, her mouth forming the word *Aggie,* but she could not do it.

He asked before her words could form, "Is there something else?"

"No. I guess not." Trixi returned to her room and waited there till the smoke cleared. Though she felt strongly about defending Aggie, she knew talking to him about the subject would just confirm it.

Trixi stayed in her room and worked on her secret project for the better part of the morning and early afternoon. She literally encased herself with it. She worked without rest till she got a call from Cookie suggesting they have lunch together. It was an excellent location to stop. Trixi gathered her things and dialed Paolo. She would have him take her to lunch with Cookie, after which he would drop her back off in Glendale, where she would return to the life that she had fashioned for herself.

Trixi trotted downstairs with her backpack in tow. As she entered the foyer, she suddenly stopped short when she spotted Aggie and her dad there. Concerned that this was the conversation he intended to have with Aggie about her, Trixi's eyes widened.

With a sneaky smirk on his lips, he remarked, perhaps laying the stage for her dismissal. "Honey, you know Agatha."

"Uhm. Dad. I. Can we talk? Please." Trixi stammered. Aggie definitely sensed the tension in the discussion. As Aggie mused, Trixi noticed a flicker of worry in her eye.

"Later, Sweetie. I'm in the middle of a business meeting. You run along. We can chat later." He made a gesture for Aggie to follow him.

"No, Daddy. Really. Please!"

"Trixi, off you go." He was firm and straightforward in his final warning. He was done hearing her out. Trixi recognized the voice, which terrified his daughters when they were children.

Trixi clenched her fists and pushed her eyelids together as she prepared herself for the worst. She made her way outside, where Paolo waited with the door to the car propped open. Even though Trixi wanted to save Aggie from her father, she couldn't.

Aggie heard the front door close behind her. She turned her head ever-so-slightly to the side and gazed back over her shoulder, where she saw Trixi had already departed. Trixi's persistent disagreements with Martin led her to the conclusion that the upcoming conversation she was about to have with her boss would somehow be relevant to the nature of their relationship. In spite of the fact that she desired for her wall of defense to safeguard her, she maintained her composure and played the dialogue in a cool and controlled manner.

"Agatha, sweetheart. Let's take this to the office. I'm sorry you had to come in on your day off, but this needs to take precedence," Martin stated as he made his way down the hall to his private study.

"No worries. When it comes to work, I'm always on call," Aggie replied, since she wished to be as accommodating to him as was humanly possible.

"Exactly, this is why I like you." Martin opened the door and motioned into the room. He pointed to the chair while he walked behind the desk to sit on his throne. "How's Justine?"

"Well, sir. Glad to be back in California, for sure."

Martin reached for a picture of his children that he kept on his desk and studied it fondly. "You are fortunate to have someone who will travel with you. My girls are my angels. I used to bring them on all of my trips when they were little, especially Trixi. Now, I simply don't see them often enough. It seems like

Traci is always off with her friends. Trixi, well, she's a handful. She's always running here and there. I'd prefer her home more, but we don't always get what we want. Agatha, do you not concur?"

As Aggie's chest constricted, she took a deep breath and swallowed hard. Because of her anxiety, she gripped her hands in front of her and began to sweat. "Having Justine come along on my trips is great, I must admit. Thank you for accommodating our closeness."

"As you stated, she is delighted to be back in California. I believe that our two favorite people appreciate this region. And this is excellent news because a position on the west coast has just become available, and I'd like you to accept it," Martin replied, after placing the photograph on his desk and clasping his hands together.

"Sir, thank you, but I am perfectly content working with artists on the east coast. I am familiar with the area, and all of my contacts are there. I am confident that the events and exposure I am securing for your artists are solid. Is it not?"

"Yes. Very much, Agatha. This is why I believe you are the most qualified candidate for the position. The west coast has a premium market. There is a great deal more occurring that requires a powerful leader. This is in no way a demotion. Due to the market's tightness and competition, agents and promoters need someone with your skill set. In addition, it is advantageous for your wife to stay at home, where you stated she prefers to be."

"I am grateful for your confidence, but I must respectfully decline." When Aggie observed his authoritative glare at her, she asked, "Or do I not have a choice?"

"Sure. You have a choice." His eyes narrowed and lingered a bit too long on her cleavage, which was exposed by her unbuttoned collar. He raised his gaze to hers. "Obviously, you have a choice, but I've already filled the position on the east coast since I know you'd want to spend more time with your beautiful wife."

Aggie nodded. She didn't need to battle the circumstance because she knew she had two options. She may accept the position or she could resign. Aggie knew his unspoken intentions, especially when he mentioned Trixi being at home, because he didn't need to speak them. Martin accused her of mingling with his daughter by using particular phrases and stressing others, but without presenting the truth.

The two resumed their discussion on the work and her additional responsibilities. The promoters she oversaw arrived at the estate for introductions within an hour. He had planned everything to prepare for Aggie to accept the role. When one of her subordinates informed her that the former west coast supervisor had relocated to New York, her suspicions were verified.

Following a series of updates, Aggie packed her briefcase and exited the office. As she reached for the front door, she overheard one of the men say Trixi. Her ears pricked up, but she did not let anyone know she was listening in on the discussion.

"I should go upstairs and see whether Trixi is still there. According to legend, she is a nymph. She'll fuck anyone."

Aggie was unable to contain her anger about their disregard for professionalism and Martin's daughter. She joined them with a march of authority. "I will replace you with the snap of my fingers if I catch any of you sticking your dicks where they shouldn't be."

Aggie then turned away and walked to the door. As she opened the door, she immediately heard the sarcastic insults of her new staff. "She's a dyke that wishes she had a cock."

Aggie continued to her car without engaging the ignorant, as there was no reason for her to do so. Aggie's backbone relaxed as she reached the protection of her vehicle, and she sagged into the seat. Her eyes filled with despair and rage, as she immediately detested her new position.

Because of her anxiety around her father and Aggie, Trixi did not enjoy lunch with Cookie. Aggie had not yet returned to Glendale after her rendezvous with Martin when she arrived. Justine had also not heard from her.

Justine prepared supper as Trixi sat at the kitchen island with her laptop open. Trixi's typing on the keyboard drew the attention of Justine, who gave her some strange looks, then asked, "What are you working on?"

Trixi glanced up from the display while maintaining her fingers on the keyboard. "Remember how I mentioned in Miami that I wanted more in my life? I decided to write a book."

Without turning around from stirring the aromatic sauce on the stove, Justine stated, "A book?"

"Yeah. After reading the book, *Emmanuelle*, it inspired me to write my own scandalous love story, which I realize sounds ridiculous. A little erotique and a poly relationship? I believe I have a good understanding of this style of narrative."

Justine giggled, "That you do. Well, I want to read it after you've completed it. I have no doubt that it will be juicy."

"Can we please not tell Aggie? I intend to surprise her with it once I've completed it."

Justine agreed, and they continued with their evening. Justine did not get a text message until after dark, at which point she walked to the side door and kneeled down. It signified Aggie's return home.

When Aggie entered her ranch-style home through the side door, she kissed Justine. Trixi anticipated being screamed at, but she also received a kiss. "I apologize for the delay. How are my women today?"

Aggie took a healthy swallow of the red wine that Justine poured for her and then patiently waited for more. "Good, sweetheart. I currently have supper simmering on the burner. Let's get you undressed and then we'll eat. I'm sure you're hungry."

Aggie grinned. "Actually, let's go out. We can celebrate."

Trixi paused, troubled by Aggie's buoyant disposition. "What are we celebrating?"

"I got a promotion."

Trixi exhaled a sigh of relief as Justine placed her arms around Aggie. Aggie directed a stern look in Trixi's direction while Justine clutched on. Her eyes revealed to Trixi that she was unhappy with the promotion and with her. Her father was aware of their connection, but they decided to put off discussing it for the time being. Certainly not that night. That evening, they celebrated.

Aggie brought her significant others to a wonderful restaurant for dinner to celebrate her promotion and hefty pay increase. Although money was not what she desired, she had no option but to take it. She maintained a polite grin while Justine celebrated. She would have more time at home to devote to her craft. The sight of Justine's happiness pleased Aggie, but it was not what she desired.

When she accepted the position as a promoter, they offered her a west coast route, but Aggie preferred the opposite side of the country. The setting and ambiance were considerably more refined than sunny California's casual lifestyle. She simply selected to reside in the state since her wife, Melody, cherished it. She made concessions when they relocated to Glendale, but since her wife's death, she despised living there.

Aggie's fury had eased by the end of the night, mostly due to Justine's euphoric descriptions of how she might schedule additional photo sessions and spread her work to other galleries while maintaining a more secure living situation.

When they got to their residence, Justine disrobed and made her way to the bedroom. Aggie stood at the island as Trixi retreated behind her computer. She tapped the marble counter top to get Trixi's attention.

When she did, Aggie quipped, "Does it make you happy too? Being able to spend your entire time here without having to get permission to board one of my flights?"

Trixi raised her eyebrows and said, "If you're trying to start an argument, it won't work. I've done nothing wrong."

"What was that then this morning? You were rather eager to talk with your father prior to my being hauled into his office, where he continued to tell me how much he cherished you and appreciated you being at home."

Trixi slammed the laptop shut in response, indicating that it touched a nerve. She seized the device and stormed into the living room. After Trixi exited the room, Aggie expelled a deep sigh. She needed relaxation, which necessitated a massage.

In the living room, Trixi worked diligently. She

intended to create a tale about a married couple who took in a young, innocent woman and devoured her immediately. Similar to her relationships with Aggie and Justine, however the tale barely alluded to their bondage and discipline. In contrast to her actual life, the lady entering the relationship was the subservient one. Due to Trixi's lack of knowledge about Aggie's ex-wife, Justine took the stage in her tale rather than her.

Her ears pricked up as she heard the unmistakable moaning of her two favorite people having a good time. It wasn't the first time that Aggie and Justine had spent some time alone. Trixi didn't like being touched when she was on her period, so she usually spent that week alone. However, that wasn't the case this time.

Trixi approached the playroom on tiptoe and peered through the open door. Aggie lay face down on the table with her legs dangling over the edge, while Justine stood behind her and massaged her back. Justine's hips moved with little jerks toward Aggie's center. It was uncommon to see Aggie as the bottom in a sexual interaction.

Trixi slid down the wall and sat with her back against it and her knees up so as not to interrupt. There was a reason they did not invite Trixi to the play date. Trixi, feeling a bit left out, placed her finger between her thighs and circled her clit for her own orgasm as Aggie sang the house into a serenade.

Aggie's promotion took her off the road to handle the high-end musicians in Los Angeles, which meant they would be on the West Coast year-round.

During the next months, they established a pattern, although there appeared to be lingering nonverbal tension between Aggie and Trixi. Since Aggie's promotion, it had persisted, but Aggie never allowed it to interfere with what they did behind closed doors.

Trixi stayed at home on a night when Justine departed for an evening photographic session. Aggie sat and read a book in the living room. Trixi kneeled next to the ottoman and kissed Aggie's leg, as if she tried to make amends.

Aggie pushed her aside and stated, "Not now."

"Are you angry with me?" Trixi questioned as she scowled and felt rejected.

"Why would you think that?" She placed her book on her lap and shifted her focus to Trixi.

"Because I sense this tension in the house. Did I do something?"

"Did you?"

"No. But I believe you think I did."

"Why do you say that?"

They were circling the answers and interrogating one another. "Do you still want me here?"

"You wouldn't be here if I didn't want you," Aggie remarked with a half-smile.

Trixi got onto her lap while wearing nothing except

a long shirt. Her knees pressed against both sides of the chair. Trixi reached into Aggie's lounge pants and felt the warmth between her legs as she kissed her. As Trixie took the breath from Aggie's lungs, she whimpered into her ear.

Next to her chair, on the side table, was an ancient wooden box. Aggie grabbed the box, opened it, and extracted a phallus made from ivory that was as old as the box itself. Aggie signaled Trixi to rise with a tap on the outside thigh.

Trixi's eyes brimmed with tears as she raised her body and Aggie placed the ivory shaft in her lap. Trixi caught her breath as she braced herself for the worst. Slowly, she ingested it with care, as there was no give to it and no soft, rubbery parts to conform to her sex. Trixi cried out in agony as she expelled the breath she held.

Nothing was forgiving to this dildo that Aggie wanted her to fuck. While Trixi knew this would hurt like hell, she nevertheless accepted whatever Aggie thought she deserved. It was not a sex-for-pleasure object. The purpose of Aggie's thick, ivory phallus was punishment. Each time Trixi sank on it, it felt like a dagger digging into her sex cavity. She wept. She wailed. And when she orgasmed, the pain was so severe, bile churned in her stomach. Trixi's tears flowed down her cheeks as she felt remorse for something she had not done. Trixi done nothing to warrant the chastisement, yet she accepted it in light of the strained nature of their relationship.

Trixi returned to her perch in the kitchen and spent the evening alone with her thoughts while working on her laptop. Trixi didn't greet Justine when she arrived home. Justine, acting more as a mediator, remarked as she suspected something was amiss. "I leave you two alone for a few hours, and there is trouble in paradise."

Trixi remained silent as Justine approached Aggie. The home was so small that nothing was private unless one whispered. Therefore, Trixi could hear their conversation.

◆ ◆ ◆

As soon as Justine entered the living room, where Aggie sat with her nose buried in a book, she exclaimed, "Why does Trixi look like you sent her to hell?"

Without responding to her query, Aggie handed Justine the ivory dildo. "Here. Clean it up"

"What in the hell did she do to deserve that?" Justine's voice rose in surprise as she comprehended what Aggie had done with the horrific phallus.

"Do what I say. It's not your place to question."

"I am and will; but seriously? What's going on? Something has been amiss between you two, and I have the right to say so and to ask." Justine said more quietly so that their conversation wouldn't be heard in the kitchen.

Aggie dropped her voice to a whisper. "I've only ever requested that her existence in this household remain a secret. Martin knows. Now I have to deal with the fallout by working over these pretentious pricks. We are all aware that Martin would not have offered me this position on his own, especially considering that he knew exactly everything I wanted when I jumped into promotions."

"And you think she told him?"

"Doesn't matter. He is certain. And that was the rule.

No one knew. That jackass said everything he needed to when he threaten my job. This is my punishment for erroneously believing this would work with her."

"Perhaps you should quit viewing this as negative. I adore being home. And if he knows and doesn't fire you, she has sort of won, correct?"

"That's the point. I didn't have a choice. Do you honestly think I want to stay here? I hate being in this house." Aggie suppressed her tears.

Justine leaned forward toward Aggie and gently stroked her face. "Sell the house. You know Trixi wasn't a mistake. The issue is not with her."

◆ ◆ ◆

Trixi retreated from the living room door frame and returned to the kitchen island. Martin did not fire Aggie for having an affair with his daughter. His problems were with Trixi, not Aggie. Because Trixi had witnessed her father and Miranda fornicating, it was his way of blackmailing Trixi into remaining silent. He used Aggie like a chess piece.

Her conflicts with her father were so ancient that she scarcely recalled them but at the same time, she vividly remembered them. It was really difficult for her to escape his grasp. And it was that fear that made her want to run away from Aggie and Justine, but she had to stop doing that.

Trixi immersed herself in her work until Justine entered the kitchen carrying the bloody awful ivory dick that tore her apart. Justine meticulously cleaned and polished it, as though she had done so previously; possibly following her own punishment. Trixi loathed looking at it because she could still feel the searing sensation it produced.

When Justine left the kitchen with it in her hands, Trixi did not see it or them again that evening. She stayed devoted to her task and slept on the couch, unwilling to join them in the bedroom.

With a kiss, Aggie awoke Trixi in the morning. At first, it scared Trixi, but when she looked into Aggie's caring eyes, she knew everything was going to be okay. Aggie bent over her, pressed her chin to Trixi's chest, and gazed up at her almost pleadingly. Aggie cracked a smile.

Aggie said, "Regardless of how upset or angry you are, everyone in this house sleeps in beds, not sofas."

"I didn't do anything. I swear, Aggie."

"Let's not dwell on this any longer. Get up and move! Justine will draw a bath for you. I need to get to work. Morning meetings."

She rose and helped Trixi to her feet. Trixi got no apologies, despite her protestations of innocence. Trixi believed she would never obtain one, a sadness she would carry with her for quite some time.

# AUTOMATIC SYSTEMATIC HABIT

Life once more settled into a pattern. A consequence of dating a woman twice her age. They cherished regularity and predictability. They enjoyed what they enjoyed. The more Trixi comprehended their relationship, the more she knew Justine was more than a mere sexual slave. She was bound by the rules of Aggie's household, which included living a boring existence. She had no voice other than to yell rouge when Trixi carried the games a bit too far, typically without Aggie.

Without Aggie, Trixi often and vigorously tested Justine's limitations. It exhausted them following hours of furious play that occurred in the dungeons. Outside of their sex lair, Trixi and Justine were best friends. They laughed with one another, ate lunch in the city, and explored the sights as if they were tourists. Trixi fulfilled her duty, which was to occupy Justine.

Aggie typically capped Justine's pain level before she reached her threshold on the occasions when Aggie joined them for a threesome. Aggie's false portrayal as a sadist annoyed Trixi. Justine and Trixi pushed the boundaries nearly every day until she serenaded her with a one-word aria: rouge.

Trixi remained infatuated with Aggie, but the animosity between them never fully subsided. The dangers of them remaining in Los Angeles were they lacked the diversion of sightseeing and socializing. When Aggie returned home from work in the evenings, their regular routine at home led them to sink into a rut of monotony.

They occasionally dined with one of their groups of pals. There was one BDSM lesbian couple among them, but most of them were vanilla lesbians who were Aggie's friends. Still, not as amazing as when Trixi joined their universe for the first time. It allowed Trixi to complete the project, which she accomplished.

One ecstatic evening, Trixi typed the letters *FIN* and printed off the three hundred-plus pages. Trixi rushed into the kitchen where Aggie and Justine were tasting the spaghetti sauce on the stove, clutching a stack of papers and announcing, "I have something to show you."

Justine looked toward her. "You're finished?"

Aggie questioned, "Finished what?"

The distinction between Justine and Aggie was their level of vigilance. While Justine inquired about her computer activity, Aggie never asked what she had been working on the computer for so many evenings.

Trixi announced as she placed the manuscript on the kitchen island, "I wrote a book."

"Wow. It looks big." Justine said, echoing Trixi's enthusiasm.

While Aggie lacked the same excitement, she frowned her brow in disapproval. "A book? You were aware of this?" Aggie instead glared at Justine rather than Trixi.

They engaged in a silent exchange until Aggie shifted her focus back to Trixi. "What's it about?"

"It's based on us. I mean, it's fictional. Similar to us, but not, I guess." Aggie's expressions caused Trixi's elation to wane.

Her brow furrowed and her focus intensified as she dropped her voice. "You wrote a book about us?"

"Not us. Inspired by, maybe," Trixi moaned as her backbone bowed in response to Aggie's repeated rebuke.

"Delete it. Tear it. Burn it. No one can know about us, Trixi."

Justine drew the manuscript over the counter with her hand. "Madam, please read it before you—"

Aggie knocked it out of Justine's hands. "I cannot tolerate this. No matter what you do, nobody will ever view this. Do you hear me?"

"Fine." Trixi walked out of the room, angry and upset, with tears flowing down her cheeks. Aggie wouldn't even talk. Trixi slumped to the floor just outside the kitchen, anticipating a conversation in which she would not participate. She waited with her knees tucked to her chest and her arms crossed.

"You should read it before passing judgment. It might be fantastic." Justine defended Trixi's position.

"I don't want to hear another word about this."

"Love, please. She's been working hard on this."

"Justine, kennel!"

"Are you serious? You are sending me away because I don't agree with you?"

Aggie increased her voice. Trixi did not need to be in the room to visualize Aggie extending her arm and pointing to the bedroom while saying "Kennel."

"Now. Not a word," Aggie demanded.

Trixi recoiled at the sound of metal striking metal as Justine locked herself in the dog crate on the bedroom floor. Trixi arose from her anguish and headed to the bedroom, where the nude slave who had been protecting her sat in a cage.

Trixie apologized as she went by her. Trixi placed her hand through the bars and patted her head. "I can't stay. No matter how hard I try, I can't be the person she wants me to be."

Justine rolled her eyes in Trixi's direction. "Again? Really? Grow up and quit acting like such a baby. Relationships aren't about running away."

Trixi attempted to protect her honor. "She continues to blame me for being imprisoned here, despite her obvious desire to go and be somewhere else. This passive-aggressive bullshit is just that. And I'm tired of feeling like her child." Trixi snatched her suitcase out of the closet.

"Fine. Go have a tantrum. Eventually, though, the door will no longer be open. I really don't want you to go. Stop running, Trix."

"Why, so we can fuck all day long? Call me. When she leaves, I'll come over and screw your brains out."

Aggie responded, "No, you won't." The focus shifted to the entrance where Aggie stood. "And put away that suitcase. Trixi, you're not going anywhere."

"What are you going to do, throw me in a cage, too?"

Aggie snapped her fingers together. "Justine."

Justine unlocked her kennel door and crept to her owner with her head lowered the entire distance. As she approached her, Aggie patted her head.

Trixi responded with sarcasm, "You want me inside?"

"Go finish dinner." Aggie smacked Justine on the bottom, prompting her to flee, leaving Aggie and Trixi to battle it out. "I don't want you to leave either."

"You're making it very hard to stay." Trixi defended her heart by crossing her arms.

"You make it difficult to refrain from stripping off your clothes and making love to you on this bed." Aggie entered the room, stalking Trixi like prey.

Trixi huffed. "Sex doesn't solve everything. It only hides the real problem."

"Which is? You drafting a book about us I do not wish for anybody to read?" Aggie halted, aggressive again.

"Why is it alright for Justine to have art shows with bondage and kink, but when I find something I am skilled at and like, you want me to destroy it?"

Aggie's chest swelled as she prepared to return fire on Trixi. She conceded instead with a passive-aggressive tone. "Fine. Touché. Publish it, submit it. Show it to the world, Trixi. I'm done talking about it."

As Aggie turned to leave the room, Trixi's rage reached its peak. Trixi shoved her into a playroom when she was halfway down the corridor. Trixi may have been little, but her wrath was enormous, giving her the power to shove Aggie onto a table and locking her into a table-mounted handcuff.

While Aggie objected, Trixi illogically snatched a bamboo cane with little metal pricks from the wall. She carried out her hatred against Aggie onto her back. Trixi's heart raced as blood rushed to her brain, causing her nerves to burn.

Aggie screamed as Trixi lashed the cane toward her.

"Stop. Treating. Me. Like. A. Child." Trixi's palm smashed down with each syllable she spoke until she cried herself to stop.

Aggie's back bled from the flesh gashes caused by Trixi's wrath. Trixi sobbed, pressing her body against her to staunch the bleeding with her shirt. Instead of shouting at Trixi, Aggie comforted her by placing her free hand on Trixi's cheek behind her.

Without freeing Aggie's hands, Trixi pushed herself out of the room, into the kitchen, only to witness Justine's wide-eyed terror, then out the front door.

J ustine rushed up to the table, and as she pulled Aggie away from it, she started wildly yelling and crying. Her cheeks heated with drenching tears. She wrapped her arms around Aggie and hugged her. Aggie did her best to soothe her during the ordeal, despite the fact that she was in excruciating pain. They clung to one another for a considerable amount of time, both of them shaking in terror at what had taken place.

Aggie was unable to respond in time to prevent Trixi from reaching out in her rage, since everything occurred so rapidly. Even though they knew Trixi had a temper, they never imagined that she would actually act violently when she lost it. She never once raised her hand in any situation and instead walked out of the room in a huff like a spoiled brat.

Despite Aggie's best efforts, Justine continued to cry. Justine's mind kept going back to the harrowing event of that night, which had taken place in the same room where they found Melody dead. She knew she needed to pull herself up and care for Aggie's wounds, but fear prevented her from separating herself from her wife's arms so that she could do so.

It wasn't until late in the evening that Justine's shaking subsided sufficiently for her to get up on her own. She lifted Aggie off the ground and carefully led her to the bathroom, where she retrieved a first aid box from the medicine cabinet.

Injuries from a BDSM beating were not ones that needed to be treated at the emergency department.

An excessive amount of paperwork and uncertainties over consent always impeded providing proper care for BDSM participants.

After assisting other prostitutes in France hurt by heavy-handed dominants, Justine acquired the knowledge necessary to treat wounds and cuts on her own. She leaned Aggie over the bathroom counter, washed her wounds, and then stitched up the deep and serious cuts with a shaky hand. Throughout the whole event, Justine kept apologizing for the unsteadiness of her fingers.

As the rage that she felt within her grew, Justine choked back even more tears. As she threw away Aggie's bloodied garment, she slammed the garbage can shut behind her. When Aggie entered the kitchen, she stooped, gripping her back. Justine's eyes swelled up again with tears.

She chittered in her direction. "Hey. I'm fine."

Justine finally spoke up at that point. "No. I'm not doing this again. I can't."

Aggie embraced her once again. Justine wanted to grasp her and not let go, but she didn't want to harm the new sutures on her delicate skin.

Aggie insisted, "This is not the same."

"I don't give a shit. No!" Justine attempted to break away, but Aggie tightly held her. She buried her head against Aggie's shoulder and instead of wiping away her tears, she let them fall.

As Justine held Aggie, she replayed the night Melody died in her memory. It wasn't simply that she passed away; it was also that they discovered her murdered body in the same room where Trixi had beaten Aggie. Her slaying was at the hands of individuals they regarded as trustworthy confidants and who they granted access to their hidden realm. It was why Aggie prohibited others from knowing their kink.

Aggie and Justine had returned from a trip to the store to discover that two of their female friends had beaten Melody to a pulp, strangled her, and raped her mutilated corpse. Aggie had hurried to save her wife, sustaining a side stab wound in the process.

While both women found themselves jailed and subjected to prosecution, Melody's body remained a horrific memory for both. Justine might not have witnessed Trixi slam the cane into Aggie, but she was unwilling to let her lover suffered the same fate.

Aggie ultimately quelled Justine's agitation to where they could have an adult conversation, unrelated to the room or the past. They entered the living room, where Aggie growled as she leaned back in her chair. Aggie turned away from Justine's attempts to nurse her. "I'm fine, beautiful. Sit. Let's talk."

Justine sat on the ottoman in front of Aggie with a resolute attitude and stated, "She cannot comeback."

"Let's not be too hasty. This is nothing I can't handle."

"That's not the point. You shouldn't have to handle it. It never should have happened. Trixi was out of control and lost her temper. As much as I love her, I will not bring fear into this house."

"I'm not afraid of her."

"I am. And if I can't trust her, then I can't play with her."

Aggie lowered her head and patted Justine's knee. "You will do as I say, and if that includes being with

Trixi, then you will be with Trixi."

Her eyes widened. "You can't be serious. Aggie?"

"I will talk to her. We'll work this out."

"As much as I live by your rules and under your thumb, I will not stand by you if you bring her back into this house. I'm sorry, but it will not happen. So if you want Trixi so fucking bad, I'm gone."

Aggie struck Justine's lips. "Watch your language. No matter how angry you are, we do not use those words in this house."

Justine sprang up, no longer able to look at Aggie. Aggie's fixation on Trixi prevented her from noticing her ongoing damaging actions. Trixi and Aggie frequently engaged in yelling bouts over petty matters. While Trixi may not have previously let her fury spill into her fists, it did occur, and Justine could not unsee Trixi's rage. Trixi fled the house with fiery eyes and a heart filled with hatred. And at that moment, Justine needed to leave because her heart simmered in the same fiery blood.

"Where are you going? Get back here," Aggie commanded.

"To my kennel, as you won't appreciate what I have to say." Justine went to the bedroom, where she locked herself in the dog cage on the floor of the room.

After what seemed like an eternity, Aggie finally entered the bedroom. Still inside her kennel, Justine remained in the same position: curled into a ball with her knees pulled up to her chest. Aggie opened up the crate and held the door open for her. "I believe that we have both regained our composure at this point."

Justine steadfastly refused to move. "My position

hasn't changed."

"Mine has. Come out."

She climbed out of the kennel while Aggie ruffled her hair. As she lifted to her feet, Aggie threw her arms affectionately around Justine.

Aggie continued, "You are correct. My affection for Trixi is clouding my judgment, and as a result, I have neglected to see your concern. You have the right to choose your Mistresses, and if Trixi makes you feel unsafe, I will sever ties with her."

"Thank you. The very last thing I or you need is another tragedy to endure. I can't lose you because of some stupid girl who can't keep her temper in check," Justine insisted.

"You won't have to. Let's call it a night. I can use a little snuggling."

After a quick change, they both got into bed and held each other until morning.

# GET BUSY WITH THE FIZZY

Since leaving Aggie's home two months prior, Trixi had neither communicated with nor texted one of them the entire time. Neither of them desired to turn the other cheek, be the bigger person, or ask for forgiveness. They were both in the wrong for what they had done to one another, but neither would accept it.

During this period, Trixi conducted research on publishing avenues for her story. Ultimately, she requested the assistance from Gracie Anderson, an agent on her father's payroll. Gracie knew just what to do after reading the manuscript, therefore Trixi allowed her to do the task.

Trixi, wrapped up in her own world and projects, didn't realize her father had planned an event at the Mansion until she woke up and found it bustling. Trixi asked people around her for details, but they were all too busy to answer her. She peered into her father's office, hoping not to observe him and Miranda or anybody else sharing a passionate moment. Trixi did not want to disturb her father, who had his nose buried in a stack of papers on his desk, so she left the room.

"Trixi!" He bellowed.

Even without looking up from his stack, he recognized her at the entrance. She entered once again. "What's going on?"

He eventually looked up. "You tell me. You were looking for me?"

"I was simply curious as to what's happening here tonight? Do I have to leave? Remain in my room?"

"Merger. We're celebrating the merger of ViP and Black Dog Records. Both companies coming under one roof. Mine. And no, you're welcome to come."

"Got it." As she was about to leave, he beckoned her back inside.

"Hey. How are things with you? You appear to be at home constantly now."

Trixi lowered her head, her heart suffering as a result of the unsaid breakup. "Fine. It's over, whatever it was."

"Good to hear."

Perhaps it was for him, but it was still terribly painful for Trixi. She left his office in a foul mood due to the turmoil in her life.

Trixi attended the party that evening, mixing with artists her age and the children of her father's coworkers. As usual, the younger generation flocked toward the music area while the older crowd conversed about business.

Naturally, Trixi's gaze followed the door each time it opened in hopes to see Aggie's arrival. When Aggie entered the home, it was as though Trixi's spirit sensed her presence. Trixi caught a glimpse of her as she entered the front door, wearing a plum-colored one-piece dress with a neckline that plunged halfway down her stomach. When she walked into the room, Trixi was sure that more than half of the people there wanted to fuck her.

On her arm, Justine wore a black and silver strapless gown that was equally delicious-looking. *Why must it be so difficult?* Trixie asked herself, wanting to be their third member; or more so, she wanted to be Justine. Trixi imbibed champagne as she pursued them through the gathering. She overheard Aggie describe Justine as her nine-year partner. Hearing that said aloud struck Trixi's heart like a two-edged dagger. She could never be Aggie's partner if Aggie continued to work with her father.

No matter how old she was, screwing one of her father's employees was a sin, even though it had happened most of her life, sometimes not by choice. And she would never acknowledge it took place. However, the pain persisted.

Hearing that the love of her life was with another person, despite having lived with them for a few years, was painful. That night, Trixi felt like the other woman, like a prostitute who wasn't good enough to be number one. Aggie paraded Justine about like a princess while ignoring her presence.

Watching Aggie ignore her the whole evening, Trixi spent much of the night brooding and looking for someone to call her own. Aggie refrained from looking in Trixi's way because she was her boss's daughter. When Justine and Trixi met eyes for the first and only time, Justine's rage was palpable.

When Trixi entered the dining room, she saw Aggie loading a dish with food. They were alone, if only momentarily. Before Trixi could say anything, Aggie objected, "Don't. Not here. Not right now"

"I came for food, thank you. And FYI, I never threw you under the bus. He has a fucking tracker on my phone." Trixi exited the room after reciting the details she learned over a recent lunch with her sister, during which she bemoaned the end of her relationship with Aggie. Since the daughters' teenage years, when they made more and more friends, their father had been monitoring their whereabouts.

Hours into the gala, Miranda Valentine poked her way behind Trixi, who was wearing a skin-tight burgundy dress with tiny straps. Miranda muttered, "We're going to a club tonight. Want to go with me and lose these oldies?"

Trixi gave her a sidelong look, still furious that she screwed her dad. "What? Daddy just doesn't cut it anymore?"

"Fine. I know you hate me, but get over it already." Miranda tossed her hair over her shoulder and said, "I'm not trying to become your mother. Besides, he goes limp before he creams."

"TMI!" Trixi vomited, then regurgitated the bile. Trixi stuffed an olive in her mouth and swallowed another glass of champagne when she noticed Aggie laughing at a joke and Justine giggling next to her. "I'd love to. Show me the fucking party."

Before Miranda released Trixi from her clutches, she posed the question. "Which one is she?"

Trixi asked, "What do you mean?"

"The one you can't have?"

"Is it that obvious?"

Miranda laughed. "Certainly, lust and melancholy are written all over your face. Now, let's get drunk and find somebody to fuck."

They sped out from the estate in a limo that transported the pop princess and her entourage through the streets of West Hollywood.

The chauffeur dropped them off in front of the trendy nightclub Daddy-O's, which reminded Trixi of a cocktail lounge from the 1950s. When Miranda smiled at the doorman, he permitted them entry into the pulsating dance club.

The velvet fabric booths around the walls welcomed the Eames designs from the club's inception in 1958. Trixi adored the ambiance of that location and could see herself claiming a throne there when she assembled her own court. Hopefully, she induced the most intense orgasms in every woman she controlled.

When Miranda arrived among the visitors, the throng dispersed like the Red Sea, and she settled in the center of the dance floor, grinding her body to the rhythm of club music on everybody who came near.

Feeling the beat of the music vibrating around her, Trixi bounced along, grooving in style with her eyes closed and her body floating in the clouds, as the little pill Miranda gave her did its magic.

Trixi let free, mulling about everyone surrounding her without focusing on anybody in particular. Trixi smirked as she surveyed the beautiful women, including Miranda, who she wanted to take to bed. When Miranda squeezed into a male-dominated sandwich between two sex-pots touching her body beneath the dancing lights, Trixi reconsidered her plan to grind into Miranda.

Trixi's style didn't scream lesbian; therefore she doubted she'd attract any. She wore her hair down and darkened in accordance with her new look. Trixi exposed her physique for everyone to see. She flaunted her riches and position among the other renowned individuals in her present circle by wearing costly outfits. When all Trixi could see around her that night were heterosexual couples twerking to the music beats, it seemed difficult for her to find a romantic partner.

Trixi scoured the room looking for a gorgeous to spend her evening and perhaps her night with as Miranda found a booth, management throwing out non-famous individuals from her section. Trixi scrutinized the eyes that were upon her. She searched for a female holding a provocative pair. Instead, vulgar guys stared at her, while their female equivalents glared at her figure.

As Trixi circled the bar, she saw someone. A young woman leaned back on the bar, elbows behind her, chest rising with assurance. Her slicked-back hair and arm tattoos said volumes. In spite of Trixi's preconceived notions she was a lesbian, Trixi drew her attention to the woman's eyes as they swept over her body with adulation. The look which Trixi wanted.

Between her and a guy waving at the bartender, Trixi wedged herself close to the woman. She advanced on the bar, lifted her breasts, and exposed her cleavage to the bartender, ensuring her body made contact with the girl's hand. When Trixi leaned into the girl, she didn't move.

Trixi apologized for breaching her space by brushing her arm with her hand while glancing quickly in her direction. Neither of them moved once again. The hand of the strong girl flattened down under Trixi's body so that it rested on her tummy. She bit her lower lip and sucked it in as she inhaled.

"CJ." The girl smiled as she evaluated Trixi.

"Trixi." She retreated shyly, being coy with the gorgeous model-like tomboy.

Trixi saw CJ stifle a chuckle as she said, "Trixi? Really? Unless you're going to cost me a fortune, I don't believe it."

The dangers of a name her parents sought to match with Traci, her sister. The majority of the time, she abhorred it. "It might cost you losing the best fuck of your life. I'm not a hooker, asshole."

Trixi grabbed the drink from the bar and started to leave when she felt a hand clutch her wrist. She spun around, ready to strike, as CJ raised her other hand in surrender.

"Whoa. Truce. I'm sorry if your name is really Trixi."

"It is, though I doubt your birth certificate reads CJ either," Trixi murmured, pondering archaic names from the ancient world.

"Touché. Carolina Jean, but I don't think either represents my vibe."

"Your vibe as a jerk? Or your vibe as a greedy little bitch who likes to stare at my breasts?" Trixi said, drawing CJ's attention from her breast to her eyes and asserting authority over what she desired.

"Well, they are quite beautiful, but I am thinking they are not your best asset; that might be your sass."

"On the contrary, it would be my ability to make you scream."

CJ smiled treacherously at Trixi as her attention remained fixed on her eyes and not her tits. "Do you want to get out of here and prove it?"

Trixi's timid and feminine blush concealed the reality that she relished the harshness. "And how do I know I should trust you? Especially when I don't even know you."

CJ extended three fingers into the air. "I promise, I'm not a creepy old man who will take you to a cabin in the woods. And how do I know you're not some vixen luring me to my demise?"

Trixi crushed her body into CJ, elevating to her ear and breathed in. "Oh, I am. And you'll be screaming the entire time."

Trixi nipped CJ's earlobe, gently pulling it as she retreated. She drew CJ out of the club with her hip-swaying swagger, entrancing CJ to follow her. She didn't bother telling Miranda, already wasted, that she was leaving. Trixi quickly missed the line of taxis waiting outside the club, ready to transport passengers wherever, like in New York.

Trixi turned to CJ with an arched brow, arms crossed, and tits raised in exasperation. "I really hope you don't plan on taking me somewhere in an Uber?"

With a low snort, CJ extracted a parking ticket from her pocket and gave it to the valet. As they waited, CJ leaned her body against Trixi's back and rested her hands on Trixi's slender hips, cuddling with her. "I have some friends in the Valley hosting a little kink fest. We don't have to go. I mean, we could go back to your place. Or hit the party. Lady's choice."

"Kink fest, huh?" Trixi's mind raced, since it might signify an infinite number of things. "What kind of kink are we talking about?"

"A little S&M, B&D. Don't know if you're into that. As I said, we can skip it if you're vanilla. You can pick the place."

Trixi rotated and pushed herself forward while maintaining CJ's grip on her hips. CJ was a demi-gentleman since she continued to touch Trixi without her consent. Trixi dug her fingernail into CJ's skin from her temple to her cheek. "If this party includes you bent over my knee, I'm in."

A velocity blue Jaguar sports car awaited their arrival with its doors open. CJ touched Trixi's lips, then moved her finger down Trixi's jaw and neck, reaching the cleavage line of her dress. "Do I get to see these?"

"If you're a good girl." Trixi yanked CJ's hand away from her body while emitting a hiss. "Touch me again without my permission, and I will break your hand."

CJ's gaze lifted upward as she realized the gravity of Trixi's comments. She inhaled deeply while smiling slightly. CJ leaned towards Trixi slowly and gently, pressing her lips against hers and inserting her tongue into her mouth while Trixi inhaled her. When CJ took a breath, she said, "Yes, Ma'am."

There was nothing comparable to the Beverly Hills houses, with acres of property around their pools and tennis fields. Even though the homes in the Valley were expensive, Trixi didn't think they were as fancy as the ones in the city. When they drew up to the grandiose Spanish-style property, she winced in horror.

CJ did not even enter by the front entrance; instead, she took Trixi through a side gate and down a pink crape myrtle-lined pathway to the pool area, where individuals skinny-dipped and others mingled in and out of the guest house in the backyard.

Instantaneously, Trixi loathed the gathering, packed with noisy conversations and a disregard for the property. As they walked toward the guest house where loud music played, a guy peed on a tree.

The sight of submissives on leashes and both male and female dominatrix walking their pets caused Trixi's eyes to widen as she entered the residence for a Valley party. A Saint Andrews cross stood in the corner, and a powerful man whipped someone while a line of other people waited for their turn. A kink free-for-all, unrefined and unlike Aggie's sophisticated New York club.

CJ grasped Trixi's hand but dropped it instantly, forgetting her rule about touching.

"Thank you." Nevertheless, Trixi seized CJ's hand as they went into the larger-than-expected guest house. Trixi attempted to avoid touching anything or anybody that would soil her clothes and skin. She hardly wanted CJ to touch her, but the notion of having a sub to torment overcame her desire to vomit at the unruly group of overindulged adolescents.

CJ murmured into someone's ear as they stopped next to her. The young woman surveyed Trixi with her eyes darting from head to toe. She pointed down the hallway with a snarling grin. CJ pointed Trixi in the direction where they were to go.

At the door at the end of the hallway, CJ grasped the doorknob and glanced behind her. "By your repulsive glare at the crowd, I figured you'd rather get to business than socializing with my posse."

"When you say business, I think money. So I'll leave if you think this is a business transaction. I'm here for my pleasure and yours."

CJ smiled precariously as she opened the door. Trixi prayed she hadn't gotten in over her head. Aggie was easy after Trixi learned all her pleasure zones. Justine was malleable, like putty in her hands. Trixi had no knowledge of CJ. She was out of her element in a wild, uncertain environment.

Despite disliking her loss of power, Trixi entered the bedroom and allowed herself to be trapped within. She walked around the room, gazing at the décor as she went. Upon the door's closing, CJ removed her shirt.

When Trixi turned around, she saw that CJ's petite but perky breasts complemented her heavily tattooed chest. She channeled her inner diva to maintain control over CJ. She tossed the shirt back to her. "Seriously, I'll tell you when to undress."

"You're really into this kink stuff?" CJ said, as she slipped her shirt over her head and straightened it.

"You said this was a BDSM party; where are the toys?" Trixi arched her brow.

CJ exhaled deeply, desiring Trixi's involvement in her little game. She hopped over to the dresser drawer, opened it, and revealed an abundance of sex toys within. Whatever Trixi could possibly dream. "Take your pick."

Trixi's lips watered as she contemplated all the treats she would employ, ones she had never seen or used on her two victims. Her fingertips slithered over everything she enjoyed. Under her breath, she said aloud, "I need to build my own collection."

"JT's Stockroom in Los Angeles," CJ boasted as Trixi took up a silicon apple and wiggled it in the air, attempting to determine where to attach it to a human given that it had a USB cord outlet.

Trixi tossed it back into the drawer with a shrug and retrieved two straps with rubber-tipped clamps on either end. She could only speculate. Trixi swallowed deeply before placing the items back in the drawer. Trixi continued to scan the room, locating herself, appraising her surroundings, and searching for an exit. Something she learned well from her former relationships.

In the corner was a padded folding table with two holes on each side. Cuffs hung from numerous D hooks along each side of the table, and one at each end. Trixi sensed the possibilities. She strolled to CJ with a promiscuous hop, yanked her shirt, and drew her near the table while tugging on her lip. CJ shuffled with Trixi without opposing her advances and with a swift movement of hands, CJ's shirt slipped over her head and back on to the floor.

Trixi clasped her hands behind her back and

fastened them to the table because she knew she could not trust CJ to not touch her. Trixi teased her breasts with her tongue as they perfectly aligned with her lips. She despised her diminutive stature, but Trixi did not have to struggle in this situation. CJ dissolved under Trixi's taste buds as she whimpered and flicked her perky nipple with her tongue.

Trixi approached the treasure chest and discovered a pair of Japanese nipple clamps. She returned to CJ's shirtless body with a little jump and positioned a clamp right over the dark circles while squeezing her nipple upward.

CJ growled as goosebumps sprang on her chest as Trixi flicked the bound breast with her tongue then nibbled at it with her teeth. Her approaches took CJ's breath away.

Trixi gripped CJ's chin in the palm of her hand, drawing CJ's face to hers. "What's your safe word, sexy?"

As Trixi's tongue stroked CJ's lips, she exhaled and replied, "I don't need one. Whatever you want to do."

"What I plan on doing, you'll need one. What's your safe word?"

"Fuck me?" CJ joked.

Trixi's demeanor reflected her seriousness, and she did not find her lack of civility for the lifestyle to be impressive. Trixi went for her jugular, clenching her teeth and whispering through pursed lips. "If you keep acting like this is a joke, I'll walk. What is your safe word?"

"You are one feisty bitch. I love it," CJ remarked while shaking her head and grinning sheepishly. "Snoopy. Now put your threats into action. Make me scream."

Trixi despised CJ's arrogance; it did not fit her. "Okay,

Carolina." She flicked CJ's ear with her finger, already irritated by her.

She knew she should have left, but Aggie's words continued to ring in her ears as she introduced Justine as her partner, as well as lover. Trixi despised it. She despised the fact that she would never be someone Aggie could flaunt on her arm. Trixi was a dirty little secret she kept locked up in her room at night, which only exacerbated her anger.

Trixi scraped CJ's face and caused havoc on her breast by dragging her bright pink-polished nails over the phoenix tattoo on one side of her torso.

CJ hissed and licked her lips again as she saw Trixi at work. Trixi grabbed the second clamp and fastened it to her right side, leaving a chain hanging in the center of her tummy. Trixi took a step back, appreciating CJ's steel-decorated, undeveloped breasts.

CJ nodded to Trixi. Her tone dripped with arrogance. "You gonna show me your tits, yet?"

Trixi removed one hand from the cuff, bent CJ over the table, and reattached it to the other side. She could no longer rise without bringing the table with her. Trixi observed CJ's line of sight at that moment, trying to locate the best place for the show.

When Trixi reached around and unzipped CJ's black pants, she discovered that CJ did not wear any underwear, an utterly repulsive act to do in a pair of dirty jeans. No one she'd even think of being interested in enjoying long term. CJ lacked the subtlety of a woman, something Trixi understood she could not alter even if she wanted CJ as her pet.

Her mind replayed the scenario. If CJ wanted to see her, Trixi would enable her to see her get pleasure from her misery. She retrieved a butt plug made of silicone from the drawer. Trixi applied lubricant on CJ despite the fact that she did not merit it and wrapped it in a condom from the pile atop the dresser.

She rammed the plug into CJ's anus due to her lewd desire to see her breasts. CJ moaned under the strict discipline. "Fuck me, Trixi."

"Oh, I'm not doing the work." Trixi doubled the size of the plug.

Under her clenched teeth, CJ whispered, "More. Give me more."

Trixi pumped it up to its maximum capacity, but she simply hissed and did not scream out in agony. When Trixi pressed the button, the low hum matched CJ's voice as she murmured, "Child's play, baby."

How could Trixi come if the victim was not writhing in pain? She realized this was her ultimate culmination. Trixi needed the screaming. She reached for anything she could find—paddles, canes, and whips. Nothing caused CJ to wince. It was much worse than her first time with Aggie, which was bad enough considering her lack of expertise in the BDSM realm. CJ was no stranger to pain. Trixi's erogenous zone was on fire because of the amount of force she had to put on CJ. It sent shivers down her spine.

"I thought your best asset was your ability to make me scream? We both were wrong. It's your tits. Now let me see them."

CJ infuriated her. Her inability to induce sexual ecstasy in the girl wounded her ego. Trixi grabbed between CJ's little cleavage, grasped the chain from the nipple clamps, and pulled them off with a roar as rage swept over her.

They tore from her body. With a bellow of excruciating pain, CJ screamed, "Fuck! Snoopy. Fucking Snoopy!"

Trixi then tore her panties from her hips and collapsed on the bed. Her sex blazed and ached for release. Trixi exposed herself to CJ as CJ wept the tears that compelled Trixi to come. Her fingers rapidly circled her clit, driving her to a climax in response to CJ's sobbing.

Trixi peered over her body and saw CJ watching her as she pleasured herself. Her thrusting hips taunted CJ as she controlled her sobbing. As Trixi reached her apex, her head fell backwards. She felt the surge of feminine essence across her fingertips. Her insides exploded with glee at CJ's misery.

Trixi sat up on the bed, pleased, and invited CJ to lick her fingers, which she did gladly. She unhooked one of CJ's hands, which she then used to seize Trixi's wrist and hold it in her mouth. As she unhooked her other hand, Trixi granted her this pleasure.

Trixi brought her lips to her chest, ready to administer some loving treatment to her breasts, but CJ overcame her, bringing her wrist to the same shackles she had inhabited. "My turn, you little vixen."

"Wait, I didn't agree with that. I said no."

"Trust me, you'll love it." CJ drew Trixi's other hand, squeezing her against the table and pushing her backward.

"Stop. Red. Snoopy. Don't do this!"

CJ's hand continued to urge Trixi backward, but she could only bend so far, particularly since she was small. Trixi arched her back which only popped her breasts forward. With a tear of her dress, CJ exposed Trixi's breasts to the cold room's air. CJ threw Trixi's body with ease, allowing her to lie flat on her back.

Trixi struggled to free herself by tugging on the shackles but she couldn't break free. When CJ stepped away from her, she used that moment to plead for her freedom. "Seriously, CJ. I don't want this."

"You don't want this? You wanted it two seconds ago when you masturbated in front of me. How fair you can come and I can't?" CJ kept her back to Trixi, who saw CJ putting something around her waist.

"Just let me go and I'll eat you out. Fuck you, whatever you want," Trixi begged.

"Whatever I want. Thanks. Because I want this."

CJ turned around with a strap-on wrapped around her waist. Trixi heard the quiet hum of the vibrator and watched as CJ rolled her eyes. Something was within her, and it will soon be inside Trixi. She closed her eyes, bracing herself for the impending invasion of her sex.

CJ slammed into Trixi with a powerful buck of her hips. The recollection of the guys Trixi once fucked without a care returned to her. Instead of stiffening her muscles in protest, Trixi closed her eyes and ground her teeth as CJ fucked her with such fury that she couldn't conceal the fact that she love it while also hating it.

The vibration, along with the powerful strokes pushing into Trixi's sex, caused indistinct murmurs of ecstasy to leave her lips. She despised it.

"See, I knew you'd love it," CJ said as she heard Trixi's groans.

The dam of tears broke. Trixi averted her head, terrified that CJ might see her frailty. She insisted, "Shut up and fuck me already."

Trixi's vulgarity with Aggie had faded, yet her loathing for CJ had reignited it. Trixi forced her eyes tight, missing the softness of a caring woman, waiting for the oncoming climax to rise inside her.

CJ's body pressed down on Trixi as she consumed her breast. Trixi couldn't contain her contentment as CJ nibbled and tugged at her delicate nipple. Her breasts heaved against CJ's lips. It felt great to be abused by CJ.

With muted groans, CJ squeezed Trixi's breasts together and buried her face in the generous cleavage, squeezing and twisting both of her nipples with agonizing force. A heinous act that males believe ladies adored. Trixi's refined women had never suffocated themselves into her cleavage. CJ made Trixi sick.

Trixi took deeper breaths, her lungs discharging hot air through her throat. She broke out in a high octave shriek, unable to halt the jerking of her body. Soon after and with a hard blast of her hips into Trixi, CJ's own aria of ecstasy sounded across the room.

After shutting off the buzzing between them, CJ lowered her weight on top of Trixi with a deep sigh. Her hand squeezed Trixi's breasts as if she owned them.

Trixi jerked away, but still bound to the table by her handcuffs, she had nowhere to go. She scowled, "Let me go."

CJ rose and extracted the dildo from their centers. She threw it to the ground and removed the cuffs from Trixi's wrists. As soon as they were loose enough, Trixi yanked them free. Not hiding her anger from the situation, Trixi struck CJ in the face with a backhand after pulling her dress up at the top and down at the bottom.

As CJ gently massaged her cheek, her head cocked to

the side and her neck popped. Trixi spun on her heel and marched towards the entrance. As she opened the door, she heard CJ say, "Babe, you have incredible tits."

Trixi stormed out of the room, oblivious to the naked and half-dressed individuals being spanked over counters in every room of the house. Trixi walked away without a backwards glance. Her backbone was solid and her posture was upright. Nobody would witness her meltdown. Not that evening. Not ever.

Trixi marched down the driveway and past CJ's car after slamming the gate shut. She grabbed her stiletto and smashed the headlight with its heel, shattering the plastic, before continuing her exit. Trixi dashed down the slope and out of sight of that God-awful location.

On her walk of shame, as she exited the subdivision, her heels clicked against the pavement. Trixi wept and sobbed with each step as she realized the error she had committed by selecting a mysterious person, going to a location outside of her comfort zone, and interacting with someone who did not share her objectives.

At the bus stop at the bottom of the hill, Trixi sat with her head in her hands on the covered bench. She despised the life she had fashioned for herself. Returning her thoughts to happier times, she recalled Aggie's kind smile and the tears shed by Justine as she thanked Trixi for pleasing her. Together, they wrapped themselves in a blanket and watched a movie. A portion of her wished she were more like Justine; content to merely exist in Aggie's presence. The other part of her desired to be loved unconditionally by someone like Justine.

Trixi, in over her head, pulled her phone from her purse and dialed the number.

Aggie answered the phone when Trixi requested help. She heard the terrified voice of a woman who still possessed her heart. Even with all that had happened, she couldn't ignore Trixi. When she hung up the phone and rose from her seat, Justine questioned Aggie's departure.

"I need to rescue Trixi," Aggie stated.

"Rescue her from where?" Justine inquired, fearing that additional drama would ensue.

"The Valley." As Justine opened her mouth, Aggie closed it with a wave. "I'll take her home. She won't come here."

"Is she alright?" Justine asked, her voice still conveying profound affection for her.

Aggie exited the room without responding. Justine stood and followed her, her concern growing. As Justine stood in the bedroom doorway with fearful eyes, Aggie stated, "I'm sure she's fine. She needs a ride."

"She has a personal driver," Justine stated, becoming increasingly irritated and less concerned.

Aggie whisked her hand across Justine's cheek before giving her a gentle kiss. "She needs a friend."

"You are not her mother," Justine huffed.

"She would not be in this situation if not for my impulsive desire to possess lovely creatures. I have a duty to her. I'll be back."

◆ ◆ ◆

Trixi praised God for Aggie's decision to leave Justine at home. She loathed the condescending glances that Justine might have given her upon her return. Her age and youth reared their ugly heads once more, and she ran to the only person who could console her. Trixi realized she had made a grave error by taking her knowledge outside of Aggie's domain.

When Trixi closed the car door, Aggie did not immediately drive away. Trixi's smeared eyeliner running down her face indicated she wasn't doing well. "Tell me what happened? We'll discuss why later."

Trixi kept her attention on the hem of her dress as she spoke so softly that she could barely hear herself. "I picked up some girl in a bar and we came out to this BDSM party. Things didn't go as planned as I ended up strapped to a table where she fucked me."

"Consensual?"

"No. I said no, but she didn't stop. It didn't hurt. Just a bruised ego, all the way around. With you. With CJ. I'm sorry."

"CJ is the girl who raped you?"

"It wasn't rape. I just want to go home. With you, Aggie."

Instead of driving down the main road, Aggie turned the corner and drove up the hill to where she believed the party was. It was simple to locate, but Trixi objected to Aggie's search for the residence.

The music, cars, and lights. Aggie arrived at the residence with an attitude. Trixi reached across the vehicle with a soft touch of her hand. "Aggie. Don't. It's no big deal."

"It's a very big deal." She stepped from the car with a

slam of the door.

Trixie followed her, tugging on her arm and her back. "Come on, stop. Let's just go home."

She pushed Trixi off of her as they hurried through the gate. "Stay here."

Of course, Trixi didn't. Aggie scampered to the residence, yelling CJ's name. Eyes surrounded them. "Who the hell is CJ?" she yelled as she burst into the guesthouse.

The fingers pointed to CJ, who stood in the corner with a smug expression of a tough girl. "Who the fuck are you?"

Trixi had never witnessed such rage in Aggie's eyes as she did when she punched CJ in the face with a right cross. CJ's jaw dislocated, producing a bone-crack sound. Everyone in the area recoiled when Trixi grabbed Aggie. "Stop!"

Aggie pointed towards CJ, who was holding her bloodied mouth. "You touch my girl again, you die. No, means no."

As they prepared to leave, CJ insisted on having the last word. "Great tits and beautiful snatch. You have a winner on your hands!"

Trixi jumped in front of Aggie and pushed her back with her hands on her chest as she turned toward her. CJ continued with the digs. "I questioned why she wandered off. Perhaps Grandma does not wet her enough."

Trixi lost control of Aggie, who then charged at CJ and threw her frail body into the wall as if it weighed nothing. "Cops will be here in five minutes to break this party up, and your ass is in jail for rape."

Immediately after Aggie spoke, the crowd dispersed.

People raced in all directions to recover their garments and poured out onto the street to avoid being caught. Half were minors and the other half were barely adults who did not wish to get caught with alcohol, drugs, or sex.

Trixi followed Aggie to her car as she went through the backyard as others rushed past her. Trixi made a forward lean. "You didn't call the cops."

"They don't know that."

When they reached the car, Aggie finally exhaled her confidence. She glance towards Trixi as her eyes lost their fury. "You say you're fine, but are you really?"

"Like I said, CJ didn't physically hurt me. Aggie, I just want to go home and make love to you and Justine. I want our family back."

As they drove from the Valley to the city, Aggie revealed she would not be taking Trixi to Glendale. She'd bring her to the Mansion. Even after apologizing and pleading to rejoin their lives, Aggie informed Trixi that they were departing in a few days for a two-week trip to Nebraska. Trixi requested an invitation which Aggie could not offer.

Aggie explained she could not share Trixi's presence with her old and ailing parents when Trixi pouted like a displeased toddler. She could-not became a would-not due to Trixi's whiney remarks. Aggie chastised Trixi for the debate about her personal life. Trixi refused to acknowledge that Justine held Aggie's unconditional love.

They pulled up to the mansion's circular driveway. Aggie shifted the vehicle into park and turned to Trixi, arguing as a parent would. "What the hell were you thinking?"

"I'm sorry. I was just having fun." Trixi's face contorted in response to a parental rebuke.

"This is not something to play with. You are too young to be picking up strangers at some bar for a quickie. Are you seriously that person?"

Trixi pulled her lips together, still facing the terror of being yelled at by a figure of authority. "I'm sorry."

"It's like you have no respect for yourself and you put yourself in danger because you have no clue what those people are capable of. You can't just spread your legs for anyone with a pulse."

Trixi's ability to hold back her tears had finally been exhausted, and as she babbled despite the tightness in her chest, tears streamed down her face. She made a fist to quell her anger. "You act like I'm some whore. That's not what this was about."

Aggie's stern voice raised even more as her face reddened. "Then tell me. What's this all about Trixi? Because I literally spend my days listening to people who brag at the water fountain about the promiscuous VanPelt daughter, who has a cute little mole on her thigh. I don't know who you are."

"That was the past. I'm not that girl anymore. You changed all of it. Please Aggie. I'm sorry I hurt you. I'm sorry for what I said, but I love you and all I want is another chance. Please!"

Aggie shook her head to express her annoyance. "I think it's best that we part ways. You're home safe. I can now sleep more soundly."

Trixi opened the door, but turned to Aggie before stepping out. "Fuck you, Aggie. You're just like all the others. Take from me what you need, then kick me to the curb when you're done. I thought you were different, but you're not. You're just another bastard who took advantage of a girl with a big heart."

As Trixi exited the car, Aggie exclaimed, "Trixi, that's not fair!"

The door slammed shut. Aggie opened the driver-side door and exited the vehicle. "Trixi! Stop!"

"Go home, Aggie. Trust me,. I'll sleep just fine." Trixi yelled from the front door, "And I'll add another notch to my bedpost for you!"

With a salute, Trixi stepped into the house with a slam of the door.

# WHAT GIRLS ARE MADE OF

Aggie and Justine left Trixi behind in Los Angeles while they traveled to Nebraska for a non-work-related purpose. Obviously, Trixi threw a tantrum, resulting in an outburst of rudeness at everyone who looked in her direction. The wait staff at the mansion scrambled to avoid her. Her wrath shouted demands to those beneath her.

After yielding to her apprehension of discovering someone in the wild once more, her primary source of delight and pleasure was the staff's dread. After her humiliating interaction with CJ, Trixi realized all she wanted to do was torment people. It did not prevent her from wanting to find someone for herself.

She felt more pain from being abandoned than from fleeing something she knew would be there once she overcame her moodiness. In the back of her mind, Aggie and Justine were sitting in Glendale, doing what they usually did: living a humdrum existence on the outside while engaging in naughty and delightful sexual activity on the inside. However, they were not. They were not in the state at all.

With them in Nebraska, Trixie had no pending obligations. She sat in her room, wondering what she did before they came into her life. Trixi knew her life had to alter when she discovered she did nothing. There was no one who could assist her with that change.

Trixi bought a Bentley-sized load of pleasure toys from CJ's favored retailer. A filthy and, dare she say, rustic hole in the wall filled with every toy she could possibly conceive. She paid for their full year's rent in a single buying binge.

She needed to search inside her social networks, which broadened as she spent more time with people her age. She invited Cookie over to test the waters of constructing a personal mini-dungeon with her new toys. Trixi revealed a few trinkets from her toy chest as Cookie, her most attractive friend, entered the room. Cookie, in jest, fawned over the flesh-colored cock that was suction-cupped to her dresser and wrapped her lips over it.

Trixi met Cookie during one of her father's galas, and Cookie became one of her closest friends. Cookie, like Trixi, dreaded the events and spent the evening with Trixi making up stories about Martin's guests, the majority of which were real because Trixi was the protagonist of their exploits.

Cookie said as she stroked the realistic dildo, "I'd love to have someone this size inside me, so long as he was muscular from head to toe."

Trixi rolled her eyes and scoffed at her. "Guys are not all that. They're hairy and sweaty—"

She cut Trixi off. "I've seen plenty of women like that, too."

It was the truth. Trixi's stomach churned at the sight of CJ's untrimmed undergrowth, which consisted of a massive, unruly shrub. Instead of continuing to discuss males, Trixi shifted the topic. "Can you ever see yourself with a woman?"

"Oh, yeah. I'm game if the woman was beautiful."

Trixi would partake in her game. "Who do you consider beautiful?"

Trixi may have equated her flaming cheeks to her

vulva if she had ever been able to view it. "There's so many. Madonna. Miley. That woman on SVU. You. Britney."

"Of course, I'm beautiful." Trixi discovered her name on her list of ladies. "You know, I'm a dominatrix."

Cookie's eyes widened. "Duh, you obviously are. You're so bossy half the time. I love it. Do you wear a leather jumpsuit similar to those seen in films? Have you dominated anyone famous?"

Trixi put her toys away with an exaggerated eye roll and accompanied Cookie shopping, where they irritated store employees by trying on everything in the boutique, only to find it all terrible while giggling behind their backs.

Jennifer Drunen was Trixi's next victim. A socialite who flitted about the room, talking about how she was nobody in a world of somebodies. She was the daughter of an investor in Martin's independent label buyout. She had attended the previous gala, but Trixi paid her little mind. Trixi led the girl to her room and subtly asserted her power over Jennifer, as her father had instructed her to play nice when Jennifer arrived.

Trixi sought to engage Jennifer in conversation about her experiences by alluding to her fetish. Attempting to discover common ground, or simply something to determine whether she had a wicked side. Trixi pretended to be looking for something to show her when she rummaged through her dresser drawer and pulled out sex toys in an attempt to pique her curiosity.

As she peered over Trixi's shoulder, Jennifer's curiosity increased. "Are those sex toys?"

"Yeah. You into kink?" Trixi inquired, while looking

over her shoulder. Jennifer towered over Trixi thanks to her tall legs.

"No, but I've heard S&M parties are popping up all over Southern California."

From experience, Trixi replied, "I'd stay away from parties, especially with people you don't know." Trixi took a big breath and concluded that she might have a chance with Jennifer. She needed to seize the opportunity with Jennifer, if possible. "If you're interested, I can show you certain stuff; I mean, if you don't mind a little girl-on-girl?"

"Show me things like what? Handcuffs and blindfolds?"

"Among other things." Trixi lifted her breasts while wearing a tank top by pressing her back on the dresser.

"I think you're trying to get into my panties." Jennifer grinned with a sheepish smile and giggles.

Trixi's finest quality, her sass, flowed into the room, drenching the black lace panties she wore. "Only if you want me in your panties."

Jennifer back flipped into the silk sheets and removed her underwear as soon as she landed. "None of that painful stuff, but you can totally go down on me."

The flying underwear struck Trixi in the face and fell to the ground. Trixi made no attempt to capture them. She was immune to the sight of underwear being thrown at her as a tease. Jennifer lifted her legs, keeping her feet firmly on the bed and her clothing draped over her knees. She looked ready to give birth. Trixi saw nothing seductive about this.

Trixi slipped the dress up, since she believed that oral sex was preferable to none. If she didn't do the same, Trixi would force herself to have an orgasm after

Jennifer left. Trixi marveled at Jennifer's bare sex. The radiantly flawless skin greeted her. Trixi grazed her fingers where a manicured garden should have been with a sly grin and followed the distinctive shape, dipping her fingers between the folds to Jennifer's shaking core. Jennifer's chest rose as Trixi's hand touched just her flesh. No hair, no stubble. Only flesh and the pleasant feeling of her wetness were present.

Trixi raised her finger to her mouth and tapped her tongue in order to sample what Jennifer had provided. Trixi did not wish to expose her taste buds to a bitter woman. As Aggie had instructed, she conducted a small taste test to ensure that she possessed pleasant delectability.

Trixi kissed Jennifer's inner thigh while her fingers trailed over her skin and caressed her fleshy folds while on her knees. Two fingers separated them so Trixi could enjoy the pink fleshy bud. Her thumb brushed across it, generating a shudder. Trixi saw with excitement the appearance of goosebumps on Jennifer's legs.

Trixi pulled her aggressively and drew the begging sex to her. Jennifer's vanilla-scented body blended with her core's musk. Trixi kissed Jennifer's thigh while lifting one leg over her shoulder, nibbling the skin and listening to the purring under her touch. Trixi raised the second leg over her shoulder and kissed it again as she moved her mouth nearer to the heat.

Trixi stretched Jennifer wide with her hands, opening her folds where she licked from her cunt to her clit, consuming as much of Jennifer's flowing sex as she could. She covered the pink, swollen bud with her tongue and sucked deeply into Jennifer, attempting to drink her up.

So quick. Jennifer convulsed around the lips of Trixi. Her body erupted, and her breathing became heavy and quick, emitted a hoarse wailing. Jennifer pulled away from Trixi, removing her legs and standing while yanking her dress down. Trixi hardly experienced her own pleasure when it abruptly ceased.

Either Trixi had become so much better at what she did, or Jennifer was the easiest lay she had ever encountered. Jennifer gave Trixi a peck with a tiny bounce when she kissed her. She ran from the bedroom to the study, where she embraced her father for the remainder of the evening. When they ultimately parted ways for the night, Jennifer extended an invitation to become best friends.

Trixi climbed the stairs to her bedroom, where she pushed the apple contraption, which she adored, to her clit and let it suck the hell out of her.

# BLOOD FOR POPPIES

After returning from Nebraska, Aggie phoned Trixi. She refused the call, only for Aggie to leave a voice mail stating that they had returned and desired to see her. Trixi, still rather enraged, refused all of her calls and slammed the phone down whenever her private mobile called. Each time, Aggie sent a message expressing much the same desire to see her.

Trixi did not meet Aggie in person until a business meeting brought Aggie to the mansion. Trixi detested the fact that when she saw Aggie in person, her heart was so filled with love that she could no longer be furious with her.

Trixi was not the one who sought her out. While speaking on the phone, Aggie walked out into the garden, where Trixi sat alone working on another story concept. They glimpsed one another, but Trixi's attention returned to the screen.

When Aggie ended her phone conversation, she moved behind Trixi to see what she was working on. "Something new?"

"Do you care?" Trixi spoke with her fingers still on the keyboard, addressing Aggie.

Aggie nudged her neck, then dropped and kissed it. "Yes, I care."

"Do you care about getting caught?"

"Extremely so." She put her face close to Trixi's neck and breathed in her perfume.

Trixi's fingers stopped, and she glanced at Aggie

while kissing her lips softly. Aggie paused momentarily before allowing Trixi to taste the contents of her mouth.

When Aggie stood, ending their kiss, she moved around the table and paced while speaking, practically begging for forgiveness. "Justine packed the manuscript you wrote to Nebraska. I read it while we were gone. I must admit that it's lovely. Yes, I see a lot of us in this book. Too much for my taste, but that's because I'm intimately acquainted with us. I breathe and live you. Every inch of your body is as familiar to me as my own. You are as much a part of me as Justine is. Society dictates that I should have just one of you. If you only understood what it took for me to have a woman, let alone the two of you, it would shock you."

"I don't give a shit about society."

"I am aware you don't. The hazards of your generation and mine. When I came out, I had a hell of a time. When I returned to the United States with Justine, everyone questioned her age, although there was not a significant difference."

"It's fine, Aggie. You don't have to explain."

She peered around the corner and counted the bodies inside the home. Trixi would have acted similarly. "When you walked into my life, Trixi, it was like a truck hit me. You are my biggest taboo, and all I want to do is scream from the highest mountain that I wanted to be with you."

Trixi tallied the number of strikes against her. "Age. Poly. BDSM. Boss's daughter. I'm quite aware of all of it."

"In a different place and time, I could share you with the entire world. Oh, Trixi. If only you could recognize how much it pains me to be apart from you."

As Trixi was ready to speak, they heard Aggie's name yelled from inside the home. "Go before they come looking for you and see us together."

"I regret I could not take you to Nebraska. That was just not something I could do for many reasons. More than I am willing to disclose at the moment." Aggie left the patio and returned to a meeting where the division heads were discussing the forthcoming season's figures and timetables.

After shutting down her laptop for the day, Trixi entered her home while everyone else in the meeting small-talked on their way to the door. The guys, who dominated the numbers, lingered around the music area in the gender-segregated room. The two women conversed in the foyer.

It was more convenient for Trixi to ascend the foyer steps from the terrace than to walk to the kitchen and up the rear stairs. As Trixi passed Aggie, the other female member of the group, Gracie, stopped her. Gracie was an agent who attended the same meetings as the department managers while being more of a publicity agent than a division head.

Gracie shifted her focus to Trixi and stated, "I heard from my contact at Anais Publishing. They intend to propose an offer for your manuscript. They want to sign you."

Trixi's jaw dropped. She gripped her chest and held her quickly increasing heart rate. "Are you serious?"

"I am. I was going to wait for the offer to share, but since you're here, I'll discuss now."

"Wow. I simply cannot believe it." Trixi's eyes flashed to Aggie's as she wished she could leap into her arms and share in her happiness. Instead, she attempted to restrain herself by smirking.

"Who knew Martin's daughter was such a talented writer?" Gracie asked Aggie more than Trixi. "You know, you should check it out. You might enjoy it, Agatha. It's a story of a lesbian couple who took in a young—"

On her own, Grace stopped. As they both held their breath, her gaze flashed between Aggie and Trixi. Trixi's jaw fell ajar. Her eyes shifted to the marble flooring as she held her breath. Gracie surmised from Aggie's sigh that the stillness between the three of them spoke volumes regarding her conclusion.

Aggie responded, "I've read it. It is quite lovely. I'm pleased to hear they want to publish it. Anais is a wonderful company. They made the right choice by including her on their roster."

When Aggie smiled at Trixi, Gracie's eyebrows raised. Trixi bit her lower lip, unable to comprehend why Aggie would not contradict Gracie's suspicions.

Gracie seemed quite uneasy and excused herself. "I'll contact you when I receive the offer. Again, congratulations!"

As Gracie left their side and exited the front door, Aggie nodded. Trixi shifted her focus to Aggie, who remained by her side. Aggie again answered, "Yes, congratulations, Trixi. That is wonderful news. It deserves to be published. I wasn't exaggerating when I said it was lovely. You transformed something that some regard to be sinful into something enchanting."

As Martin led his group of pompous guys out, one of whom Trixi had fucked a month prior to Aggie, he hesitated when he noticed Aggie conversing with his daughter in the foyer.

Before he could respond, Aggie stated, "Gracie just informed us they approved Trixi's manuscript for publication. I merely wished her well. Your daughter appears to be exceptionally talented."

Again, he was unconvinced by what they had to say as he observed them both with suspicion. Trixi shook her head, realizing she had to intervene. "It's no big deal. I'm gonna run upstairs and call Miranda and tell her the news."

When Trixi said Miranda's name, her father took a few steps back. Miranda wasn't acceptable on Martin's list of booty calls, although having sex with artists wasn't particularly prohibited. He instructed Trixi to place a copy of the book on his desk.

He evicted his staff but extended an invitation to Aggie to remain in the home. Standing in the doorway, he waved out the door to his male minions. As he turned around to face both of them, his cheerful mood altered. "Let's cut the bullshit. Go to the music room, Agatha. I'll be there in a second."

Aggie left Trixi alone with her father as she walked down the hallway toward the music room. Trixi attempted to speak. "Daddy, please—"

"Do not threaten me with Miranda or any other person! Remember whose home this is. Remember who purchased five thousand dollar works of art that I've never seen? I will shred you into a thousand pieces like that credit card." He approached Trixi, towering over her with his immense stature.

"I'm sorry." Trixi shook her head and begged with her eyes, knowing that if she spoke, she would reveal all she had worked so hard to conceal.

"Go upstairs. I need to deal with this."

"Daddy!"

"I won't say it again. Upstairs."

A whole minute passed before he lifted his hand to assert control. The memories of her father's influence over the ladies in his home, which she had forgotten, surged back to her. Trixi retreated, unwilling to experience it again. As she withdrew, her head dipped with each step until she eventually turned and hurried upstairs to her room.

Aggie sprung to her feet as soon as Martin entered the room and instantly defended herself by mentioning Gracie and the book. Anything she could do to convince him she was not with Trixi and that the situation was a mistake. Regardless of her words, Martin wandered the music room in silence.

He approached the piano and ran his finger down its perimeter. Martin's prized treasure, a 1901 ebonized "Steinway Model O" grand piano. His wide hand swept across it as he bent down to inspect its surface.

Aggie observed as Martin admired the enormous grand piano. Martin swung his hand again and asked, "Do you know how many asses have touched this piano?"

She pushed her lips together, shook her head, and then responded, "No, sir."

Over his shoulder, he heard her voice. "I'm not talking about playing while sitting on the bench. I am speaking directly on top of it." Martin struck the upper board. He added, "Trixi's been up here."

"Sir, I—"

"Oh, I'm not saying you. No, certainly not. I am aware of everything that occurs in my music room. And every other room in this residence." Martin pointed to the cameras in the room's corners. "I believe her name was Cherry. Yes. Yes. Cherry West. You must be familiar with her, right?"

"Yes, sir. She's no longer with the label, but had a

bright future."

"Had. Yes."

Aggie stepped forward, having had enough of his blackmailing threats. "I can guarantee you that I am not sleeping with your daughter."

"Currently."

The knot in her gut tightened. Her throat constricted, which brought on the verge of choking. "Sir?"

Martin slowly made his way away from the piano and walked up to his chair, where he sat down and crossed one leg over the other. Before talking, he removed a cigar from the pocket of his jacket, lit it, and took a few puffs of smoke from it. "I didn't get to where I am by people pulling wool over my eyes. Sit, Agatha."

When he signaled for Aggie to sit on the black leather sofa that was across from him, she did so. "If you'll allow me, I'll explain."

"No. No. Nothing needs to be explained. When you began working for me, I feared we might have conflicts because of your lesbian orientation. Righteous and proper. Always desiring your wife's presence, yet nothing ever transpired. You were responsible and kept your nose clean."

Aggie squirmed in her seat, feeling uncomfortable with the topic. "Because I love my wife; she travels with me."

"Does she know about Trixi?"

Aggie remained mute. Due to their unwillingness to back down, a stare-down ensued. Martin took a second drag from his cigar.

He concluded by stating, "That's what I thought. Here's the deal; I am always aware of Trixi's location. At her mother's, your hotel, and your Glendale home—"

"Then you will know she has been there for some years." Aggie finally acknowledged to herself and him the relationship's legitimacy.

"Of course. You know, I was quite alright with it. Better sucking the twats of some lesbians than whoring around with half the men on my staff. I'm kind of happy you're like one of the guys."

Aggie stood up as he spoke. "No disrespect here but —"

He waved her back to the sofa. "Sit down. Can't you hear a compliment?"

"No, sir. I hear insults directed not only at me but also at your daughter." Aggie reluctantly retreated to her seat.

Martin pointed his cigar at Aggie. "You made her happy. Or your wife. Or hell, you both. She returned frequently, enthused by life and then? You know, you tell me the rest."

"Are you asking me why Trixi's no longer staying with us?"

"No, what I'm saying is that my baby got hurt by—" He waved his hand, tossing an air of lack of concern over her. "Whatever it is you did. I don't like it when I have to console my daughter in the middle of the night because she's broken-hearted. So, what is it going to take for you to leave my daughter alone? Another piece of ass? Just tell me and I'll have her sent over."

Throughout her lifetime, Aggie learned how to read people. She read between the lines, saw things that others glossed over. Even heard the unspoken words that men, like Martin VanPelt, said that had a completely different meaning. "I can't do that, sir. And I am nothing like you because I actually love the women I fuck."

His brow raised, probably because people didn't defy him. "Excuse me?"

"I love your daughter, and I won't stop trying to make her happy, especially if it keeps you away from her." Aggie stood with a rigid backbone, sweating palms, and a pounding heart, but with confidence in her remarks.

He stood, imposingly powerful, to loom above her. Just as he was about to speak, Aggie interjected, "Don't attempt to fire me. Tomorrow morning, you will find my resignation on your desk."

She then exited the music room and proceeded towards the foyer. As she grasped the doorknob, her heart raced, and she urged herself to be courageous. She hurried up the stairs in an instant to reach Trixi's bedroom door. She took a deep breath.

◆ ◆ ◆

Trixi raised her head from the desk and looked at the door, preparing to shout at a maid coming to clean her room. When Aggie opened the door, Trixi's eyes brightened with hope, delight, and concern. She sprang from her chair and ran to Aggie.

"What are you doing here?" Trixi inquired, swarming the door before shutting it behind her.

Aggie inhaled deeply. A lengthy sigh that drowned out her heart's rapid throbbing. Aggie flashed a half-smile as she surveyed her surroundings. "I have never been in your room. Nothing like what I had imagined. It's pink. And fluffy."

Trixi disregarded the slur and returned the conversation to what transpired between her father. "Did he fire you?"

As she stepped away from the door, her eyes danced around the room before glancing at Trixi. "No. However, he inquired how he could prevent me from seeing you."

"What did you say?"

"He couldn't." She laughed. Aggie's presence in her room demonstrated that he could not stop her. Aggie questioned, returning the conversation to the bedroom. "Why is it so pink in here?"

Always a change in subject signified her unwillingness to explore a topic. Trixi wanted to probe for her father's response, but Aggie's presence in her room told her all she needed to know. Trixi approached her to where she could smell Aggie's perfume, a citrus scent that remained long after a workday. Trixi lifted herself onto her toes and kissed her while maintaining her eyes open. Trixi wanted to know whether she hesitated. She didn't.

Trixi put her arms around Aggie's neck and gave her another passionate kiss. Aggie's hands rested on Trixi's waist, making her simple to push away. Trixi had learned Aggie's motions throughout the years. If Aggie had wrapped her arms around Trixi, squeezing her into her and holding her against her body, she desired Trixi, and sexual activity was forthcoming. The instances in which her hands remained on Trixi's waist meant she acknowledged her affection but did not wish to return it.

Trixi lowered her feet flat. She moved her hands from Aggie's neck to her chest, which lifted and sank as they gradually separated. Trixi attempted to interpret the emerald gaze as she pushed a stray red hair off her face and murmured, "Is this the end for us?"

Aggie shook her head but remained silent, looking aside to avoid responding. Aggie massaged her foot into the extremely pink and fluffy cashmere rug. She chuckled. "For the love of God, tell me what is up with all this pink."

"It makes me feel girly." Trixi giggled as she let Aggie dodge the elephant in the room with an answer.

"Can't you do that with make-up and dresses?"

"That makes me feel sexy." Trixi shrugged. "I like soft pink furry things."

Aggie expelled a large amount of breath as she perched on the side of the bed. Trixi felt as though she carried the weight of the world for something she was unaware of. Aggie wouldn't tell her. Trixi kneeled in front of her and placed her hands on her knees. Trixi raised her gaze towards Aggie as she opened her legs.

Aggie advised Trixi not to do what she desired by shaking her head but she did not resist and let her legs spread open. Trixi's hand rose, carrying her skirt with it. Aggie reclined, leaning back onto her arms. She exhaled as she spoke, "I wish you wouldn't."

"Stop me then."

She would have stopped Trixi any other time, but this time, Aggie's teeth dug into her lower lip, forcing it inward as Trixi grabbed for her panties and pulled them off. Trixi discarded her unattractive work underwear and lifted her skirt to reveal her femininity. Trixi wedged her lips between Aggie's knees and squeezed her clit till the room echoed with groans.

Trixi knew the future would not be the same as it was in the past when Aggie no longer hid her pleasures vocally. She did not let her inner anguish alter the outcome of the situation. Trixi savored every wonderful moment of her sex, taking her time to raise their temperatures and Aggie's pulse. When it occurred, it was a magnificent experience. Aggie's body trembled, causing her hips to buck and grind into Trixi. When she wrapped her legs around Trixi, puffs of air with a rich alto voice escaped her lungs.

Trixi pulled herself up from Aggie. In an instant, Aggie kneeled with the young, gorgeous siren, grabbing Trixi with silent affection and placing a deep, lusty kiss on her lips.

Aggie muttered, "I have to leave. Please keep your door locked for me."

She lowered her skirt before exiting the room, leaving Trixi and her underwear on the floor. Trixi sank her face into the bed where Aggie had just came, attempting not to cry. The scent of her sex was still lingering on the sheet. Trixi screamed into it, releasing all of her rage and pain. It didn't help. As the sun fell over the room, so did her tears. Trixi did not turn on a single light as her room became completely black.

# ALIEN SEX FIEND

Aggie never stated that the relationship was over, although she did not need to. Trixi knew. Even though Aggie shook her head no when asked about their fate, Trixi didn't know what to do. She had not even pulled herself off the floor before falling asleep in a bizarre stance that resembled a drunken stupor.

If she were to appear intoxicated, she definitely needed to drink to fulfill the look. Trixi retrieved a special stockpile of bourbon from her closet, which she had stolen from the bar to prepare for Cookie and Trixi's need to relax. Trixi drank directly from the bottle while she printed the document for her father. It burned as it passed through her digestive system, warming her insides.

With nothing in her stomach, the consequences of starvation hit quickly. She wasn't exactly a lightweight. Trixi retrieved some documents from the printer and inverted them on the desk. Took another drink. She dumped as much as she could into her mouth and let it slide down her throat as she ingested more. Trixi swallowed what was in her mouth in order to take a breath. She wiped her lips with the back of her palm, then emptied the printer tray once again.

The room spun. Trixi sat down at the desk and opened her computer. Despite her inability to focus her eyes, she could access the company's website. After many clicks, she located Aggie's profile picture and gazed at it intently. Trixi felt adored by Aggie's beautiful smile and loving gaze. Her brows furrowed as the image became hazy. Trixi shook her head to focus, but when it didn't help, she slammed the laptop shut.

When the printer stopped, Trixi grabbed another drink and staggered down the stairs while holding the manuscript in her hands. She stumbled around the house before reaching her father's study and opening the door.

Trixi didn't even know who sat across from him when she smashed the papers on his desk. They dispersed throughout and above all of his work. "I hope you choke on it."

Trixi became dizzy as she spun around and fell over into a chair to stabilize herself. She fled with whatever last dignity she had.

As Trixi sobered up long enough to take a shower and get dressed, she relived a few instances from her life. Or more so its occupants. The significant individuals she desired or had in her life. Natalia or Cherry West was the first woman to grace her palette, and she showed up with a great deal of baggage.

When Natalia entered her life, Trixi had no interest in relationships. Natalia was lovely and tasted like cherries, which was peculiar in and of itself. Trixi may have envisioned herself with Natalia, but the relationship failed when Natalia got too clingy. For no apparent reason other than creative differences, her father fired Cherry West.

Trixi could not count the countless guys she fucked between Natalia and Aggie. Aggie had been her dream girl, her heart, and all she could have ever wanted in a woman, but she was uncertain whether their relationship had ended permanently. As a role model and teacher, Aggie taught Trixi something that no one else had; a world in which she wanted to live.

Trixi needed a Justine. Someone who would bow before her, worship her as a queen, and be so dedicated to her that only death could separate them. A great aspiration for Trixi. As much as she adored Aggie and occasionally lusted for Justine, Trixi's thoughts wandered as she stood under the shower head, awakening from her morning haze.

CJ.

Her equal or nemesis? She didn't know. As much as Trixi despised CJ for being such a vile creature, she thought about her in countless ways. Trixi, with a chuckle and a shake of the head, did the worst thing she could think of, second only to drinking a half bottle of bourbon on an empty stomach. She returned to Daddy O's in quest of CJ.

Trixi had Paolo steal the keys to the beach home and transport her belongings earlier in the day. She did not wish to stay in the Mansion's vicinity. She wished not to run across her father or Aggie. Angry with both of them, she would remain near to her beloved location. The beach.

Trixi was ready for a hunt by the time Paolo returned. If she found CJ, she didn't know what she wanted to do with her. She would choose the answer based on her emotions at that moment.

He drove Trixi to Daddy O's and left her off at the establishment's entrance. When Paolo opened the car door for Trixi, she gently stroked his face. "Thanks. Now, if I'm not outside in approximately twenty minutes, please come inside and fetch me."

"Yes, Ma'am."

Trixi sauntered away from the automobile, yelling her name at the doorman and tossing her father's name as if she owned the place. They opened her the door. Trixi arrived with a sense of belonging, a lifted head and chest, and an alluring stride. They may have viewed her as petite, but her self-assurance made her a giant.

As Trixi approached the dance floor, she caught sight of CJ, who was leaning her elbows back on the bar and staring out onto the main stage. Clearly seeking someone to spend the night with, like Trixi. CJ's eyes widened and her spine tightened as she turned her head towards Trixi.

Trixi stalked her, approaching her with a predatory stride. CJ threw up her hands in surrender as she realized Trixi aimed her movements at her.

She apologized as Trixi walked next to her. "I don't need Granny on my case."

"Fuck you and you deserved it." Similar to the previous time, as Trixi leaned on the bar, she turned around. "Buy me a drink."

CJ ordered a mango margarita on the rocks for Trixi, then turned around, put her elbows behind her back, and leaned back on the counter again.

"You're right," CJ told Trixi as she turned her head and leaned toward her. "I deserved it. I'm sorry, but after ripping my nipples off, you did kind of deserve it, too."

"If you had learned how to respect a lady properly, I would not have treated you like a heathen."

The bartender appeared with Trixi's drink, which she quickly downed to satiate her thirst. CJ arched a brow in response to her need for another. She lifted her hand to summon the bartender, a beautiful woman who relied on her appearance for tips. While they waited, CJ inquired, "Are you here to take in the scenery, or do you need something specific from me?"

"You."

CJ shrugged and rolled her neck in various directions before returning her attention to Trixi. They exchanged silence for a moment while staring at one another. During Trixi's previous visit, CJ displayed an interest in her. Trixi did not find CJ even remotely attractive because she liked soft women who looked like women.

CJ had small tits, slicked back hair with tattoos on her arms, and a boyish physique and attitude. Underneath it, her lovely blue eyes glistened in the room's swirling light. Her lips were quite full and kissable, with a round baby face. The longer Trixi observed her, the more she desired her; at least for a minute, if CJ could control her abhorrent behavior.

"If you agree to play by my rules, I guarantee you will not be disappointed."

CJ grinned. The bartender served Trixi another margarita, which she promptly swallowed. CJ asked, "What are your rules?"

"Ditch the attitude, for one. It's so not attractive."

CJ did not wait for Trixi to finish speaking. "And?"

"You submit to me. Submit fully and completely."

"And?"

"You don't fuck me until I let you."

CJ rolled her eyes while displaying an authoritative demeanor. Trixi grasped for CJ's cheeks as she turned her head and buried her claws into her flesh. "Cut the crap, Carolina. I'll be out in the Bentley. You have five minutes to decide. If you're not in the car, it will be the last time you'll ever see me. I'll only make this offer once."

She pushed away from her, releasing her face. Trixi turned on her stiletto heel and walked away without looking back. Trixi expelled a long sigh when she closed the door behind her. It was fantastic to have such confidence. Trixi had five minutes to determine whether it worked. It may have only taken CJ one minute to decide, but since she was at a club, she would pay the bill if she consented.

Trixi waited in the backseat of the Bentley. In the driver's seat, Paolo remained silent as well. Trixi couldn't—in fact, she refused to—gaze at the door. Trixi checked her phone messages while she waited, hoping alleviate her anxiousness after instructing Paolo to go in exactly five minutes.

A message from Aggie. *Each rose contains thorns that make it difficult to appreciate its full beauty. Until we dethorn it, we can only enjoy it from a distance.*

Trixi was ready to respond when the car door unexpectedly opened, causing her to put away her phone. CJ joined her in the back seat. They did not speak immediately. Paolo glanced at Trixi before understanding that they had company.

"Para a casa de praia, Paolo!" Trixi instructed her loyal chauffeur to transport her to the beach home in his native tongue in an effort to appear worldly and keep CJ guessing. Trixi peered at CJ. "I'm glad you made the correct choice."

CJ smirked, still arrogant and confident. "Do I get any say in what happens tonight?"

Trixi laughed. "Oh, I forgot to tell you. It's not for the night. I'm taking you for the entire weekend."

CJ joked. "Kidnapping. I didn't know it was one of

your fetishes."

"You came voluntarily. And for your say in what we do, I'll give you hard limits. You receive five. Choose carefully."

CJ exhaled deeply and nodded. She observed Paolo inspecting the rear view mirror. "Does he speak English?"

"Yes."

Concerned that their chat was being overheard, CJ regarded Trixi. BDSM and kink were not frequent subjects of conversation among outsiders. When Trixi didn't bat an eye, CJ responded, "Okay. Five. Straight up, no scat. No breath play."

Trixi lifted her arm and placed her palm on the back of CJ's neck before raising it again. She rubbed it softly before sliding her fingers down CJ's arm and over her shoulders. She felt no bra straps, much to Trixi's amazement. Trixi contorted her body towards CJ. "I hope that voyeurism is not among your limitations."

Trixi slipped CJ's shirt over her head and lowered her mouth to the small but perky breast without waiting for her assent. Trixi did not need to see CJ's eyes to deduce that she questioned Paolo watching them. He should have known better after all the numerous times Trixi had gone down on someone in the backseat.

Her chest dropped as CJ relaxed. After getting her nipples to erection, Trixi asked, "What's the third limit?"

As she glanced down at Trixi, CJ said, "I think that's all I have."

Trixi laughed and said, "So I can piss on you?"

"You don't seem like that type of girl, but as long as I'm not required to drink it, I'm OK with it. If that's your kink, go for it."

"Now, my rules." Trixi once again lowered her head to CJ's breast and bit her nipple with her teeth. CJ growled as Trixi released her grip.

Trixi said, "No talking unless I ask you a question. This includes no shit-stirring or requests to see my breasts. You will view them when I deem it appropriate. My thighs, hair, and breasts, which I know intrigue you, are off-limits until I give you permission to touch them."

"They are beautiful tits," CJ said.

Trixi obligated her to seal her mouth with a firm squeeze. "One more time, and I'll gag you."

She raised her hands and, in jest, air-twisted the lock on her lips shut.

Trixi then kissed CJ's breast then licked her tight nipple. When Trixi looked up, she noticed that CJ's blue eyes were lit up. Trixi continued, "You will have normal safe words. If you want me to slow down, use the color yellow. Red if I should quit. And don't even consider saying green for go because I will kick you out of my house before you can say *please*."

After Trixi's forceful requests to their rendezvous, CJ just nodded, not daring to test her with words. Trixi lifted her head and placed CJ's lips to her own in order to determine if they were as soft as they appeared. With a delicate kiss, Trixi pulled away to say, "And I will not piss on you."

CJ smiled erratically and raised her hand as though in school. Trixi glared at her sarcasm. "What?"

"I didn't want to speak without permission, so can I have permission?" Her tone and words induced a grin from Trixi. When she realized Trixi had given her permission to speak, she responded, "Thank you."

Trixi raised her eyebrows. "For what? Not wanting to piss on you?"

"No, for kissing me."

Trixi continued to lean on her until Paolo arrived at the beach house and proclaimed their arrival.

When Paolo unlocked the passenger door, Trixi shoved CJ out of the car without even allowing her to put on her shirt. She smiled at Trixi's desire to bring her into the opulent beach home, which was far too large for just one person. Earlier in the day, when Trixi texted her father that she had taken the keys and would spend time there, he consented. It was Trixi's for at least a month before his yearly beach party.

As CJ wandered aimlessly inside the mansion, she took in the beauty of the VanPelt beach monstrosity. Before leaving Trixi alone, Paolo inquired if she had any other needs. When Trixi told him to go, he persisted on remaining. "Nonsense, Paolo. She's a pussycat. Don't worry about me."

Yes, Trixi was rather concerned, especially given her previous encounter with CJ. This time, they were on Trixi's territory, and she felt significantly safer.

Trixi walked out onto the terrace after Paolo left, where CJ gazed out at the water. Trixi observed CJ's tattoos as she stood shirtless with her back to her. In the upper left corner, there was a heart with the name Luisa written on it. Trixi's curiosity piqued. She recognized the name, but it had been years since she had heard it uttered, and she despised the sound of the girl's voice.

"Do you enjoy the view?" Trixi inquired.

"I love the ocean. I live–" she stuttered, correcting herself. "Lived on the beach, up the coast, actually. Great surf in Malibu."

"Does up the coast mean that when I hang you over this banister naked, someone you know may see you?" Trixi inquired, alluding to her intentions.

CJ raised a brow. "It's possible."

"And would that someone's name be on your back, under the heart?"

"That would be probable."

Trixi shook her head and drew CJ into the residence. As they ascended the stairs, CJ finally made the connection and spoke. "Wait a second! You're Trixi VanPelt, daughter of ViP Music guy, which means you're the one—"

"And you're getting gagged." Trixi grumbled as she dragged CJ into the territory she claimed as her own. Trixi rummaged through the dresser drawers, where Paolo had placed all of her sex toys.

CJ stopped Trixi as she attempted to use the ball gag. "Whoa, wait. Please."

"I said, no talking."

CJ retreated while pleading with Trixi not to gag her. "Just give me two seconds."

"One."

"I'll shut up as soon as you let me say this."

"Two."

CJ retreated even farther as Trixi approached her. "Stop. Red!"

She leaped onto the bed to avoid Trixi, although Trixi had never touched her. "Look, I'm still going to follow what you asked, but seriously, I need two seconds here. I kind of want this even more now, knowing who you are and not because you're rich and have all of this."

Trixi waited for her to finish with her hands on her hips.

"There's this myth. More like you're infamous in my house... world." CJ shook her head while attempting to compose words. "I used to live with Cherry West... Natalia and her friend Luisa–"

"Who is on your back?" Trixi stated, having known it from the start. She added. "Get down! I won't gag you."

CJ sprang off the bed and landed in front of Trixi. "You caused a lot of shit in my house."

"You said you used to live there? What happened?" Trixi inquired as she placed the ball gag back in the drawer and closed it.

"Luisa wasn't over Natalia when we all moved in with each other. She said she was, until one night Natalia kissed her. I never told her I saw it. It's a long story, but ultimately, I got thrown out of the house because I'm a fucking mess."

Trixi exhaled. "How did I contribute to this drama?"

"Again, long story. Natalia was in love with you. Me in love with Luisa. And Luisa is in love with both Natalia and me. It's a totally fucked up situation. And now I will shut up, and you can have your kinky way with me."

Trixi sincerely thought that the Gods did not wish for her life to go well. They continued to hurl bullshit at Trixi, and she had to sift through everything to find anything even vaguely favorable. Trixi strode across the room. At one time, Trixi believed she was in love with Natalia. Natalia may have been a potential partner.

She exhaled a chuckle, thinking how amusing it was that she was the third person in a love triangle with Natalia and Luisa. Trixi shook her head and turned to CJ as she stood shirtless in the middle of the room, ready for her to wreak havoc on CJ's body. "Take off the rest of your clothes. This is going to be fun."

Trixi entered the bathroom and started a bath, as CJ dropped her jeans and quickly removed her clothing. As the water warmed, Trixi hollered to her, "Carolina, dear. Come join me."

Trixi tilted her head to the side, towards the bathtub, as CJ entered the room. "Get in. I don't like dirty little girls to sully my sheets."

CJ acquiesced to Trixi's request and hopped in. Trixi arose and obtained the necessary supplies. Her delicacy would be required to tame this girl's palate to a reasonable level. Trixi grinned as she returned to the tub with shaving cream and a razor and placed them next to CJ, who opened her mouth to protest.

Trixi held up her finger. "This was not on your list of limits. My rules, remember? And my rules say I don't want to enter a jungle. Shut up and sit back."

After shutting off the water, Trixi set out to clean the girl. She lathered up her crotch, sometimes dipping her finger between the folds. Trixi applied the razor to her skin with care and began the long process of shaving her entire body, including the somewhat darker hair on her arms. Trixi desired CJ to be velvety smooth.

Trixi appreciated her work and arose from the floor to turn on the shower after a tedious ritual. She returned to assist CJ in exiting the tub and took her to the shower, where Trixi instructed her to lather soap into every nook and cranny of her body. Leaning against the shower's glass wall, Trixi observed and oversaw her bathing procedure. She compelled CJ to wash her hair. Trixi did not know what CJ put in her hair to make it sleek and to remain in place. Trixi did not want CJ to dirty the bedding with that when they would subsequently soil the velvety sheets with several other unpleasantnesses.

When CJ completed her assignment, she switched off the water. Trixi presented her with a towel. Trixi inquired as CJ dried herself. "How long have you been into BDSM?"

"Off and on for two years, I guess." CJ grabbed the towel from Trixi and returned it to her after drying her hair, leaving it untidy, but clean.

Her hair had a chestnut brown tint when it was not held in place by all the junk. Trixi brushed her hair away from her face as she reached for it. Her blue eyes captured her attention. Trixi did not want to move, but CJ's comments prompted her to do so. "If I could touch you, I'd kiss you right now."

Trixi threw the towel to the ground and leaned forward to kiss CJ. Her mouth slightly opened as she begged Trixi to kiss her.

That's when Trixi stated, "If we kiss too much, you will fall in love. Remember, I'm notorious for creating drama in the lives of others."

Trixi then grabbed CJ by the breast and twisted, dragging her from the bathroom to the bedroom, while CJ struggled to keep up. This was the beginning of all the wonderful sensations Trixi showered on CJ that evening. She poked and prodded CJ. Licked her and sucked her. Punished and tortured. Forced to have many orgasms; all for Trixi's fun and enjoyment. They both lost track of CJ's and Trixi's climaxes, especially when CJ performed incredible things with her tongue.

Trixi viewed the sunrise while seated on the bedroom's balcony. Just as fatigue set in and Trixi closed her eyes to take a little nap, CJ yell from the bedroom.

"Red, Trix!"

Trixi sprang to her feet and ran in to check on her. Still in the exact position Trixi left her in, upside down on this wheel with X-shaped limbs. As Trixi approached her, CJ stated, "I really need to pee."

"Red because you need to take a piss?" Trixi questioned, gazing downward at CJ's sex, which was perfectly positioned for her pleasure. CJ's head pointed downward, with her hair falling toward the ground. She resembled a lady connected to a knife-throwing death wheel. CJ wasn't in any danger; she was unnecessarily using the term red.

Trixi stroked her finger over CJ's sex; her folds were open and ready for Trixi. As well as her hips, CJ's face contorted. CJ begged with her eyes closed. "Please. Red. Please, Trixi."

"You said I couldn't piss on you. That doesn't mean you can't piss yourself." Trixi laughed while continuing to stroke her silky skin with her fingertips.

Trixi turned CJ on her right side and unhooked her from the wheel after CJ pleaded with her a million times. CJ hurried to the restroom and sighed aloud as she relieved herself. Trixi just let her go because she didn't want to contact Paolo to clean the carpets.

When CJ returned to the bedroom, Trixi pursued her. She brushed CJ's hair back and planted a passionate kiss on her lips.

CJ nearly lost her breath from the intensity. "What was that for?"

"Because I am exhausted, and debating whether you should sleep in the cage or in my bed."

"Did the kiss warrant you shoving me into a cage?"

Trixi exhaled with her palm pressed against CJ's

cheek, and her thumb stroked her lips. Trixi's heart sank when she realized she couldn't capture CJ, knowing she wasn't a genuine submissive. They were both dominant personalities that required someone like Justine to fulfill that aspect of their life. They may share and engage in wild sex with one another. Long-term, they required the presence of the ideal submissive goddess in their everyday life. Trixi would never consider CJ to be that person.

CJ would give Trixi that night, and even the weekend, if she could, but CJ's temperament would not allow her to live on her knees.

When Trixi did not respond, CJ averted her gaze downward, and she appeared dejected. Trixi hooked her finger beneath CJ's chin and drew her eyes back to herself. "Are you ready for some sleep?"

"If I'm sleeping with you."

"Get in bed, Carolina."

As they nestled up in bed, CJ asked, "Can I go down on you? I like to fall asleep with the taste of a woman on my tongue."

Trixi used her teeth to draw her lower lip inward. "You've been good. Have at it, slugger."

It did not take long for CJ's enchanted motions to propel Trixi to the gorgeous chorus of her climax. The blissful waves lulled Trixi into a pleasant slumber that did not last long. The sound of CJ dozing next to Trixi awoke her. Trixi first believed someone had invaded her home. She awoke CJ when she discovered CJ snored like a semi-truck's horn.

"What? What?" CJ abruptly sprang up and looked around.

"Are you fucking kidding me? You snore?" Trixi said,

exhausted and enraged. CJ disturbed her beauty sleep.

"I'm sorry. I can't help it!"

Trixi pointed to the door. "Out!"

"You want me to leave? Because I snore?"

"My room. There are seven other bedrooms. Find one that's not here."

CJ stomped out of the bedroom and down the hallway while huffing. It did not matter to Trixi where she ended up. CJ had to leave. As Trixi rolled onto her back, she dramatized her exhaustion by huffing. Before spending the night, Trixi needed to remember to have potential submissives fill out a questionnaire.

# FIX ME NOW

The notification on her phone awoke her. Gracie texted Trixi that she had information on the book. Trixi immediately phoned to hear the wonderful news. Anais Publishing offered Trixi a handsome sum for the book and a ten-thousand-dollar advance for a second book, if she can deliver the manuscript within six months. If Trixi did not create the second book, she would be required to repay the advance.

"Can you write another book that fast?" Gracie asked.

Trixi rubbed the back of her neck and slowed her breathing as she gazed at her bedroom door and thought of CJ. Her face lit with a grin. "I can."

"Great. You'll need to swing by the office or I can come by the house for you to sign. Whichever is best for you?"

Trixi didn't answer. As much as Trixi trusted Gracie with the arrangement, she lacked the legal knowledge necessary to sign the contract with confidence. "I'll call you back and let you know."

Trixi emitted a girlish cry of delight as she hung up the phone. She felt pleased to have produced something she could call her own. Aggie had her work. Justine was an artist. Trixi finally had her writing. Trixi wanted to share the news with someone.

Trixi left the phone on the bed and searched the house for the snoring little vixen who curiously had her heart at the time. She followed the sounds downstairs and discovered CJ naked on the couch in the living room. She stroked the hair off CJ's face with her finger. Trixi despised CJ's imperfections. She was not Aggie, whom Trixi adored with her entire being.

As Trixi saw CJ sleeping, she pondered her narrative. Who was she? Where did she come from? How did she wind up with Trixi's worst enemy, the nagging and bitter anime character, Luisa?

Trixi touched her sex and slipped her finger between her folds to awaken CJ. CJ sighed and wriggled, eventually awakening. When Trixi's eyes opened, she withdrew her hand and licked her finger. CJ said, "That's a nice way to be woken."

"I need to go somewhere," Trixi stated while sitting next to CJ at the coffee table while still wearing her pink fluffy robe.

"So you want me to leave?" Her eyes swelled with despondency.

"No. I called my driver. You can stay if you promise not to rob the place while I am gone."

"Ye of such little faith in me." CJ scooted up on the sofa. Her bare physique appeared at ease in her environment.

Trixi scrutinized CJ with the purpose of describing her in words for her next book. "You know, I trusted you once, and you literally fucked me over. So. I have good reason to not trust you."

"I said I was sorry. You really need to let shit go." CJ grinned, but her eyes expressed genuine regret for her actions. When Trixi got up from where she had been sitting, CJ grabbed her hand to keep her from going. "You can't just wake me up with a tease, then leave me blue-balled."

"There are a million and one toys upstairs. Go fuck yourself and tell me all about it when I get back. I gotta go." Trixi leaned forward with CJ and gave her a good morning kiss.

After changing, she would give her a farewell kiss, but Trixi understood she needed to cease doing so. CJ might fall for Trixi despite her wisecracks, but it was Trixi who was falling for CJ. And that would be detrimental to both of them.

Trixi drove up in front of the ranch house in Glendale. Both Aggie's and Justine's vehicles were parked in the driveway. Trixi has never previously shown up unexpectedly. She cautiously approached the door, unsure of what she would find when she knocked on the door, as they sometimes viewed random door knockers with contempt.

Trixi knocked with a tense chest on their red wooden door. The last time she visited their home, she fled after whipping Aggie senseless with a bamboo cane. Trixi had seen Aggie since then without a word being spoken, but she hadn't confronted the true head of the household. Justine.

The door opened to Aggie's anxious face. She strolled onto the porch without first asking Trixi to come inside and questioned as she closed the door. "Trixi, is everything okay?"

She had a million things to say, but none of them came naturally. Trixi acted confident, almost cocky, around people her age. She transformed into a timid version of herself in the presence of Aggie. "Everything's fine. I mean, not really fine. I needed your help with something and I know I could have called you, sent this via email or something, but I wanted to see you, too."

Aggie smiled as she walked Trixi around the side of the home, which was more secluded from the street. Once out of sight, Aggie pressed her palms on Trixi's cheeks and dragged her into a rapacious kiss. Trixi's knees went weak. Aggie had that effect on her with every kiss. Even more so since it had been so long since they'd actually spent any time together.

As Aggie retreated, she inhaled deeply into Trixi. "I wanted to see you, too. To touch you, to bathe in your scent—"

"Then let me in. Aggie, I belong here with you."

She separated herself from Trixi, holding back tears. Aggie took a few big breaths before asking, "What did you need my help with?"

"You're not denying it. You know I do."

"Trixi, please."

Trixi grumbled and extracted the contract from her satchel. "Fine. This is the contract for Anais. Gracie sent it over. I'd like you to look it over before I sign it. Make sure it's all legit."

"Gracie could have done that for you," Aggie said with wonder of why Trixi brought it to her instead of just letting Gracie handle it.

"I trust you... with my life." Trixi nearly shed a tear as she spoke the words.

The agreement was lengthy. Not something Aggie could consider on her front porch and decide. As she took it from Trixi, she sighed. "Okay, give me a day."

"No. Now. Please," Trixie said directly and clearly.

"Do you not think that I might have been in the middle of something?"

"Let's see. You're home, which means one of two things. You're in the middle of a book or you were in the middle of Justine. Both of which can wait. And besides, after that kiss, I know you aren't the one keeping me away. I need time to fix what I've broken."

Aggie retreated and headed towards the main door.

Trixie pursued her. Before opening the door, Aggie gave Trixi one more kiss. "I don't think you can."

When the door opened, fond recollections of them committing heinous acts in the home flooded Trixi's heart. In the living room, Justine stood naked in the doorway leading to the rest of the home. The defender of the hidden sanctuary. While Aggie may have been the dominating partner in the relationship, everyone in the BDSM universe understood that the power resided with the submissive.

Justine gasped when first seeing Trixi. Her eyes blazed with fury. Trixi knew why Justine despised her. It was for the same reason that Trixi despised herself. One syllable passed through Justine's voice chords. "No!"

Aggie pressed ahead. Trixi followed in her footsteps. As they passed the border into her world, Trixi noticed a temperature shift. The rage in Justine's blood set her body ablaze. Justine would seem intimidating to Trixi if the latter didn't realize how mild-mannered she actually was. Trixi nonetheless followed Aggie down the hallway to her office.

Her desk, which was formerly cluttered with documents, photographs, and appointment calendars, now lay vacant. She sat behind her unadorned wooden desk and nestled herself in as the contract lay before her. "Sit. I'll look over it."

"What happened in here? Where's all your stuff?"

Aggie expelled air from her heaving chest. "I had to return it after I quit."

"You quit? When?" And then it hit Trixi. Aggie quit the day Trixi asked if her father had fired her. No, he hadn't fired her. She quit. Trixi questioned, "What happened when my father called you into the study?"

"Trixi, please. Let me read this for you."

Her pride taking over. Trixi walked around the desk and swiveled Aggie's chair to face her. She leaned closer, putting her palms against the armrests. "Tell me what happened."

Aggie ascended, pushing Trixi backward. "He told me I was just like him, like all of them. Said he understood the need to feel younger by using pretty, young girls to boost my ego."

Trixi's eyes widened as her hatred for her father intensified.

Aggie continued. "He offered me someone else, so I would leave you alone. Like everyone was for sale, someway."

"Mother—" Trixi intended to complete her sentence, but Aggie stopped her by extending her hand.

"I told him I was nothing like him and I wouldn't work with someone who believed I was. I insulted him by saying the difference between him and I was the fact that I love the women I fuck."

"You actually said the word *fuck*?"

She chuckled and smiled briefly. "I did. Right after that, I quit."

"You also told him you love me?"

"I did. And I do, but I opened a huge can of anger in this house and I'm struggling to fix it."

Trixi grabbed for Aggie, pleased by her confession of affection. Aggie retracted her hand and instantly felt horrible about doing so. She drew Trixi to her and then used her body to pin Trixi against the wall. She attacked her, placing her mouth on Trixi's. Their tongues intertwined to the rhythm of their hearts. If there was tension in the home, it intensified when

Aggie shut the door, pulled Trixi onto her desk, and tore Trixi's clothing off.

Aggie squeezed her body between Trixi's legs. Her front hand crashed into Trixi's female body. There was nothing elegant or romantic about it. She used her full hand to tear through Trixi and seize her heart from within. Aggie's body bowed over as she repeatedly penetrated Trixi while placing Trixi's breast to her lips.

Trixi inhaled deeply and opened herself wide enough for Aggie's full fist to strike her for destroying her family and life. Trixi quivered in pain and moaned with ecstasy until Aggie removed herself from her, only to lower her head and taste Trixi's abused sex.

She tried to contain her sound waves of splendor as she came, hoping Justine would not be a witness to Aggie's fixation with her and Trixi's obsession with Aggie. Trixi's feet dangled off the edge of the desk when she sat up. Her moisture would leave her aroma on the ancient wooden desk, therefore marking her territory. They peered into one another's eyes for a time before Aggie gently kissed Trixi on the lips.

"Let me look at this contract. You should get dressed."

Trixi giggled. "What? I don't get to please you?"

"Not this time, my love."

Aggie sat down and smoothed the papers that they had jumbled during their frolic. Trixi sprang from the desk, collected her clothing, and threw them on while smoothing them.

As Trixi approached the door, Aggie asked, "Where are you going?"

With her fists on her hips, Trixi said, "To figure out how to fix things?"

"Just let it be, Trixi."

"If you fought my father for me, then I am fighting Justine for you." Trixi then opened the office door and raced into the kitchen, where she saw Justine perched on the island reading a book.

When Justine saw Trixi arrive, she immediately stood to protect her home and territory. Even though she was naked, Justine stood tall and confident. She crossed her arms in front of her, aloof and unreceptive to Trixi's apologies before Trixi even offered them.

If Trixi were to leave her body and witness the scenario from above, she would see herself presenting her case before a nude, subservient lady who wore the pants in the family. "I know you said that one day the door wouldn't be open to come back. I thought it would be Aggie that closed it, not you."

"Things change," Justine stated, unable to look Trixi in the eye as she did so. As Trixi rounded the island, the woman's gaze shot downward. When Trixi attempted to grab Justine's hands, she retreated. "Don't!"

When Justine refused to let Trixi touch her, Trixi fidgeted. Her emotions prevented her hands from remaining at her side. She leaned against the island, grasping the marble counter in order to feel anything. "When I met you, I was terrified of you and your relationship with Aggie. She brought me back to the hotel that first day. I was expecting an afternoon fling; not to be thrown into the middle of a love affair with two amazing women."

When Justine was silent, Trixi paced. She was at a loss for what to do next. "I fell in love with Aggie." Trixi sank on her knees and exchanged positions with the lovely submissive in front of her. "I fell in love with you.

You've taught me so many things, Justine. I can't just walk away from you or Aggie."

"All you did was walk away. Every time I turned around, you were running from us."

Trixi grasped her hands, but Justine retreated again. Trixi stated, "I was scared!"

"You were loved!" Justine argued back.

Trixi's voice rose, begging for her to understand. "I didn't know what that was. All I saw was you and Aggie and this world I couldn't be in."

"You were a part of it. Day in and day out, you had a home with people who loved you and wanted you."

"And yet, you forced me to remain invisible because this—" Trixi alternately flicked her hand between them. "This isn't supposed to be. Try putting yourself in my shoes."

"I have. And I didn't run away."

After several exchanges of angry words, they finally paused to catch their breath. Trixi returned to her feet. There was no point in her pleading her case while on her knees. "What do you mean?"

Justine took two glasses from the cabinet and set them on the table. She poured them each a glass of wine and took a drink. "When Agatha brought me with her from France, she was married to another dominant. They had a beautiful relationship with memories and inside jokes that I didn't understand. Their relationship was hard enough under judgmental criticism. Add a third to the mix, they chastised us." Her eyes were brimming with tears. Before they could fall, she turned aside, grabbed a towel, and dried them off with a pat.

Again turning back, Justine threw the towel in front of them on the island. "For the longest time, I watched as they lived their life together, wishing I could be part of that, but never once did they come home and not love me. Never have you been unloved in this house, Trixi. Until now."

Her heart sank to the bottom of her stomach. These comments from her were like a dagger to the heart. Trixi's body shook as tears formed. Trixi begged, "I'm sorry."

Trixi urged Justine to stop talking, but she refused. "It took a long time for us to allow another person in. I was afraid of you, too. She told me to trust her and to trust you with our secrets and our bodies. And I did. I let myself fall in love with you."

Trixi knew what she would say next, regardless of how much she claimed to love her. Trixi's head sank. The rest of Justine's tears fell because of the sadness in her eyes. "You betrayed that trust the moment you lifted your hand in anger. We can not come back from that."

Trixi's heart raced, and her breathing became deeper and more labored. Her chest contracted as she struggled to take a breath. "Justine, please. You need to know that I love her. And you. I didn't mean it."

"But you did. And I can't trust you. And if I can't trust you, it makes for some horrible situations that I will not put myself or let Aggie put herself in. I'm not sorry for making this decision, Trixi, but you broke the most important rule of this lifestyle. And that is unforgivable."

Trixi tried to close her eyes, but nothing could stop the tears that came out of from the disgust with herself. Regardless of what Trixi attempted to assert, Justine was correct. She violated a fundamental rule by allowing her anger to influence her judgments that night. Trixi vented her anger on Aggie though Aggie never yelled out to Trixi, using a safe word that may have averted an internal reaction. Leaving Aggie bloody and helpless, Trixi's hand held its strength while she pounded mercilessly on Aggie's back. It made Trixi painfully ill to realize that she contained so much rage.

Trixi peered up at Justine from the island counter, her eyes pleading for Justine to provide her one more opportunity to prove she was worthy of trust and love.

Justine shook her head. "No. I can't."

Trixi, mustering the strength to move, stood erect and straightened her spine. If she were to leave her life forever, she would do it with as much confidence as possible. Trixi gracefully left the premises and made her way to the Bentley, where Paolo waited for her. She ignored the fact that Aggie was inside reading her contract. Trixi broke down and tore herself apart upon entering. Not even her closest confidant could find the right words to say or do the anything to make her feel better.

# I'M ONLY HAPPY WHEN IT RAINS

Trixi took her time returning to the beach home for a variety of reasons. The city received much-needed rain, which impeded traffic. She also requested that Paolo take the longer route home, as she needed time to recover from a shattered heart.

She thought CJ might still be there, but she didn't want any company right then. Trixi first had to collect her thoughts and emotions before confronting a person she hardly knew. Trixi absolved CJ for her misdeeds, despite the soundness of Justine's argument. Why was Justine unable to forgive her? She used her pain as a teaching tool. Regardless of where she traveled or who wore the handcuffs, she would never allow her fury to do harm to another creature.

Aggie and Justine introduced Trixi to their world. A realm about which Trixi had only heard tales and seen depictions in films. She never in her life would have imagined herself holding a whip next to a lovely woman shackled to a massive wooden X. Trixi may have imagined herself with several lovers, but they would not have been sophisticated women who had sex in antiquated dungeons.

While Trixi remained heartbroken at the loss of the one person she had ever genuinely loved, she tucked that love down into her heart and sealed it away. Aggie would remain there forever, and nothing Justine could say would alter Trixi's affection for Aggie. Trixi loved Justine as well.

Trixi had stopped sobbing and stiffened her back by the time they drew up to the home that evening. There was a recognizable electric blue Jaguar in the driveway, with a repaired headlight. When Trixi strolled past the vehicle, she also spotted a substantial amount of clothing heaped in the backseat. The indicators of a homeless person living in their car.

CJ was in the den watching a movie on the enormous plasma screen when Trixi entered. She sprung from the couch. "I'm sorry. I got bored and didn't know when you were coming back."

Trixi motioned her to sit. "Chill. What are you watching?"

"Transformers. The new one. This girl is killer hot." CJ returned to her seat but paused the film upon Trixi's return.

Trixi inquired, ignoring everything she had said. "When you said you used to live with Natalia and that other one—" Trixi cringed at the thought of Luisa, but continued, "Where do you live now?"

She lowered her head. As she said, shame replaced her happiness and joy. "Nowhere. My car. A parking lot."

"How do you have money for food and gas?"

"I work at Daddy-O's. Or may have since I left with you."

"If you don't have a job, I'll get it back for you. For now, get your shit out of the car and wash it all. Take one of the bedrooms. You can stay, for now." Trixi turned and left the room. "Don't piss me off."

"Why are you doing this for me? I mean, it wasn't like I was all that nice to you," CJ asked.

Trixi hesitated at the top of the steps. She turned

around, visibly distressed. "Nice? You raped me. And just because I enjoyed it doesn't make it right. You were a horrible person and if you do it again, I'll cut off your tits. For now, you are my muse." Trixi retreated up the steps and disappeared from view.

Trixi allowed CJ to settle into her room while she isolated herself in her bedroom and plunged into the literature she had brought over. She knew reading would make her a better Domme, including *Belle de Jour* by author Joseph Kesse, *Histoire d'O* by Pauline Réage which she read in French to practice the language of love, and *Delta of Venus* by Anaïs Nin.

During the following several rainy days, Trixi and CJ established an intriguing pattern of playing house. Trixi worked on her second book despite not having yet signed the deal for her first. Trixi did not sure whether Aggie would contact her over the matter. She allowed time for the problem to heal.

As Trixi inquired about her connection with Natalia and Luisa, a still-existing love triangle, CJ gave a great deal of background information all at once. The emotional abuse she suffered as a child and adolescent was one of the many revelations that led to her downward spiral of using sex as a bandage for her pain. She continued to wear the bandage due to issues with the triangle she frantically attempted to fit into.

CJ used Trixi to hide the agony. That night, when CJ lashed out at her, she used Trixi. A similar outburst of rage like Trixi's that shattered Aggie's friendship with her. CJ's rage stemmed from the lady she loved being with another. Sometimes, damaged individuals discover one another and help each other recover from their mistakes.

All of what CJ said, Trixi would use as a part of another amazing adventure of a lesbian seeking love in such a messed-up world.

Daily, Trixi wrote. They adored shared meals. Trixi admired CJ's culinary skills. In between rain showers, they enjoyed their favorite long walks on the beach. And at night, Trixi paddled CJ's backside and put her into a scrumptious play zone. Even though she let Trixi exploit her body, CJ wasn't submissive. Her body's torments didn't faze her; it was almost as if she had become immune to pain. That immunity existed way before Trixi. Orgasms were much more fantastic. Pain had little effect on her, but the sensation of a woman's tongue on her clit threw her over the brink.

If only oral sex could satisfy Trixi, her life would be perfect. CJ and Trixi might have a happy ending. Unfortunately, she required something that CJ could not provide.

Trixi concluded they were slobs after living together for a week during a stormy stretch of weather. She had spent her whole life in a mansion with servants following her wherever she went. They invariably returned the clothes she threw on the floor in her closet after the laundry. Because there was always someone trailing after her, the strands of lost hair didn't exist at home. Even with Aggie, Justine maintained a spotless home.

Trixi regarded the toothpaste smears and stray strands of hair in the sink with a wrinkled nose. She reached for her phone out of disdain.

He answered.

"Paolo, send someone to clean this house today." Trixi disconnected before he could debate her.

As Trixi made her way to the kitchen, she heard Aggie's phone vibrate. She had forgotten she still had it, since it had been inactive for so long. A message.

*Trixi, my beautiful girl. I long to see you. I miss waking up to you, safe knowing you're mine. It hurts tremendously to be apart from you. I've reviewed your agreement and believe you should sign it. If this is your only copy, I will need to see you in order to return it. If not, I'd still like to see you. I miss your adorable face.*

They walked a very fine line. Trixi made love to Aggie in the mansion's bedroom. Aggie mounted Trixi on her desk, despite Justine's protests. Seeing her again could lead to another fling; an indiscretion because the creator of the rules forbade it. Trixi grinned at the thought of being the bad girl who invaded Aggie's thoughts, although she despised still being at odds with Justine.

Trixi responded: *I am at the beach house. If you miss me that much, join me. And no need to bring the contract. P.S. This phone will self-destruct in five seconds.*

She then hit the send button and threw the phone into the garbage disposal while flipping the switch. The sound of metal grinding against plastic brought a smile to her face. A momentary sigh of relief and happiness.

With her personal phone, Trixi called him again. "Paolo! Send over a plumber, too."

Aggie arrived by herself on Friday evening. Trixi gave her the damaged mobile phone upon her arrival, although it may have been a foolish act. They fought and shouted at one another. Aggie was the mature adult, whilst Trixi stamped her feet until she got what she wanted. Something she learned through seeing the haughty pop singers at her father's record company. Also, something Aggie oversaw on a daily basis as their manager.

Since she was no longer employed by Martin, Aggie compromised by using Trixi's personal phone instead of a burner. After resolving the argument, Trixi placed her arms around Aggie's neck and sprang to kiss her. Aggie welcomed Trixi's offer but resisted taking her into herself, preventing Trixi from becoming one with her.

Trixi asked Aggie, as she fell to her knees and peered into her beautiful eyes. "Do you trust me?"

Aggie heaved a sigh after a moment of indecision. "Yes, but I am not the one submitting their life to you."

"And she's not willing to give me a second chance. Are you? I mean, if she was?"

"I don't know what would have happened if you hadn't left that night, but when that door closed behind you, Justine locked it faster than I could say I was alright. There is history and memories. No matter how much time passes from them, she can not forget," Aggie said while pacing the room. A discussion they should have had earlier.

Trixi followed in her footsteps. Trixi unlocked the glass door leading to the terrace when Aggie stopped in front of it. Aggie walked out. Her chest tightened as if lead filled it. The enclosed patio hid them from the foggy twilight. Trixi asked, "Did this have anything to do with your wife?"

Aggie cocked her head, astonished that Trixi had brought up the topic. When Trixi refused to back down, Aggie's stature diminished. Aggie eased into the discussion by taking a seat in one of the lounge chairs beside the pool. "Melody. Yes. My angel. As soon as it became legal, we were married. Prior to meeting Justine, I never felt the need for a permanent companion despite our open marriage. Melody was ecstatic when Justine joined our group. We had a beautiful relationship."

Trixi had sat with her, holding her hand while she spoke. When Aggie paused, Trixi asked, "What happened?"

"Perhaps we were a bit too open about our relationship or careless about who we let in on our secret. Someone we trusted took our open marriage far too literally. When Melody refused the offer, the women we considered being our friends had overpowered and restrained her."

Trixi cringed and fucked herself internally as Aggie continued to speak. "They abused, raped, and sodomized her to the point of bloody death."

Trixi's head fell into her hands. She objected. "Don't say it. Don't continue, Aggie."

Glancing at her companion, Trixi hoped Aggie would cease speaking. But she didn't. Aggie stated, with tears in her eyes, "When Justine and I returned from the store, we found them still taking advantage of her, even after they had suffocated her."

As she told the story, Aggie fought back the tears by closing her eyes. Trixi did not want to touch her after hearing this. Aggie placed her hand just above Trixi's leg. Trixi said, without intending to be heard, "It makes perfect sense."

"There was no disputing what happened. I still have cameras in every room. As we watched the events unfold, we could see the anger in their eyes when Melody rejected their advances. It took Justine a very long time to accept another person in her life."

"And I fucked it up." Trixi rose to her feet, but immediately kneeled in front of Aggie. Not looking for forgiveness, Trixi said to her, "Aggie, I am so sorry for what I did. I get why she hates me. I want you to know that I love you and never meant to hurt you or her."

"I know, my love." Aggie wiped a few tears from Trixi's eyes and tenderly kissed her on the forehead. "You asked if I would give you a second chance if she changed her mind. Yes, my darling, because I know you love me. They did not act out of love. Only greediness. Lust. I'm not sure but there definitely wasn't any love. I am madly in love with you, my beautiful girl, and I want nothing more than to bring you home and make sweet love to you."

"But it can't happen," Trixi stated matter-of-factly.

"Not yet. Trust me. Believe me. I want you to marry us. Yes, you have vexed me so many times. Oftentimes, I attribute that to your youth. And please do not hate me for saying so."

Trixi laughed, smiling up at her. "I don't. You're right. I am childish. Stubborn. A spoiled rich kid that gets what she wants or throws a tantrum. I know this about myself."

"Maybe that's why I love you."

Trixi kissed Aggie's hand and the fabric that covered her leg. "I'm willing to wait for Justine to come around. See I am sorry—"

Aggie got up from her chair and paced again. Aggie still had to tell her something. She took a deep breath as she leaned against the patio railing. The moon and stars hit the ocean just right to make a layer of shine on the water. Trixi walked up behind Aggie and put her arms around her. "Whatever it is. Don't say it. Please. Just give me this weekend. Stay with me."

They stood there for a few minutes before Aggie pulled away from Trixi, took out her phone, and made a call. Trixi didn't move and gave her space. Trixi couldn't hear what Aggie said when the call began. She muttered to the person on the other end of the phone line.

◆ ◆ ◆

"I'm assuming you're with Trixi." Justine said on the other end of the phone, her voice dripping with venom.

Aggie walked to the edge of the patio, even though the evening mist pebbled on her arms. "I'm sorry for leaving without talking to you. I needed to do this without your commentary."

"I'm really over this unhealthy obsession you have with her."

Her voice got louder as her frustration grew. Aggie said, "Stop. Just stop."

"At this point, you need to make a choice. I'm not doing this and if you want her so badly then I want a divorce."

As she spoke with her teeth clenched, her voice got even stronger. "Don't threaten me."

"Then you need to come home."

"I'll be home on Monday."

"I don't know if I'll be here."

"You will be."

◆ ◆ ◆

She put the phone down. Still with her back to Trixi. Trixi's chest tightened as she worried that wanting to spend one last weekend with Aggie would cause them to break up. Not what Trixi wanted to happen.

Aggie smiled as she finally turned around. A forced and unnatural smile. Trixi worried about the ache in her eyes. She couldn't keep Aggie. She said, "You should go."

Aggie walked over to Trixi, her smile becoming more genuine. Aggie's eyes revealed her affection for Trixi. "I am a big girl and can handle my relationships."

"You need to go home," Trixi said, displaying the same erratic temperament as the Texas climate. Trixi wanted her one minute and then wanted her to leave the next. "I don't want to be the reason you break up."

"You're not breaking us up. I need this weekend with you; probably more than you need it with me."

"Why do you say that?" Trixi inquired, wanting to know what she had previously had difficulty communicating.

Again, Aggie hesitated. "Because I don't know when I will see you again." When Trixi's eyebrows rose, her concern intensified. Aggie said, "We're moving back to Omaha. My father is not well and my mother can't take care of him by herself."

Trixi's eyes grew wider. This weekend was a farewell romp, not a mercy fuck to appease Trixi. Her eyes fell to the ground as tears formed in the ducks. When Trixi presented them to Aggie, the dam burst and a torrent of waterworks formed on her cheeks.

"Please. Don't cry. Let's just go inside and enjoy the weekend."

"So you can fuck me and leave?"

Aggie gestured toward Trixi with her hands. "That's not fair."

"I call it like I see it."

"And that's not what you wanted when you asked me to stay?"

Their similarities were striking. In frustration, not anger, Trixi let out a huff that spun into a scream. "You tell me you want me in your life, just not yet. I figured we could work toward fixing it, but how is that supposed to work when you're in the middle of a fucking cow town?"

Aggie responded by yelling back, "I wasn't the one who scared the shit out of my wife. I'm dealing with the fallout of your moods. The one thing I asked for was no drama. That is exactly what I have and had since the beginning."

"And if that wouldn't have happened, would I have gotten kicked to the curb anyway when you went to take care of your dad? Because I remember being told to stay home the last time you went."

"No. I told my parents about you." Aggie cried. "They told me I was stupid to try this again. Even though Justine was dead set against you coming back, I told my parents that I fell in love with someone so wonderful. I'm not giving up on you or on us, because I believe it will work and we'll be able to have this wonderful life together."

Trixi clutched her and snuggled into her, wiping her tears and snot from her nose. Aggie made her feel so young, like a wounded child in need of her mother's comfort. "I'm sorry I ruined this."

"Trixi, you are such a beautiful butterfly. You've

grown so much over these few years. It's time you spread your wings and fly. I'm doing what I can, but I don't want you to wait for me. Take another submissive. A woman devoted to you."

Trixi's chest rose as she took a deep breath. "I can't."

Aggie led Trixi up the stairs to the bedroom by the hand. As the door closed behind them, Aggie grabbed Trixi's wet cheeks and planted a lengthy, passionate kiss on her. Breathtaking in every way.

Trixi breathed into her, delighting in the union of their souls. Under their kiss, it was their farewell sonata. The last time their bodies would dance to the sweet tune of an unspoken addiction they shared.

Aggie rescued Trixi from herself and her insanity on numerous occasions over the years, when Trixi's outbursts could have landed her on the street. Aggie repeatedly bandaged Trixi's wounded ego in a maternal manner. Trixi loved her in each of these instances. More compassionate than her own family. Letting her go felt devastating. In between their final kisses, Trixi wept.

As they collapsed onto the bed, Aggie rolled on top of Trixi, seizing control of her. Trixi permitted Aggie to direct their bodies because she had always wanted Aggie to make love to her alone.

Without chains or harnesses. No pain. Aggie slowly removed Trixi's clothing, making passionate love to every inch of Trixi's bare skin, savoring every delicious morsel along the way.

They did not rush the pleasures that rolled through them throughout the night, as they were skin to skin. They exchanged their devotion for one another without speaking a word; only their heavy breaths and the sounds of desire were audible.

By dawn, they were exhausted. No sleep, just the peaceful rest that came from being close to each other. As Trixi huddled under Aggie's protective arm and rested her head on Aggie's chest, the sun peered into the bedroom and Trixi's heart swelled with dread.

Nothing had changed. Regardless of how many orgasms or kisses they shared, Aggie had to leave. She shed a tear, which landed on Aggie's skin.

Aggie lifted Trixi and wiped her eyes after sensing sadness on her own body. "My butterfly. You are going to fly high, and I will admire your beauty from afar until I can keep you as my own. And when that time comes, I hope you will still love me as much as you do right now."

Aggie then climbed out of bed and dressed herself. Trixi watched her as she submerged herself in a pool of misery. Nothing she could say could alter the course of events. Aggie leaned into the bed, wiped away Trixi's tears with her fingers, and gave her a final kiss.

As Aggie prepared to depart, Trixi grasped her hand and held it close to her chest. "I will always be yours, Aggie. Forever."

...TO BE CONTINUED

## STAY IN TOUCH

For more information on Cyan LeBlanc's work, you can follow along with works in progress, short stories, upcoming releases, and more at our website:

www.posiesandpeacocks.com

# MORE BOOKS AVAILABLE ON AMAZON

◆ ◆ ◆

**Cause & Effect (a girl/Mistress novel)**

Open Your Eyes
The Queen and I
Something Wilder
My Final Muse
Thirty-Three
Dark Waters Ahead

Printed in Great Britain
by Amazon